THE ROM COM MOVIE CLUB - BOOK TWO

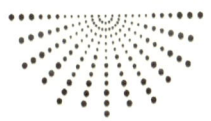

BERNADETTE MARIE

5 PRINCE PUBLISHING

Published by 5 PRINCE PUBLISHING & BOOKS, LLC

PO Box 865, Arvada, CO 80001

www.5PrinceBooks.com

ISBN digital: 978-1-63112-303-0

ISBN print: 978-1-63112-304-7

Cover Credit: Bernadette Soehner / Marianne Nowicki

11-30

To Stan,
"You have bewitched me, body and soul,
and I love, I love, I love you.
I never wish to be parted from you from this day on."
Pride and Prejudice

ACKNOWLEDGMENTS

T, N, G, S, J, You are all everything I ever wanted! "You complete me." ~*Jerry Maguire*

Mom and Sissy, I think *he* believed this to be true of all three of us. "To me, you are perfect." ~*Love Actually*

Cate, "We'll always have Paris." ~*Casablanca*
  Wait! What I mean to say is we'll always have Panera's. (haha) Thanks for sticking it out with me! Through all the misguided words and Old Lady Chics.

Marianne, Colleen, Grace, Sophie, and Cayla, You make me shine! And to Whitney, you make me sound amazing. Thank you! "I can't see anything I don't like about you." ~ *Eternal Sunshine of the Spotless Mind*

Carrie Winfield, Lindsey Haggerty, and MeganHammond, You make me want to do this every single day!
  "I don't want to sound foolish, but remember love is what brought you here." ~*If Beale Street Could Talk*

To my Readers, Thank you for coming back time and time again. Keep coming, and I'll keep writing. "As you wish." ~*The Princess Bride*

OTHER TITLES

BY BERNADETTE MARIE

THE KELLER FAMILY SERIES

The Executive's Decision

A Second Chance

Opposite Attraction

Center Stage

Lost and Found

Love Songs

Home Run

The Acceptance

The Merger

The Escape Clause

A Romance for Christmas

THE WALKER FAMILY SERIES

Walker Pride

Stargazing

Walker Bride

Wanderlust

Walker Revenge

Victory

Walker Spirit

Beginnings

Walker Defense

Masterpiece

At Last

THE ROM COM MOVIE CLUB

The Rom Com Movie Club - Book One

The Rom Com Movie Club - Book Two

The Rom Com Movie Club - Book Three

FUNERALS AND WEDDINGS SERIES

Something Lost

Something Discovered

Something Found

Something Forbidden

Something New

THE DEVEREAUX FAMILY SERIES

Kennedy Devereaux

Chase Devereaux

Max Devereaux

Paige Devereaux

STAND ALONE TITLES

The Happily Ever After Bookstore

THE MATCHMAKER SERIES

Matchmakers

Encore

Finding Hope

THE THREE MRS. MONROES TRILOGY

Amelia

Penelope

Vivian

THE ASPEN CREEK SERIES

First Kiss

Unexpected Admirer

On Thin Ice

Indomitable Spirit

THE DENVER BRIDE SERIES

Cart Before the Horse

Never Saw it Coming

Candy Kisses

ROMANTIC SUSPENSE

Chasing Shadows

PARANORMAL ROMANCES

The Tea Shop

The Last Goodbye

HOLIDAY FAVORITES

Corporate Christmas

Tropical Christmas

Date for Hire

THE ROM COM MOVIE CLUB - BOOK TWO

CHAPTER ONE

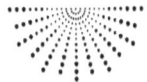

YES, SHE'D PUT PINE-SCENTED FLOATING CANDLES IN THE CLAW foot bathtub, because Lisa always thought it was a nice touch.

Yes, she'd made ice cubes out of punch for Tina to put in her sugar-free, caffeine-free, color-free soda.

Yes, she'd made the special peppermint candy cookies her grandmother used to make, just for Ruby.

In lieu of the usual college T-shirts which they would always wear with pajama pants for rom com movie night, Mindy had a box for each of the girls under the Christmas tree with a sweater to wear with their pajama pants. Of course they were ugly sweaters, and she couldn't wait until the girls saw them.

Mindy had chosen *Bridget Jones' Diary* as the holiday movie, and it seemed appropriate to have uglier sweaters than even the ones depicted in the movie.

She had real gifts for each of her friends as well, because this would not only be their Christmas Rom Com Movie Club night, but it would be their time to celebrate each other before the holiday.

Now that both Lisa and Tina were married, they'd have family to be with at Christmas. Ruby had already told everyone she was going to Hawaii with her mother for Christmas, and they weren't going to celebrate at all, which was no surprise. Ruby could be a Scrooge, but her mother could be a bigger one.

Mindy would end up at her parents' house with her sister and her family. Her grandmother would be there, and probably an aunt and uncle or two. She would endure the many questions. *Why aren't you married? Why don't you date more? I know a nice guy, would you like to meet him?*

She didn't want any of it, but she was a rule follower and the keeper of any tradition, so she'd put up with it, even if she'd rather fly to Hawaii and be Scroogey with Ruby and her mother.

As she pulled a tray of chocolate chip cookies from the oven, the doorbell rang. Right on time, she thought as she set the tray on the top of the stove and hurried to answer the door.

Her three dearest friends stood together on the porch, each with boxes and bags in hand.

"Come in. Come in," Mindy said stepping back from the cold.

"How Lisa got married outdoors a month ago, and today I have on long underwear under my pajama bottoms, a sweatshirt, a coat, scarf, hat, and gloves amazes me," Ruby complained as she handed Mindy her stack of gifts to hold while she toed off her boots.

"Yes, and next week there are two days predicted to be in the sixties," Tina said, setting her bags on the ground and slipping out of her coat.

"Why would we want to live anywhere else? Colorado gives us all four seasons every day of the year. We're lucky," Lisa added her optimistic view.

Ruby growled as she pulled off her coat and hung it on the rack by the door. "Bite me. I want seventy every day of the year."

Lisa shook her head. "Boring."

Once everyone was free from their winter wear, they moved

to the living room where they tucked their gifts under the Christmas tree.

Tina shook her head. "Seriously, Mindy, you should go into professional holiday decorating. People pay good money for perfect trees and lights like this."

Mindy laughed. "I had help with the lights."

"Still, I've never seen a more curated tree."

"You should see my mother's house. She has a tree in each room, each with a theme."

Ruby shook her head. "Your mother has a tree filled with porcelain dolls."

Mindy laughed at that. "And she curated that tree after you freaked out about her doll collection. So, Rube, that's your tree."

The four of them laughed as Mindy pulled the three boxes from under the tree and handed them each one.

"Okay, this goes with our movie night," she said.

Tina pulled her sweater from the box first, and wrinkled her nose. "*Bridget Jones' Diary*, huh?"

"You got that from the ugly sweater?" Mindy asked.

"You have your tells, Mind."

"Oh, hell no," Ruby held her sweater up which had an elf hat and legs that protruded from the sweater itself. "Are you kidding me?"

Mindy held up a hand. "For the record, I wrapped them all, walked away, mixed up the boxes, and then put a name on them. I didn't choose one certain sweater for any one person."

"Liar," Ruby snorted.

Each of the women pulled their sweater out of the box and slipped it on while they laughed.

Then Lisa, with her blinking Christmas tree sweater on, looked at Mindy. "If you don't have one, I'm taking this off."

Mindy grinned. "I'll go get it. And tonight I have a pink champagne face mask, and a sparkling red nail polish."

Tina was the first to stand. "I'm ready for a facial. Let's start there."

As was tradition, they'd all come bare faced and they put on the pink facial masks that tingled. Then, they polished their toenails and fingernails and started the movie. Glam came before drinks and snacks.

Crowded onto the sofa in the family room of the little home, they watched as Bridget Jones pulled up to her mother's house and proceeded to walk through a crowd of guests, while her "uncle" grabbed her butt.

"I had an uncle like that," Ruby said, tight-lipped because the mask had hardened. "He never tried anything, but he was—bleh."

"He's dead now, right?" Lisa asked. "I mean, I would think if he tried that on you now, you'd stab him."

"Damn right I would. Knee to the balls, and a knife in the heart while I looked him in the eye," Ruby said with confidence.

Mindy felt her cheeks heat under the facial mask she wore. Ruby could always take it that inch too far that made Mindy uncomfortable. But, that was some of her charm. Ruby was raw and uncensored, and sometimes Mindy wished she were more like that herself.

When the doorbell rang, the four of them exchanged looks.

Tina held up her hands. "I don't live with my mother-in-law anymore, so I know she didn't send her boys over here to deliver anything," she said referring to the night Aaron, her husband, and Ryan, Lisa's husband, brought over cookies while the women were all masked up as they were now.

Mindy stood, hobbled to the door on her heels, so as to not mess up her wet toenail polish, and looked out the peephole of the door. The man on the step was turned around as if he were looking at the lights on the trees outside. Hesitantly, Mindy opened the door just a crack.

"Can I help you?" she asked.

When the man turned, her heart caught in her throat. It was

dark on the porch, and green and red lights shadowed his face, but it didn't matter, because she could see that he was heavenly perfect.

Dark eyes smiled at the same time his perfect mouth did. "Hi," he said with a hint of humor. "I think I caught you at a bad time."

"We're good."

"Mindy, right?"

She stared at him, studying him. "I'm sorry, do I know you?"

"Victor Hayes," he said the name as if she were supposed to know it. "My grandmother was Victoria Hanson, she owned the house next door."

"Vic?"

His smile widened. "You remember me?"

"I remember you being ten," she said, her lips held tight by the constriction of the mask.

When he laughed, it was deep, just like his voice, and it surged through her. "And that's how I remember you, too." He leaned in. "Remember when we played married couple in the treehouse across the street at Mr. Smith's?"

Mindy swallowed hard and nearly choked. "*You* remember that?"

"My first kiss."

Holy shit!

"So what are you doing here?" Mindy asked, now fully aware of how she looked with her mask on and the reindeer with the blinking nose on her sweater.

"I just moved into my grandma's house. I'm going to renovate it."

"It's been empty for years."

"Yeah, I have my work cut out for me. But I locked myself out. My phone is in there too. Can I use your phone to call my mom?"

It sounded childlike when he said it.

"Um, sure," Mindy said as she stepped back and let him in.

He eyed the pile of shoes at the door. "I've interrupted a party. I can go ask Mr. Smith to let me use his phone."

"It's dark out. Mr. Smith will have already barricaded himself in his house. But, no laughing when you see us."

"You all look like this?" he asked, scanning a look over her.

"Yep," she said and wondered what kind of impression she possibly could have made on the handsome man she'd once kissed in childhood.

CHAPTER TWO

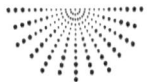

VIC FOLLOWED MINDY THROUGH THE KITCHEN, WHICH HE'D BEEN in many times during his childhood, and he was surprised to find it hadn't changed all that much. In fact, only the appliances were updated.

When he looked toward the family room, which was still dark with wood paneled walls and thick carpet, three sets of eyes were turned his way, and each of them had on a pink mask, just like Mindy's.

"Hi," he said with a wave in their direction.

One of the women stood and walked right toward him. She had bright red hair piled atop her head, and a no nonsense gait to her walk. Her sweater had an elf on it, and its legs hung off the sweater. It was hard not to stare.

She held out her hand and green eyes studied him from behind that pink mask. "Ruby. And you are?"

"Vic," he said, sure to keep his eyes on hers, and not the elf. "Next door neighbor. I just moved into my grandmother's house," he continued to say as if her one question warranted all those answers.

"Nice to meet you, Vic. Would you like some wine?"

He looked at Mindy, who was holding out her cell phone. "Um, I…" Mindy nodded. "Sure. Thanks."

Vic took the phone, mouthed the words *thank you*, and dialed his mother. When she didn't answer, he left her a voice mail.

"Do you mind if I text her too? She doesn't know the number, so she's probably ignoring the call."

"Go ahead," Mindy agreed. "I'm going to go wash my face," she said and disappeared down the hall with two of the other women, but Ruby stayed in the kitchen with him, cracking facial mask and all.

"They're pansies. Men come around and they all rush off to wipe off their faces," Ruby laughed as she poured him a glass of wine.

"You guys do this often?"

"Every month since we were in college." She handed him the glass and then poured one for herself, but her glass had a red shoe charm on the stem. "So, you moved in next door, huh?"

Vic texted his mother from Mindy's phone and nodded to Ruby. "Yeah. My grandma died four years ago, and no one can seem to let go of the house. So I finally offered to buy it from my mom and her siblings. It'll be a good starter house."

"Starter house, so there's a wife? A fiancée? A little family?"

Vic laughed and waved his hand to ward off that comment. "Oh, no. Not me. I'm the youngest of four, and the other three are married with kids. Seriously, I don't envy them that. I like my freedom, thank you very much," he said as convincingly as possible. He was building his business, and now renovating a house. Who had time for the distraction of relationships and marriage?

"All of your sisters are married?" Mindy's voice came from behind him, and when he turned to look at her, he had to remember to breathe.

Her dark hair pulled back from her now fresh face caught him

8

by surprise. She was just as he remembered her—and boy did he remember her.

"Um, yeah. They're all married with little kids. I'm the cool uncle, not that they know it yet."

She smiled and it radiated through the room. Suddenly, he was glad he'd locked himself out of his house.

"So what are your plans for the house?" Mindy asked as she poured a glass of wine, this one with a cherry charm on the stem.

"Well, it's stuck in the seventies. I mean, there are still avocado green appliances."

It was Ruby that choked out a laugh when he said that. "Do they work?"

"Yeah."

"That's so cool. Can I see it?"

Vic shrugged. "Of course. As soon as my mom gets here with a key, I'll take you all over. I mean, I have to demo the kitchen, so it'll all go. Let's just say, I'm more afraid of the wiring hazards that dwell within the walls."

"Sure," Ruby agreed. "Some of the shit in these older houses isn't to code anymore. One extra jolt of power, the whole house goes up in flames."

Mindy stared at her. "Seriously. You're going to say something like that and think I'm not going to have nightmares?"

"You should think about it," Ruby said. "But then you're not improving this house. You're keeping it as a shrine."

"I am not."

Ruby puffed out a breath. "You sleep in the guest room so that your grandmother's room isn't bothered. Only two years ago you finally took the plastic off the sofa in the formal living room."

Mindy felt her skin grow warm as she shifted a look toward Vic, and noticed he was smiling.

"Knock it off," she warned Ruby, and then she took a long sip of her wine, which only made her choke and cough.

Vic put his glass down on the counter and patted her back. His big, warm hands on her distracted her from choking.

"I'm good," she managed. "I'm fine."

"You're sure?"

No, she wasn't sure. Looking into those dark eyes, she could use a dose of mouth to mouth, but she wasn't going to even think that way. Ruby was already flirting with him, and he lived next door. They had history. Okay, no, they didn't. They'd had a childhood that had long ago been forgotten—but it hadn't, had it?

Mindy nodded. "Fine. I'm fine."

Vic looked toward the family room where the movie was paused. *"Bridget Jones' Diary?"* he asked.

"You've seen it?"

"Hasn't everyone?"

"We watch rom coms when we get together. This one has a Christmas theme."

He nodded slowly. "Hence the ugly sweaters."

Okay, he was a keeper, Mindy thought. At least when her house went up in flames, due to old wiring, maybe he'd throw something through the window and pull her to safety.

She felt her skin heat again.

"Yeah," she finally answered.

Vic leaned his hip against the counter and angled in toward Mindy. "Do you think she really smokes?"

Mindy looked toward Ruby, who had walked out into the living room and was setting her wine on the coffee table. "Ruby?"

Vic chuckled. "No. Bridget Jones. I mean, I felt as if the cigarette smoking in this movie was, I don't know, fake."

Mindy couldn't help but laugh at that. "I always thought that too. Like, she holds it funny."

"Yes," he agreed, tapping her arm with his hand in a quick gesture. "It's weird."

He sipped his wine and kept his eyes on her. When the heat from it grew to be too much, Mindy looked around the room to have someone to draw away his attention, but they had all gone back out to sit on the sofa, and Ruby had gone to clean off her face.

They were alone in the kitchen, and he was leaning in to talk directly to her.

Mindy took another sip of her wine, careful to not choke again.

Vic took a sip from his glass. "Mindy Baldwin. I just can't believe you live next door to me."

"Right?" She wasn't sure what made her say that, as if it were some prize to have her there.

He leaned in even closer. "If I remember right, you spent every summer here with your grandma."

"Mondays, Wednesdays, and Fridays," she confirmed. "My mom worked on those days."

Nodding, Vic smiled as he sipped again. "That's right. And my sisters and I stayed with my grandma all week, and some weekends." He snapped his fingers as if he were remembering something. "Curt Smith. Was that Mr. Smith's kid's name?"

Mindy nodded. "Yes. Curt and Brian."

"That's it!" he said, again touching her as if he didn't know it was causing her temperature to rise every time he did it.

"Curt was our age. Brian was a year older. They played baseball competitively. I remember going to their games a few times with my grandpa."

Mindy remembered that they were the kind of boys who liked to put dirt down her shirt, or try to look up her skirt. Her memories of Curt and Brian weren't necessarily as fond as Vic's.

"I'm glad I had to come over. I think it'll be fun to get to catch up as adults," he said, still smiling at her.

"Yeah," was all she could say.

"So what about you? Married? Kids?"

Mindy shook her head as she finished her glass of wine. "No."

"I find that hard to believe. You were a catch."

"Me?"

"Yeah. I remember everyone in the neighborhood having a crush on you. I mean, I stopped spending summers at Grandma's when I was twelve, but I remember you turning heads."

For some reason that made her laugh out loud. "You're kidding me, right? I mean I followed my sister around all the time. I was just the annoying little sister."

His brows drew in. "That's not what I remember at all."

The doorbell rang and Vic eased back from their intimate stance. "I'll bet that's my mom."

He finished his glass of wine and headed to the door. "Did you want to come see the kitchen?"

Ruby must have heard that from the other room, because Mindy didn't have a chance to reject the invitation before all three of her friends were at the door.

"Yep!" Ruby nearly shouted as she pulled on her boots. "I may have to take pictures and post them on Instagram."

Vic lifted his eyes to Mindy and smiled. Why did she think having him next door was going to be very distracting?

CHAPTER THREE

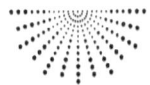

Vᴵᴄ ᴛᴏᴏᴋ ᴛʜᴇ ᴋᴇʏs ʜɪs ᴍᴏᴛʜᴇʀ ʜᴀɴᴅᴇᴅ ʜɪᴍ. Tʜᴇɴ ʜᴇ sᴛᴇᴘᴘᴇᴅ around his mother and moved past her. "Hey, Mom, you remember Mindy Baldwin, right?" he called out to her as everyone followed him up his front walk.

His mother scanned a look over her, wide eyed, and then a tight smile formed on her lips.

"Right. Mindy. Well, you were pretty little the last time I saw you."

"I was."

"It looks as if my son interrupted a slumber party," Vic's mother said to Mindy as Vic pushed open his front door with the key his mother had brought for him.

"We have a movie night each month, and pajamas are part of the attire," Mindy told her.

"That sounds like fun. I remember your mother used to have friends over all the time. She'd have slumber parties too," Vic's mother said, but there was a strain to her voice.

"She's mentioned that."

"The sweaters are for Christmas only?"

Mindy laughed. "Yes. They're quite hideous, but they're supposed to be."

"And what do you do with them after tonight?"

Mindy shrugged. "Keep them for the next ugly sweater event. People have them all the time."

Mindy watched as Vic's mother puckered her lips. Mindy wasn't getting the best vibe from the woman. Maybe she was mad that Vic had called and interrupted her night.

A moment later his mother smiled at her, though it looked strained. "I have an ugly sweater party at my office in a few weeks. I just might have to borrow that reindeer."

Mindy studied Vic's mother to see if she were serious, but her smile didn't quite make that clear. "I'd be happy to lend it to you."

"That's very sweet. I'll let Vic know, and he can get in touch with you." She lifted her head from their conversation and looked toward the kitchen, where Vic had turned on the light and the three of Mindy's friends had followed him. "Vic, I'm leaving. Your dad wants me to pick up ice cream on my way home."

Vic emerged from the kitchen with the key in his hand. "He doesn't need ice cream," he scolded.

"Maybe frozen yogurt."

He shook his head. "That's not any better. You'd better just go home and make him a veggie tray."

"Like he'll buy that over me getting him ice cream."

Vic leaned in and kissed his mother's cheek. "He'll get over it and still be alive to be mad about it." He handed her the key. "Thank you for saving my ass."

"Of course. I love you."

"I love you too."

His mother turned to Mindy. "It was nice to see you again. I can't believe it's been so long that you're all grown up." She smiled. "My mother and your grandmother were quite a pair on this cul-de-sac. And to think now you and Vic live next door."

Mindy looked at Vic, and he was looking at her. They exchanged smiles.

"I think it'll be fun," Vic said. "We have a lot to catch up on."

"It'll be nice for sure, Mrs. Hayes."

"I'm sure." His mother let herself out the front door and Vic shook his head as he closed it behind him. Mindy wondered if he'd felt the tension in his mother as she had. Or maybe there was something else.

"My dad just was diagnosed with diabetes, but she's no help," he said, scrubbing his hands over his face.

"He's okay?" Mindy asked, wondering if that was why his mother seemed out of sorts.

"Yeah, it's new, but you can't let that shit slide. Grandma had it, and in the end, that's what killed her."

"I'm sorry to hear that."

He shrugged. "All you can do is learn from their mistakes, right?"

Mindy wasn't sure what to say to that. She looked around the entrance to the house she'd only been in a few times. "It looks like I remember in here."

"Yeah, kind of like your grandma's. It'll look a lot different when I'm done with it."

"You're going to completely change it?"

"Of course," he said folding his arms in front of him. "This is old lady chic, I'm not an old lady."

Mindy chewed her bottom lip. Was he saying that she was one since she hadn't changed a thing in her grandmother's house? Mindy was sure he didn't mean his comment as a jab against her *shrine*, as Ruby had called it. But it jabbed at her anyway.

"Where do you start?" she asked.

"I started in the bedroom. I figured I needed that space to be mine. I didn't have to do a lot. Some paint. New carpet. New doors on the closet. I took out her furniture and put in my own."

"Yeah, I guess if you brought home a date, they wouldn't want to see doilies on the tables," she said jokingly, but his face didn't register humor.

"I don't just bring home dates," he laughed, but it didn't have humor to it. "I'm not a bachelor pad kind of guy."

And why was he sharing that with her? What did it matter? Mindy wasn't even a dating kind of woman.

"How can you tear this out?" Ruby's voice came from the kitchen.

Vic grinned at Mindy and with a nod in the direction of where her friends were. He led Mindy through the door into the preserved seventies kitchen.

A smile lifted Mindy's cheeks as she looked around the clean, but dated room.

Avocado green everything and linoleum flooring filled Mindy with a warmth. It wasn't that she liked the colors, but there was a peace that filled her with nostalgia.

"I suppose I could charge admission and keep it as a museum," Vic teased as Ruby picked up a piece of plastic fruit from a basket on the counter.

"Dear God, even plastic fruit," she burst out with a laugh. "I'll give you three dollars and fifty cents for the tour."

Lisa shook her head, grinning at their friend. "You're a cheap skate. Something like this is worth a five."

They all laughed and then Vic pointed out all the amenities, including the bright orange phone that still hung from the wall. The cord to the handset stretched at least six feet or more.

"What does your mom think about you changing all of this?" Mindy asked as she followed her friends through Vic's house.

"She's behind it. She knows a thirty-year-old man is not going to live in a house like this in the state it's in. And anyone else who moved in would be changing it too."

"Well, it certainly is quaint," she said smiling up at him, because she found that he exuded that kind of response from her.

After they had toured the house they all headed back for the door.

"Thanks, man. This was an awesome tour," Ruby said as she slipped on her gloves. "I'll send Mindy back with my entrance fee."

Lisa pushed Ruby out the door and Tina followed.

"It was nice to see your mom. I guess I'll see you around, neighbor," Mindy zipped up her coat.

"Just in case you girls don't finish all those cookies on your counter, bachelors consider those a diet staple."

Mindy pressed her lips between her teeth. "I'm sure there will be leftovers. I'll make you a doggie bag."

He winked at her and suddenly she was ten again, and she wanted to lift up on her toes and kiss the boy in front of her. But that would be the worst mistake she could ever make.

"Thanks again for the tour."

"I'll have you all over when it's done."

"That would be nice," she said, forcing herself to walk out of the door, but not moving on until she turned and gave him a small wave.

Okay, so Victor Hayes lived next door now. Victor Hayes, who Mindy hadn't seen since he was a pre-teen. Victor Hayes whose kiss at ten-years-old held her for a very long time.

CHAPTER FOUR

BECAUSE THE BATTERIES IN MINDY'S GARAGE DOOR OPENER HAD died, and she hadn't made the trek to the store yet, she was scraping ice from her windshield as her car warmed on Wednesday morning. Sure, she could have opened the door from inside, but Tina had been on her phone when she'd gotten home talking about the new ultrasound they'd had that day. Tina wanted to have a gender reveal party, and she wanted Mindy to make revealing cupcakes for them.

That was a lot of pressure. Not the cupcakes, but to be the only person who knew what the gender of someone's baby was, well, that was a secret that Mindy wasn't sure she wanted to keep.

In the end, she forgot she'd parked her car in the driveway.

The crunching of snow under boots had her looking up and watching as Vic made his way toward her, an ice scraper in his hand.

"Good morning, neighbor," he called to her.

"Good morning."

She watched as he began to scrape the windows on the passenger side of the car.

"Why aren't you parked in the garage?" he asked.

"Batteries died in my opener, and I was on the phone with Tina, and got sidetracked to open the door from inside. So, here I am."

Vic scanned a look over her and grinned. "Why don't you let me do this and you sit in the warm car. You look like you're dressed for work, not a snow day."

"Oh, you don't have to…"

He held up a gloved hand and walked around the front of the car. "You brought me left over cookies from your movie night. I most certainly can do this." Moving past her, he pulled open her car door.

Mindy studied him. Over the past few days, she'd given a lot of thought to the boy she'd once known—the man, who now stood in the cold looking down at her.

Victor Hayes had always been a cute kid, and the handsome man he'd turned into hadn't gone unnoticed by her or her friends. But she remembered him riding his bike too fast, wading knee deep in the creek down the street and catching frogs, which she also remembered him taunting her with. There were worms dug up to put on fishing hooks, which were dangled in front of her too. The fact that he played house that one time and kissed her, well, that must have been a sympathy moment, because in the past few days, Mindy couldn't remember him being a soft and gentle kind of kid.

Obviously, that hadn't gone with him into adulthood. He stood next to her open door as she looked up at him. His mouth was in a half grin that made the breath that was carried on frozen air hitch.

"You're going to let all of the warmth out. I'll be done in just a minute and you're on your way," he said.

"Don't you need to get to work?" she asked.

"I work from home. The spare room is my office. It's next to get the makeover."

Mindy just nodded. "Thanks for your help."

"What kind of battery?"

Mindy blinked as she sat down in the driver's seat. "Battery?"

"For the opener."

"Oh, right. 9-volt."

Vic nodded. "I have one. When you get home I'll bring it over."

"You don't—"

"I'll watch for you," he said as he shut the door and continued to scrape her windows.

THE PAINT FOR THE OFFICE HAD BEEN DELIVERED AS WELL AS THE flooring. The green screen Vic used for video calls would soon be a thing of the past. But at the moment, he couldn't risk anyone seeing the gaudy wallpaper behind him that boasted roses in all different sizes.

He dressed for work, but admittedly, he wore slippers. No one, ever, would see his feet, so it didn't matter. And though shag carpet should feel good under one's feet, he couldn't stand the thought of walking on it. It had been the same carpet that had been there since the room was his mother's, and she stopped living in the house when she was nineteen.

Over the weekend, it would get a new floor. Thank goodness someone invented floors that could be snapped together and they looked amazing. Vic had considered real hardwood floors, but he just didn't want the upkeep, especially in such a dry climate.

Before his next Zoom meeting, Vic scanned his planner. He was still a paper planner kind of guy, even though everything was on his digital calendar that was synced between his phone, computer, iPad, and every other digital device he owned.

He opened his top right drawer to take out a colored highlighter to mark off a task on his planner, and there was the pack of 9-volt batteries. He plucked one of the batteries out of the pack and put it right under his computer screen. When he saw Mindy drive up to her house, he'd take it over to her.

Vic leaned back in his desk chair and rested his hands behind his head. He'd lived in the house for a month, and he was surprised that it had taken that long to finally even see Mindy, and he'd had to go to her door for that.

His mother had told him she'd lived next door, and for some reason, he still had pictured her as an awkward teenager, because that had been what she was the last time he'd seen her.

But, even that image brought a smile to his mouth.

Her hair had been pulled back into a ponytail the last time he'd seen her when they were kids. She'd had a mouth full of braces, and he'd never forget that she had a zit on her chin, because she'd been awkward about how she kept trying to cover it.

At the same time, she'd had her arms crossed in front of her as if she'd been hiding her breasts too. Then again, Curt and Brian had made mention of them, so she must have been self-conscious.

Their summers playing together had ended the year before. Suddenly she wasn't outside in the cul-de-sac drawing with chalk or riding her bike. If they saw her at all, she was on the porch with a book.

He wondered if she still read all the time.

Vic looked at his watch. He had a half hour until his next meeting. Picking up his phone, he walked to the kitchen for another cup of coffee. As it brewed, he rested his hip on the counter and scrolled Facebook on his phone. He typed in Mindy Baldwin, and smiled when she was the first of many listed.

He clicked on her profile, sad to find that it was very private, and not much popped up. Well, what did he have to lose? He clicked the friend request button, and laughed when less than a minute later it said she'd accepted his request. Was she sitting at her desk, or wherever she worked, watching Facebook?

His fingers itched to talk to her, so he opened the Messenger app and pulled up her name.

I hope you don't mind me friending you, he typed and waited for her reply as the coffee finished.

I don't mind. I don't post too many things, she replied.

I have the battery on my desk for you. I'll watch for you to drive up.

A full five minutes passed. It was enough time for Vic to watch his coffee finish brewing, and to carry the mug back to his office, and get situated before she replied.

That's very nice of you. And thanks for the help this morning. I might have been late if I'd had to do it all myself.

The sentiment seemed to warm him to the core. Vic liked that they were starting up a little friendship, because it would be nice to be friendly with the neighbor.

That warmth turned to heat and Vic laughed to himself. Initially he'd meant that thought to be a genuine thought of friendship. If he needed a cup of sugar, Mindy would lend it to him. If they were outside in the spring, they'd talk over the fence. But for some reason, it landed different in his chest than it had in his head. Mindy Baldwin had always been that memory in the back of his head that popped up once in a while. He'd often wondered what kind of woman she'd turned into. Wasn't it interesting that he'd have a chance to find out?

When his computer chimed, he realized he'd spent more time than necessary on that thought. It was time to get back to work. Home renovations didn't pay for themselves.

CHAPTER FIVE

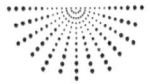

THERE WERE PERKS TO WORKING FROM HOME AND HAVING grateful clients that liked to do nice things for you.

When Mindy pulled into her driveway, Vic was still standing on his driveway after having received the dinner that his client had sent over.

When you ran an ad campaign that had brought in thousands of dollars in revenue in one night to a struggling restaurant, they not only paid your fee, but they sent dinner over too.

Vic waved at Mindy as she parked in the driveway and climbed carefully from her car.

"I have that battery for you," he called over.

"Thanks."

"Are you busy right now?"

He watched as her brows rose. "I just got home."

Deciding it was better to not yell across the yard, Vic walked toward her. "How was your day?"

"Fine," was all she said, and he wondered if she wasn't enjoying his friendly neighbor banter.

"I just need to take this in and I'll bring you that battery," he said.

"You ordered dinner? I thought you said your ancient appliances worked."

Okay, so she did have a sense of humor. "They do. This is a gift from a client."

"A client that's coming over to have dinner with you?" She scanned a look over the number of bags in his hands.

"No. No. They just don't know I live alone." Vic studied her for another moment, noting the line that had formed between her brows. "You don't have dinner plans do you?"

Her lips pursed. "Is that an assumption?"

"What? No," he stammered. *Shit!* "Sorry. I didn't mean it like that. Let me start over. If you don't have plans for dinner, I'd love to invite you to partake in this delightful meal with me."

The corner of her mouth turned up. "And what is it you're having for dinner?"

"It's Italian. I don't know what's in here. It's a feast that will last for days. But I know the restaurant, and it's good food."

Mindy stood there in the cold studying him. She was probably trying to decide if he was a maniac, a nuisance, or safe enough she could share a meal with him.

"It happens that I don't have dinner plans, other than a bowl of cereal or something."

Vic wrinkled his nose. "Seriously?"

She shrugged. "Just feels like that kind of night."

"So you'll eat with me?"

"Yeah."

"Awesome. Your outdated kitchen or mine?"

He saw her wince at that, but before he could apologize, she nodded toward his house. "Let me just go in and change and I'll be over."

Vic nodded. "I'll leave the door unlocked."

He watched until she went into her house, mostly wondering what her entire outfit looked like. She had on boots and a long skirt, but he'd only seen her with that big coat on.

Shaking off the thought, Vic went back into the house to set up dinner, leaving the door unlocked as promised.

MINDY WALKED INTO HER HOUSE, DROPPED HER BAG ON THE FLOOR, and leaned up against the door as she closed it. Was it going to be the norm now that Vic had knocked on her door, that he'd be lurking outside every time she turned around?

He was nice enough, and from what she remembered of him, he was a good guy. But she didn't need a good guy in her life. Good guys always had baggage too. At thirty, she was content with her life. She had a house, which was out of date according to everyone she knew. She had an amazing career and a newer model car. People were envious of her friendships, and her family dynamics weren't horrible. So, she had everything she needed, right?

Mindy let her head fall back to the door.

The last three guys she dated wanted to take things hella fast. Where was the written play book that demanded that on a second date they could feel you up and by the third you had to sleep with them?

It wasn't as if she were a prude, but seriously, her body wasn't a conquest. Sex was on the table when her heart was committed. And no one had quite fit that bill in years.

Maybe she should be a little more free with the sex. Maybe she wouldn't be so pent up and worrying about the next door neighbor if she'd had sex in the past two years.

Mindy let out a low growl. This is what happened when a man gave her even the hint of interest. As far as she knew, Vic was just a nice guy trying to rekindle a friendship from childhood. It was her overreacting that made her think he was out to get into her pants, or up her skirt.

God, he'd met her again after all these years standing in the doorway with a facial mask on and in her pajamas—oh, and that ugly sweater, which she'd take over with her so his mother could borrow it.

Dropping her coat to the floor, Mindy stomped off down the hall to change. A simple dinner invitation had turned her into a mess of a person. If she didn't correct her attitude, Vic wouldn't talk to her again, and funny enough, that wasn't what she wanted. She did want to talk to him again. She did like him being right there. She did want to be friendly with the neighbor—and he hadn't hinted to anything sexual.

Pulling her hair up with her hands, she walked to the bathroom and secured it in a band. Then she walked to her bedroom and changed out of her work clothes. She wasn't going to put on sweat pants, though that would be the go to, but she did slip into a faded pair of jeans and threw on a sweat shirt with Nashville written on it.

As she walked through the kitchen, she picked up a container of cookies from the counter, and because she was trained to consider it, she took a bottle of wine from her rack, which she knew would go well with Italian food. At the door, she set the items on the small table, shrugged on her coat, and put on her boots. Acknowledging that she was going into someone's home, she picked up her slippers too, so that she could change out of her boots when she got over there.

Deciding against her gloves, since she was just going next door, Mindy headed out for dinner with the neighbor.

When she got to Vic's house, she pushed open the door. It was unlocked just as he'd said it would be.

There was soft jazz playing, and she looked down at the bottle of wine in her hand and reconsidered the gesture. Maybe she'd just leave it by the door with her boots, she thought, but before she could commit, Vic appeared from the kitchen.

"You brought wine? That's better. I only had beer," he said taking the bottle from her.

"It pairs well with Italian," she suggested, but her voice was shaky.

"Did you bring more cookies too?"

Mindy nodded. "I bake—a lot."

He laughed and took the container from her hands. "Just so you know, I'm A-okay with you bringing over baked goods any time you need to unload them." He grinned at her and suddenly she was very aware of how warm the house was as she stood there with her heavy coat on.

"You can hang your coat up on the rack. Did you bring your slippers?"

"I didn't want to trek through your house in my boots."

"Huh, I wouldn't have considered it. This shag shit is going, and soon. I got new flooring today to put in the office."

"Nice," Mindy said as she shrugged out of her coat. "I'll still keep the mess of my boots by the door. I also brought this for your mother," she said, handing him the ugly sweater.

"For my mother?"

"She said she had an ugly sweater party coming up and was going to ask you to get it from me. I just thought I'd bring it by."

"She said that, huh?" he hummed as if he wasn't sure what to do with that.

Vic took the sweater and turned back to the kitchen. Mindy hung up her coat, slipped into her slippers, and followed him.

The kitchen table had been set, and he'd put the contents of the takeout containers into serving bowls.

"They sent pasta, meatballs, sausage, bread, and salad. There are three different pastas," he laughed. "Just know, I'm sending some of this home with you."

"Why?"

"I can't eat it all. And if I'm lucky, I'll have Mexican food this weekend."

Vic took down two glasses from the cupboard, rinsed them at

the sink, and then opened the bottle of wine with an ancient corkscrew that he'd pulled out of a drawer.

"Why do you get food?"

"Ad designer. If they're grateful, they send bonuses."

"Food bonuses?"

"Most of the time. Sometimes it's sporting event tickets, or dinner gift certificates. But, during the pandemic, restaurants started sending food. They just keep doing it, and I eat well." He poured the wine and handed her a glass. "And now that I know you're alone next door too, I'll be calling to have you help me with my bonuses."

Mindy took the wine and sipped. She certainly hadn't anticipated spending more time with the next door neighbor, but for a woman on a budget, free food was intriguing.

CHAPTER SIX

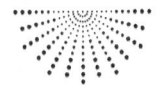

WITH HER HANDS ON HER BELLY, MINDY SAT BACK IN HER CHAIR. "I don't know when I've eaten so much," she groaned and Vic smiled. Had she noticed that dimple in his cheek before?

"You had a salad and one scoop of spaghetti. How are you full?"

"You expect me to eat more?"

"I'm just saying. We have food for three days."

Mindy lifted the napkin from her lap, wiped her mouth, and set it on the table. "Then I guess I'll take a container for lunch tomorrow," she teased.

"You'll take more than one container. When do you get off work?"

Mindy picked up her glass of wine. "Why?"

Vic's brows rose. "Because we're having Italian for dinner tomorrow too," he said as he picked up the pasta bowl and carried it to the counter.

"You don't have to have me over two nights in a row," she said, picking up the salad and following him to the counter where he pulled containers from the cupboard to store the food.

"I would love to have you over two nights in a row. I mean, we sat at the table and only talked about our grandmothers. We have twenty missing years to catch up on."

She was staring at him when he turned and looked at her. He smiled, and she dropped her eyes to the salad she held.

"Do you have one of those containers for the salad?" she asked, trying to keep her eyes averted.

Vic handed her one, and a lid. "I guess I should ask, would you please come to dinner tomorrow?"

Mindy chewed her bottom lip. "Sure, but can I pay you for dinner or something?"

"Are you kidding me? This is just bonus on bonus. Free food and conversation. Besides, you brought wine."

Mindy put the salad in the container and fastened the lid. "I'd understand if you wanted to have dinner with other friends too."

Vic leaned his hip against the counter, crossed his arms, and studied her. "Are you not enjoying my company?"

He was smiling, surely he didn't think she wasn't, did he? "Oh, I enjoy it. I just—"

His hand reached to a curl that had escaped from her ponytail, and he tucked it behind her ear. "I'm kidding. Please come over and have dinner with me. No strings attached."

Mindy swallowed hard. "Okay."

"We'll have an agenda too. Come prepared to talk about what you've done between the time you were thirteen and now. I want to know all about your job. And then, this weekend, over Mexican food, you can tell me about your friends and your movie club."

Finally a smile tugged at her cheeks. "You've lived over here a month, and I've never seen you. Now I've seen you multiple times, and you're making plans?"

"I haven't been out of the house much the past month. I mean, yeah, I go out, but I don't have too many people in. I don't want them to see that sea green tile in the bathroom."

Mindy laughed. "I like the mermaid theme."

"What color is your bathroom?"

She wrinkled her nose. "Bright yellow."

"Tub too?"

"Tub, toilet, sink, backsplash, and even though I bought the shower mat, it matches too."

Vic shook his head. "If you like what I do over here, and you ever want to go modern, you let me know. I'll help."

"I haven't been able to let go that much, yet." She thought about Ruby calling her house a shrine, and now she wondered if it was.

"I'm not being forward, but I want to show you my bedroom."

Instantly her cheeks went hot. "O-kay," she drew out the word and followed him from the kitchen, down the hallway to his bedroom.

Mindy stood at the door and Vic flicked on the light.

It was masculine in dark grays and deep blues. The furniture probably came from IKEA, it certainly wasn't the heavy antique stuff she'd kept in her house.

"This looks really nice," Mindy said, making sure she didn't cross the threshold.

Vic kicked back the throw at his feet, exposing the unmatched flooring where the new floor met shag carpet in the hallway. "I'm doing each room separate, so I have to leave parts undone until I can tie it together."

"That makes sense."

"I'll show you my next project," he said, turning off the bedroom light and opening the door next to them.

Mindy couldn't help but laugh out loud when he turned on the light. "Oh, wow." This room she stepped into. "Is this your office?"

"Yes, hence the green screen."

"I'm sure your colleagues would love to see this wallpaper."

"Hell no."

"And shag carpet? Tell me you're documenting all of your remodeling."

Vic pulled his phone from his pocket and scrolled through his pictures. "Here." He handed her his phone.

"I'm okay to scroll?"

"Any which direction you'd like," he said, and that had her looking up at him.

Really? A man that would just hand over his phone and say something like that?

Mindy scrolled through the pictures of Vic's house. His bedroom was the only room he'd finished so far, but he'd obviously done a lot of decluttering.

"In the month that you've been here, I didn't see you carrying out most of this stuff," she admitted.

"Because most of it's in the garage. I'm waiting for spring to get the roll-off."

"That makes sense."

She scrolled through the pictures and stopped when they were no longer about the house, but a blonde smiling up at her that made her hands shake.

"Oops, I think I went too far." Mindy handed him back the phone.

Vic looked down at the screen, smiled, and tucked his phone back into his pocket.

"I'll start on the office this weekend. I suppose if you're wanting to pay me back for the food, you could drop by and help me tear out this carpet."

Mindy wrinkled her nose. "I have to make cupcakes on Saturday."

Vic laughed. "You have to?"

"Tina's gender reveal is on Sunday."

He nodded. "And what is she having?"

Shaking her head, Mindy held up a finger. "I'm not even telling you."

"As if I'll tell anyone."

"I'll bring you a cupcake."

Vic leaned back against the wall, crossing his feet at the ankles and his arms in front of him. "I guess I'll wait to find out then. But when you're done with baking cupcakes will you come over?"

After seeing the reaction he had to the blonde on his phone, Mindy wasn't sure that was the best idea. "I'm not very handy."

"I doubt that."

"Are you sure no one is going to get upset that I'm here?"

His brows drew in. "Who would be upset?"

"I don't know, a girlfriend, a non-girlfriend?"

His eyes narrowed and then a grin curled up the corners of his mouth as if he understood what she was asking. "No one in the whole world will care that you're here."

"I'll let you know then." Mindy nervously tucked her hands into her pockets. "I should be getting home."

"Wait," he said as he walked to his desk and picked up the battery. "This is for you." He handed it to Mindy.

"I really appreciate this."

"We can't have you out in the cold each morning scraping off your window."

"Thanks for dinner."

"What time works for tomorrow?"

"Oh, you know, I have a late meeting. Maybe I should—" Vic inched closer, and again moved the curl, which he'd earlier tucked behind her ear, back into place.

"I think you shouldn't make excuses. I work from home on my own hours. So I can wait for you all night."

Okay, so she wasn't going to be able to talk her way out of leftovers. "I can message you."

"Do you have your phone in your pocket?"

"Yes."

"Open it to your contacts," he said.

Mindy took out her phone and opened it to the contacts, then she handed it to him. He used his thumbs to type into the phone. A moment later, he held it up in front of himself and took a picture.

Mindy laughed. "Did you just add a photo to the contact?"

"Of course. Maybe you have a lot of Vics in your list."

"You'll be the first," she said, still laughing.

Vic handed her phone back. "Now text me."

Mindy opened a message and typed. *I'll text you when I leave work tomorrow, and I'll have dinner with you.*

When his phone dinged, he smiled down at the message. "Perfect," he said, saving her contact information. Then he lifted his phone and Mindy covered her face.

"Oh, no. Not tonight," she said turning and walking back toward the kitchen.

"How am I supposed to know which Mindy it is that's texting me?"

"Put a picture of the wallpaper up," she said as she headed to the door.

"I could do that. Maybe the shag carpet?"

Mindy pulled on her coat, slipped off her slippers, and put on her boots. "I appreciate dinner," she said as she reached for the doorknob, suddenly feeling the need to get out of his space because there was a lot going on inside of her.

"Don't forget to text me on your way home tomorrow."

She nodded and walked out, heading back home carefully over the frozen ground. She certainly couldn't afford to fall on her ass in front of him now.

CHAPTER SEVEN

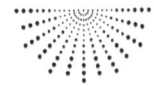

THE BOOK WAS GROWING HEAVY IN VIC'S HANDS AS HE LAID IN BED. Closing it, he set it on the nightstand and turned off the light when his phone buzzed.

Turning back on the light, Vic picked up his phone and smiled down at the text.

I thought you'd like to see my mess, Mindy's message read, and then was followed by a picture of her yellow bathroom, and another specifically of her bright yellow sink and tiles. She stood facing the mirror with the phone in front of her face to obscure it. Then again, since she was only in a tank top and a pair of shorts, maybe she wasn't aware she'd put herself in the picture at all.

I have a sledge hammer when you're ready to take on that project, Vic responded.

When she didn't reply right away, he wondered if he'd overstepped that line between funny and insensitive. Was he supposed to at least reply with goodnight or something?

Just as he started to text back, another text came through. This time it was a picture of a modern bathroom with a glass bowl sink, open shower layout, a wood plank wall and gray tile on the floor.

What do you think? her text read.

I like it! he replied, studying the photo. *It means taking out the yellow tub.*

She sent a rubber duck meme, and that had him laughing. *This is what that tub makes me think of.*

He touched the picture as if it made him nearer to her. *I'd have to agree. I've got a guy that gets me good deals on remodeling supplies. I can get you a quote whenever you're ready.*

I'll let you know, she added. *I'll be over around six-thirty tomorrow, does that work?*

And she'd changed the subject and committed to dinner. *That would be perfect. I'll see you then.*

IT WAS NEARLY SEVEN WHEN THE DOORBELL FINALLY RANG, AND VIC walked to the door with a full glass of wine in his hand.

"I'm so sorry I'm late. If you have other plans, I'd understand, and—"

Vic cut her off by reaching for her hand and pulling her into the house as the snow flew outside. "You are fine," he said. "Everything okay?"

She brushed the snow off her coat and looked up at him, her cheeks bright red. "My car got stuck. It took me twenty minutes to get it to move," she said, and he was sure there were tears in her eyes. "I came right over. I told you I'd be here at six-thirty, and you've been waiting."

Vic set the glass of wine on the entry table and pulled Mindy to him. Snow from her jacket melted into his shirt, but it didn't matter.

Her rigid body softened in his arms, and he thought he might have given her that peace she needed.

"I'm sorry your drive was bad. You're safe? Your car is okay?" he asked, pressing his cheek to her wet hair.

"Yes," she whispered against him. "It's just been a very long day, and then the snow…"

"Well, you're home and warm. I have the fireplace going. We can eat in the family room in front of the fire."

He felt her draw in a few deep breaths before she eased back. "I should go home and change. I can be back in—"

"I have things you can wear. Stay here and get warm," he said wiping her wet bangs from her face. "And don't ask me why, but I have some hair ties you could use too."

Mindy laughed and it caused a small flutter in his chest. "You say not to ask, and that only makes me want to."

"I'll show you pictures someday when I'm feeling like being exposed," he said. "Take your coat and boots off. I'll go get you some clothes and put them in the bathroom."

MINDY TOOK OFF HER COAT AND HUNG IT UP. THEN SHE TOED OFF her boots, making sure they were left on the small carpet by the door so they wouldn't leave a puddle.

With her arms wrapped around herself to keep warm, she walked toward the bathroom, where Vic was setting clothes on the counter.

"There's a brush in the drawer and the hair ties," he said.

"You have leftovers from other women?" she asked, raising a brow.

The corner of his mouth lifted. "I said don't ask questions."

"I can't help it. It's kind of an intimate item."

"You think so?"

She shrugged. "I'd say if you had extra tampons under the sink, that's exactly what it is."

She watched as the tips of his ears grew red. "There are no tampons in this house," he confirmed.

"Then expect me to ask more questions about the hair ties."

Vic shook his head. "I'll warm up dinner. Take your time. If you need a towel for your hair, you can use the ones that are hanging up. They're freshly laundered."

"Did you clean house just because I was coming over?"

He leaned up against the doorjamb, and shook his head again. "My mother dropped by. But she gave me a thirty minute head start. So, the house got a quick clean."

That caused Mindy to laugh. "I do the same thing."

He stood just a moment longer before giving her a smile, flashing that dimple in his cheek, and walking away.

Mindy closed the bathroom door and then winced when she turned to the mirror and saw what she looked like. Her hair was wet and pieces stuck to her face. The makeup she'd put on that morning was gone, and black smudges darkened her eyes.

So much for looking nice for an attractive man. Well, she wasn't looking to date the man, and it was probably better. If he still considered her the girl from the neighborhood, they'd both be better off.

Opening the drawer in the bathroom, she found the brush and a small container of hair ties. They all looked new, and there wasn't hair attached to any of them, so perhaps they hadn't been left from random women who stopped by.

Mindy brushed her hair out and knotted it on top of her head, securing it with the tie. She reached toward the door to make sure she'd secured the lock, and then stripped out of her clothes. She folded them neatly and left them on the bathtub. They certainly wouldn't dry all folded up, but they wouldn't make a mess anywhere else either.

The pile of clothes Vic had left for her consisted of a pair of gray sweatpants, which would need to be rolled up at the legs and rolled down at the waist. And to accent it, a bright green CSU sweatshirt.

When she was dressed, she took a tissue from the box on the

counter, and scrubbed at the black smudges under her eyes. After she'd fought it enough, she sighed, and decided she'd done all she could do to be presentable.

Stepping out of the bathroom, Mindy could smell something cooking. It wasn't the leftovers, there was something else.

"Are you baking bread?" she asked as she walked into the kitchen.

When Vic looked up at her, he smiled wide. "You look cute."

"Cute?"

"Yeah, cute," he confirmed as he handed her a glass of wine. "And yes, I'm making bread. I bought a loaf from the store that you just pop in the oven. I'm no cook."

"So the ancient oven works."

"I told you," he laughed, and held out his glass of wine toward hers. "Here's to the end of the day."

"I could drink to that," Mindy said before she sipped her wine.

"So what do you do?" Vic asked as he leaned up against the counter.

She held up the glass of wine. "I'm a wine buyer for a beverage company."

Vic's brows rose. "Seriously?"

"Yep."

"That sounds amazing. Are you deep in wine samples?"

Mindy took another sip of her wine, watching him over the rim of her glass. "I have a nice selection," she admitted. "And what do you do? You said something about ads and restaurants."

Vic smiled from behind his glass as he sipped. "That about sums it up. I'm an independent ad agency."

"Independent ad agency. As in it's just you."

"Yep. I work in the room with the roses on the wall and create ad campaigns for local restaurants, some chains, a few salons, law offices, and really anyone who will pay me."

"Now that sounds amazing and creative. Lisa has a YouTube

channel, and is a food blogger. That's how she makes a living. I'm not as creative."

"You're making gender reveal cupcakes."

Mindy shrugged. "I guess that's my creative outlet."

"Your cookies are divine."

Mindy tucked her lips between her teeth so that she wouldn't smile, because she could already feel the heat creep up her neck when he'd said that.

The timer on the oven chimed and Vic put his wine down on the counter. Mindy watched as he picked up oven mitts, opened the door to the oven, and pulled out the loaf of bread.

As she sipped her wine, Mindy realized just how comfortable she was in his presence, in his clothes, in his kitchen, and that made her a little uncomfortable.

CHAPTER EIGHT

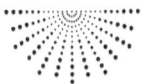

THEY EACH BALANCED A PLATE OF PASTA ON THEIR LAPS, THEIR FEET kicked up on the coffee table, which was something Vic had brought with him. If it had been his grandmother's he wouldn't have dared to put his feet up on it.

"What should we watch? There's a hockey game on. Every different version of NCIS. And a handful of movies," he said, surfing through the channels.

"You pay for the big channel package, huh?"

Vic shrugged. "When you work from home, you can get a little lonely. When I'm creating, I have the TV on. Usually for background noise."

"Lisa says the same thing. Before Ryan came along, I know Tina, Ruby, and I would make sure to get her out of the house once a day. If she ever caught on, she never said a word."

He laughed. "I think that's why my mom calls me as often as she does. But doing the renovation helps keep my mind occupied too. And I go out with friends a few times a week. You know trivia night at the bar. Bowling on Sunday nights."

Mindy turned her head and smiled at him. "You bowl on Sunday nights?"

"Yeah. Does that make me seem old? I thought it seemed like an old man thing until I started doing it with some buddies. It's fun."

"No judgement. I love to bowl."

Vic nodded slowly. "What does your work week look like?"

"Tuesday through Friday, with the occasional Saturday thrown in there."

Twirling noodles around his fork, he considered his upcoming week. "Lunchtime at the bowling alley off the highway on Monday? I have a coupon," he said with a wink and enjoyed watching Mindy's eyes go wide.

"Oh, I'm sure you have other people who—"

Vic puckered his lips. "Do you not want to spend time with me? Whenever I ask you if you want to do something, you think I should ask someone else."

Her face went sullen. "I just assume…" she stopped, worried her lip, and then looked back up at him. "I'd love to go."

He couldn't help but smile at that. "Are you sure?"

"Let's call it a personality flaw, if you will. I'm a rule follower to a fault. I blush when someone is suggestive or curses, which is usually Ruby." That made him laugh, because in the few moments he'd been around Ruby, she was straight forward. "And I usually assume someone is only asking to spend time with me out of pity or desperation."

Vic considered her. "This is good information to have. For the record, I'm kind of a rule follower too. Walk the line. Be nice to others. Keep your word." He lifted his fork to his lips and then set it back on his plate. "Ruby's personality is refreshing, if I dare say so, and I've always liked spending time with you. It's not out of pity or desperation that I've asked you to share dinner or go bowling with me. You're a good memory to me, and I'm glad we can make more of them now that we're neighbors."

Mindy blinked a few times and Vic took the bite he'd been

balancing on his fork. She finally smiled, and he assumed that was a good sign.

Mindy looked back down at her plate, took a bite, and then focused on the TV when Vic began to scroll through the channels again. He noticed she perked up when he came to *That Thing You Do!* so he stopped scrolling.

"A favorite?" Vic asked, amused by her sudden change of expression.

"Totally. You've seen it?" she asked and Vic shook his head. "Are you kidding me?"

Laughing, Vic picked up his wine and took a sip. "I'm a sports guy, not a movie guy."

"Oh, well, you don't have to watch this now, but I recommend it. Anything with Tom Hanks is gold, but he wrote this one. So it's double gold."

"No kidding? He wrote it?"

"Yep. His wife plays a cocktail waitress in it. It's about a band that signs a recording contract. Anyway, it's awesome."

"One of your rom coms?"

"Are you teasing me?"

"Nope, you just mentioned that you all meet once a month to watch rom coms. I just wondered."

Mindy puckered her lips, but the smile broke through anyway. "Tom Hanks is the rom com king."

"Is he now?" Vic took another drink and chased it with a bite of bread. "And who is queen?"

"The answer should be Meg Ryan, because they go hand in hand. Hanks and Ryan, ya know?" she asked but Vic only shrugged. "Anyway, I really think the queen is Sandra Bullock. I mean, she's romance gold. Even in her serious roles, there's romance. But she can play hard ass, she can play sweet and innocent, and she can just be the bitch in charge."

Vic wanted to scoop Mindy up and plant a wild kiss on her after that. Everything she'd just said must have been Rubyinfluenced, because when Mindy got passionate about the movies and the actors she was talking about, there was a whole new side to her. Would he see that come out when they bowled? Was this some hidden competitive nature?

"Favorite Bullock movie?" Vic asked.

Mindy blew out a breath and her eyes darted back and forth as if she were mentally calculating which one would be the winner.

"*While You Were Sleeping* is legendary. *The Proposal* is hands down amazing. But I think, and don't tell my friends this, but I think *The Blind Side* is my favorite of her movies."

"*The Blind Side*? That's a football movie."

"I know. But I love that character. I love everything about her."

"That character is a real person."

"Which Sandra Bullock does very well."

"Agreed," Vic said. "*The Blind Side*," he repeated, "I'll give you that one."

Mindy picked up her wine and took a sip. "Okay, let's be totally honest."

"It's the only way to be," he teased.

"The movie is great."

"It is."

"And she was brilliant."

"Indeed."

Mindy grinned wide behind her glass. "But Tim McGraw, oh-my-God, I could watch that man all day long."

He didn't mean to laugh as hard as he did, but he couldn't help it. And the harder Vic laughed, then the harder Mindy laughed, until they both had to put down their food and drink before it spilled.

When they thought they were under control, taking those deep breaths that were supposed to stifle the laughter, one of them would look at the other and it would start again.

"So I should have rephrased it?" Vic asked, still trying to catch his breath. "Which Tim McGraw movie was your favorite?"

Mindy fanned her eyes which had begun to tear. "Swoon," she said on another laugh. "If only I could be so lucky as to have a man like him."

The laughter in Vic died down, and for some reason the seriousness of the conversation pulled at him now. "What about him? You mean the character? The real man?"

Mindy's laughter died down too, until she was staring at him. "Oh, well, I don't know really. The character was just supportive, which made Tim McGraw even more hella sexy." She thought for a moment. "But as the super star musician he is in real life, I guess I don't know much about him."

Vic nodded. "So maybe you mean a supportive man—that's what you want in your life?"

She was somber now as she looked into his eyes, and he felt a comfort between them. "Yeah, I guess that's what I mean."

"You've never had a man like that?"

Mindy licked her lips and then pressed them together. "No."

Her answer was firm, and Vic didn't like it. His mind went back to the girl he'd known all those years ago. The girl he'd kissed in that tree house. They were thirty now, and she sat on his couch confiding in him that she'd never had a supportive man in her life—as a partner that was.

Because it was how he was wired, he wondered how he could be that person to her, even as a friend and next-door neighbor. Obviously learning the little things like what a draw Tim McGraw was in a movie, helped Vic be more supportive.

"I have more bread if you want some," Vic changed the subject.

Mindy shook her head. "I really should be getting home before it gets too late."

What did it mean, that he really didn't want her to go?

"Right. I'm glad you don't have far to drive."

She laughed as she stood with her plate in her hand.

"I'll take that," he said reaching for the plate but she pulled it back.

"The least I can do for another night of free dinner is put my dish in the dishwasher."

Vic wrinkled up his nose. "That's the only ancient appliance that doesn't work," he admitted.

"Then I'll wash my plate."

Vic shook his head. "You'll do no such thing. Like I said, if you want to pay me back for dinner, you can help me pull up that carpet."

Mindy shook her head and grinned at him. "I still have to make cupcakes for Tina, but what time do you want me here on Saturday to start?"

CHAPTER NINE

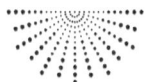

Cupcakes were baked and cooling by seven o'clock Saturday morning. She would wait until tomorrow morning to pipe in the gender revealing color. And because she couldn't get her mind to settle, she baked cinnamon rolls next. Again, she couldn't just show up at Vic's house without something in hand.

Are you okay? The text from Lisa read when Mindy picked up her phone off the counter after it had buzzed.

Was that a cryptic message? *Yes*, she replied. *Why?*

I just haven't heard from you in a few days.

Mindy blew out a breath as she leaned against the counter. Was it possible she'd been more preoccupied than she'd thought? *I guess I've been busy. I'll see you tomorrow though.*

She thought it was funny that Lisa of all people was the one that had been missing her. The newlyweds didn't get out of the house much, and who would blame them? It was supposed to be a hot and sexy time for them, wasn't it?

How was Mindy supposed to know? She'd never had a relationship like that.

Have you talked to the guy next door again? Lisa asked, and Mindy laughed.

Maybe this wasn't a text of concern at all. This was an investigation.

Maybe.

Lisa then sent the smiling face emoji with the raised eyebrow. *Details?*

Mindy shook her head. What kind of details was she supposed to give? The kind that said, no big deal, or the kind that said I had dinner with him two nights in a row and wore his clothes home—even though that wasn't quite how it would come across if she texted that to Lisa.

I had dinner with him because one of his clients sent over a ton of food, and he had a battery for my garage door opener.

Those three little dots appeared and then disappeared before Lisa's next text came through. *Ryan says that's a ploy from the neighbor to get you into bed.*

Mindy felt that hit her right in the stomach and make her sick. She didn't feel that way at all, but now it was going to be on her mind when she showed up with cinnamon rolls and his laundry folded neatly in a pile for her to return.

Maybe that was how Ryan worked. I don't think that's the case here. We're just old acquaintances getting to know one another, again. Yeah, that was it.

This has a Breakfast at Tiffany's vibe, Lisa typed and added the two champagne glasses emoji.

I'm no socialite. Heck, if she didn't have her friends, Mindy figured, she'd have no life at all.

No, but you're Audrey Hepburn cute AF, and the neighbor is a looker.

Mindy shook her head as she read the text. The compliment from her dear friend made her smile, and her assessment of the neighbor was spot on, but Mindy wasn't going to read anything into it. They were just two homebodies sharing some space in old lady chic houses. And that thought made her laugh.

I'll see you tomorrow, Mindy typed. *Cupcake announcements are almost done.*

Lisa sent a blue heart and then a pink heart with a question mark.

Mindy laughed. *I'm not telling anyone. ANYONE!*

Then Lisa sent the smiling face emoji with the tongue sticking out. *I still love you.*

I love you too, Mindy replied and set her phone back on the counter.

She finished the cinnamon rolls, put the cupcakes in a container to keep them covered, and decided she'd killed enough time. Picking up everything she had to take over to Vic's, she headed out the door before eight-thirty.

WITH HIS EYES CLOSED, VIC RESTED HIS HANDS FLAT ON THE counter and listened to the coffee maker whir. The creative mind was never at rest, and he'd worked until two o'clock in the morning on an ad campaign for a new resort that was going in near Castle Rock.

The hotel had some amazing, themed suites, and it had spurred him into creating, what he considered, one of his best campaigns ever.

He'd present it to them on Wednesday. So until then, he'd stew over it and perfect it.

When the coffee finished its noise, he opened his eyes, and pulled the pot from the maker and filled his cup. The knock at the door startled him enough, he jerked back, and hot coffee splashed out onto his bare chest and dripped on his bare feet.

"Who in the hell?" he muttered to himself and then looked at the clock. Eight-thirty in the morning and someone was knocking at his door? He put the coffee pot back on the burner.

There wasn't time to put on clothes. He had to know who

thought their political campaign was so important, or their roofing company was so amazing, or...

He pulled open the door with a curse and his breath caught when it was Mindy standing on his porch, her arms loaded down with items, and a travel mug of coffee, he assumed, in her hand.

Her wide eyes scanned a look over him, no doubt taking in the mess he was. He hadn't looked at himself in the mirror, and hadn't even made it to the bathroom yet because coffee was that important.

No doubt his hair was on end, he hadn't shaved in two days, and his teeth hadn't yet been brushed. Never mind that he was standing in front of her in a pair of loose shorts, and yeah, it was morning—her eyes had caught that little detail he thought when her cheeks flushed red.

"I'm too early. I'm so sorry. I was up. I made the cupcakes. I brought cinnamon rolls. I'll leave them. You could eat them when you're ready," she spewed out the words and handed him the container and his clothes. "I washed the clothes. I hope you're not allergic to the soap. I didn't use softener. I didn't want to ruin them or anything. Thanks for the loan. Just let me know when you're—"

"Shhhh," Vic said and her eyes went wide again. "I just forgot it was Saturday."

"Oh. But seriously I can come back."

He shook his head, stepped back from the door, and nodded for her to enter.

"You really made cinnamon rolls this morning?" he asked, looking at the Tupperware container in his hand.

"Yes. I had to make the cupcakes for tomorrow so—"

"And you did that all this morning?"

She nodded. "I couldn't sleep."

That made him laugh. "I couldn't either. I was up all night creating a campaign for a new lodge."

"That sounds exciting."

"Let's get settled, and I'll show you."

He watched her shrug out of her heavy coat, and slip off her boots. She was dressed in a pair of overalls that had seen a few paint jobs, he noted. With her hair pulled up on top of her head, he realized he wasn't immune to her absolute cuteness.

Vic walked to the kitchen and set the tray of cinnamon rolls on the counter. He told Mindy where to find anything she needed, and then excused himself for a few minutes.

Considering she'd come over to help him demo a room, he didn't see any reason to actually shower, but he brushed his teeth, and ran his fingers through his hair enough that he at least didn't look as if he'd only just rolled out of bed, as he had. He wiped himself down with a washcloth and added some deodorant and cologne. Who knew the girl next door could make him so self-conscious.

Vic slipped on a pair of jeans and a T-shirt. Still barefooted, he padded back out to the kitchen where Mindy sat at his kitchen table, a cinnamon roll in her hand, and looking over his scribblings from the night before.

When he picked up the coffee pot, her head lifted.

"I hope you don't mind I was looking at these. Is this your creative process?"

Vic nodded filling a cup, and finally took a sip of his coffee, unsure where he'd put his other cup.

"I admire this," Mindy said. "Seriously, all I can do is bake. I just don't have this same creative mind."

"You used to," he said as he picked up a cinnamon roll, skirted the island, and leaned against it on the other side. He watched her look up at him with a confused glance, and he smiled. Oh, he'd remembered those dark eyes from so long ago. He was rather surprised to have them looking up at him in his own kitchen.

"I don't remember ever being creative."

Vic bit into the cinnamon roll and his mind was drawn into the flavor. "Did you make this from scratch?"

"Yes."

"And you don't think you're creative?" he asked with his mouth full. "Betty Crocker has nothing on you."

The corners of her mouth curled up. "I appreciate that." Mindy pulled a piece from her roll and popped it into her mouth. "Now, what do you mean I used to be creative?"

Vic licked the icing from his fingers and carefully carried his coffee and the rest of his cinnamon roll to the table, sitting in the chair next to Mindy. Their knees brushed as he adjusted, and he wondered if that little connection sparked in her too.

"I remember a girl who would organize games and play scenarios. I think I was privy to more than one Baldwin sisters play, the driveway was always covered in chalk drawings, and I think it was that creativity that landed me that kiss."

He watched her throat work as she swallowed.

"You don't think I contrived that, do you?" she asked. "That was just childhood."

Vic shook his head. "That was creative, and I'm having a bit of a foodgasm here, so I'm going to hold firm on the creative statement."

CHAPTER TEN

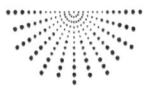

AFTER ANOTHER CINNAMON ROLL AND ANOTHER CUP OF COFFEE, Vic felt human again as they emptied out the office in order to prep for demolition.

"Why is it an empty room looks grungy?" He stood in the center of the room turning in a slow circle.

"I don't have an answer for you, but I think it's worse than it was with your office in here."

"Most definitely." Vic shoved his hands in the front pockets of his jeans. "My mom knows I'm doing this room, but I wonder what her reaction will be."

"Why is that?"

"It was her room when she was young. She picked out the rose paper and the carpet."

Mindy wrinkled her nose, and he found that endearing. If she didn't like the rose pattern, then why hadn't she updated any part of her house?

"You know, I didn't set the profile for your contact as the rose like you said I should."

She turned her head to look up at him, her brows drawn inward. "What did you use?"

"I was going to use that picture of you in a tank top, but—"

"My what?"

"I assume what you wore to bed."

"How did you see that?"

Vic pursed his lips to keep in his smile. "You sent me the picture of the sink in your yellow bathroom. You're in the mirror."

Her cheeks went red hot. "Oh, God. I didn't send that to you did I?"

Now he smiled. "Um, yes, you did."

"Erase it off your phone."

"I will not. It's my picture, and it's a nice picture, though I like your face too and that was obscured by the phone in front of you."

"I'm not kidding, Vic. Take it off your phone."

Now he remembered that young girl from next door to his grandmother. He'd seen that face before, and he'd heard his name used in that way. Usually it had been saved for when he dangled a worm in front of her, or tried to get her to touch a frog.

"I'm tempted to ask you to make me," he said grinning at her, but she didn't look amused at all.

Instead of fists flying his way, or fingernails raking across his skin, which he suddenly remembered happening once, Mindy turned and walked out of the room.

"Hey," he called after her, but she didn't come back at him.

Well shit! What choice did he have now but to go after her.

She was at the front door pulling on her boots when he got to her.

"Where are you going?" he asked.

"Home."

"Mindy, I didn't mean—"

"To what? Objectify me?"

"What?"

"Men are all alike. They get you comfortable and then they think that they can do or say what they want."

Vic wasn't sure what he'd done to fall into that general pile, minus teasing about not erasing the picture.

He reached for her arm, and when she turned, he pulled back so she wouldn't think he was manhandling her.

"I'll erase it. I was kidding. And I'm not trying anything on you. I like your company, and it's nice that we have a little history." Vic ran his fingers through his hair, and then clasped his hands behind his head as if to hold himself together before he let them drop to his side. "Mindy, I don't want to make you uncomfortable, and I haven't been asking you over to get my way with you. Seriously, I like your company."

Her lips twitched, and he wondered if she was going to cry. He hadn't meant to make her do that.

"Erase it."

Vic took his phone from his pocket, turned it so she could see the picture, and hit the erase button.

"Now erase it from the folder that says erased photos."

Vic nodded, scrolled to the folder in question, and erased it there too.

"There. It's gone. Can we forget this?"

She batted her eyes, but her breathing seemed to have returned to normal. "I'm sorry I flew off the handle at you. I just don't want you to think that because when we were ten and we kissed, that you can just have your way with me. I'm not looking for anything from you."

"I get it." Boy did he get it.

"I enjoy your company too, and we have that common bond between our grandmothers and living in outdated houses."

That brought a smile to Vic's lips, though he tried to control how wide it grew. "Right."

"Not that I don't find you attractive, because I do, but I'm not comfortable in relationships, or in casual sexual situations."

Now he bit down on his lip as she continued talking.

"I mean, I'm no prude," she said. "But I didn't mean to send you something suggestive and give you any ideas."

Vic reached for her hand. "If it's any consolation, I loved seeing your bathroom. In one short week, I've come to love getting your texts, and having you share meals with me. I wouldn't do anything to jeopardize that."

She didn't pull from him, and he took that as a win.

"Stay and help me. Please. Besides, I have a Mexican feast being delivered for dinner."

Mindy looked at where his hand still held hers. Her gaze moved from his hand to his face, landing on his mouth, before shifting to his eyes.

"Do you like wine?" she asked.

"I do."

"Okay, we'll celebrate getting that hideous room started," she smiled. "I'll choose us a good wine for when the food gets here."

Vic ran his thumb over her knuckles, wondering if he was the only one who felt something when they touched. It wasn't worth bringing up, especially after her little speech.

"That sounds like a plan. Let's go tear up that shag and rip down those roses."

FIVE HOURS LATER, AND A FEW TYLENOL FOR THEIR ACHING BACKS, Mindy stood in the middle of the bare room with her hands in the pockets of her overalls.

"We're going to have to repair that wall," she pointed to where the drywall was damaged from the wallpaper.

"Yeah, I noticed that. I'll want to do that before we put down the flooring." Vic ran his hand over the back of his neck. "I'll have to learn how to do that."

Mindy turned to him. "Where are you going to work from?"

"I guess the kitchen table." He blew out a breath. "I made a much bigger mess than I expected to."

"We can eat dinner at my house tonight," she reached for his hand and gave it a squeeze when he tucked it into hers. "I'm sure there is an entire YouTube channel dedicated to fixing walls."

Vic laughed, as he linked his fingers through hers, and it sent warmth surging through her. "That's how I learned to do most of the fixes I've made."

"And I sometimes watch Lisa's channel to make dinner," Mindy laughed. "I can't help tomorrow. I have Tina's gender reveal."

He nodded. "That's okay. I should focus on my presentation and setting up a place to work for the week."

Mindy jumped when her phone buzzed in her pocket. Vic let go of her hand as she pulled her phone out.

Dinner? I'm thinking Chinese. I'm starving for some sweet and sour chicken, Ruby's text read.

Mindy winced. *I have dinner plans. I'll have to take a rain check.*

YOU have dinner plans? OMG are you banging the neighbor?

Mindy bit down on the inside of her cheek. *Grow up.*

This is so Sweet Home Alabama, Ruby texted. *That fateful kiss at ten, and now love blossoms years later.*

Mindy shook her head. *Go away. I'll see you tomorrow.*

"Hey," Vic's voice was soft and Mindy turned to find him in the doorway, a hand on each side jamb. "I just got a text that said dinner is on its way."

"Why don't I go home and set the table."

He nodded and then looked around the room. "Thanks for your help with this. It would have taken me a week to get all of this torn out."

"My pleasure," Mindy smiled at him and suddenly felt stupid about the fit she'd thrown over the picture earlier.

Was she so conditioned to turn away from affection and appreciation?

A part of her wished she thought like Ruby. *OMG are you banging the neighbor?* Thinking about her text made Mindy chuckle.

"What are you thinking about?" Vic asked, still standing in the doorway.

"Are you familiar with *Sweet Home Alabama?*" she asked as she walked toward him.

"The song?"

She laughed. "No. The movie."

He crinkled his nose. "Guy with the yellow airplane and glass store?"

Mindy's laugh grew more intense. "That's what you remember about it?"

He shrugged. "Did it have a sport in it?"

Instinct had her placing her hand on his chest. Once she did, she reconsidered, but then thought it would be too strange for her to pull back.

"No, it didn't have a sport. They played pool, but that doesn't count," she said, smiling up at him. "Never mind." She let out a breath. "I'll wait for you at my house."

Vic took a step back, and Mindy slipped by and headed home.

CHAPTER ELEVEN

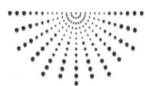

IT WAS FORTY-FIVE MINUTES BEFORE VIC RANG MINDY'S DOORBELL. It was the owner of the restaurant that had delivered the meal, and then he'd wanted to talk about the next campaign.

Vic hoped the man hadn't realized that Vic was just a bit off his game. He hadn't invited him in further than the entry because the rest of the house was a mess with the remodel of the office.

Then, just as he'd been heading out to Mindy's, his mother had called.

"Will you be able to pick up Uncle Don at the airport next week?" she'd asked, and he wondered why they had to have that conversation at that moment.

"Sure. Send me the details."

"I sent them to you last week. It's in an email with the menu for Christmas Eve and Christmas morning."

"Right."

"And we're having lunch tomorrow, here at the house for your father's birthday."

"Uh-huh," he'd replied remembering he was going to have to text the guys to let him know he'd miss bowling.

"You sound preoccupied," she'd said and the irritation in that tiny statement still rattled through him as he stood on Mindy's front step.

He supposed the reason it shook him was because usually he had time for his mother, but tonight, he just wanted to be with Mindy.

When she pulled open the door, he noticed she'd changed her clothes. Now she had on a pair of flannel pants and a sweatshirt.

"Sorry that took so long. The owner of the restaurant wanted to talk, and then my mom called," he said as he handed Mindy the box of food.

"It's no problem."

Vic toed off his boots and hung up his coat before following Mindy to the kitchen.

The dining room table was set with china. The very thought that Mindy used her grandmother's accessories that came with the house, made Vic smile.

"You didn't have to go all out. We could have eaten from the containers," he offered.

"Other than movie night, once every four months, I don't entertain. I thought it would be a good use of the china."

"Was this your grandmother's?" Vic asked as Mindy set the box of food on the table, and he began to take the containers out of the box.

"Yes. That old lady chic we were talking about," she admitted.

He smiled when she said it, not daring to tell her he'd been thinking the same thing.

"Do you think it's bad that I haven't changed anything? Ruby gives me hell for it every time she's here."

Vic looked around. He wondered what personal effects were Mindy's, though he would think that nothing was hers, originally.

"I've only been in these few rooms. And I don't know that it's bad. If you're comfortable..."

Mindy shrugged. "I guess I would just feel bad if I removed her from her own house."

"I get that. I'm struggling with that too. The basement is still all wood paneling, and my grandfather's tinker shop is still intact down there."

"Tinker shop?" Mindy raised a brow.

"He didn't work on cars or do woodworking in the garage like most men did then. He built models, like cars and spacecraft. So his tinker room was the male version of a craft room, I guess."

"Got it. Male ego and all."

"Exactly. No reason a man couldn't have a craft room."

Mindy's smile spread wide on her mouth. "Or a woman with a tinker room. I rather like that term."

THEY ATE THEIR FOOD ON DISHES WITH PINK AND GOLD ROSES. They drank wine from crystal glasses, which Mindy paired with the meal from her vast selection of wines. And they ended up together on the loveseat in front of the fireplace after dinner with a cup of coffee and a plate of chocolate chip cookies between them.

"Do you like *Elf*?" Mindy asked as she pointed the remote at the TV.

"I've never seen it."

She turned her head to look at him, eyes wide, and her mouth open. "You've never seen *Elf*? How have you never seen it?"

"Does it have sports in it?"

"Is that your prerequisite to seeing a movie?"

Vic shrugged. "Is having romance in a movie yours?"

"Of course."

He laughed when she answered right away. "Well then, I suppose we could have our own movie club. I'll learn about romance movies and I'll introduce you to sports movies."

"*Elf* is a Will Ferrell movie too, so it's a comedy. Do you watch comedy?" He took a breath and Mindy shook her head. "Let me guess. Only if it has sports in it?"

"Don't think I'm a nerd, but I read a lot. So I don't watch movies or TV shows very often."

Mindy lifted her coffee mug to her lips and smiled from behind it. "I would never think a man who reads a lot a nerd. Well, I mean, yes I would, but I think that's a sexy attribute."

Vic raised a brow. He desperately wanted to say something about her thinking that reading was sexy—meaning he was sexy, but he didn't dare.

It had been twenty years since he'd seen her, and they were just kids then. A few dinners over the past week didn't warrant his excitement over her thinking his hobby of reading was sexy.

Mindy sipped her coffee and lowered her mug. "Who's your favorite author?" she asked.

"There's a local author who writes time travel. Andre Gonzalez?" he said, and Mindy shrugged at the name. "I'd be happy to lend you one of his books, but you won't find a lot of romance."

She kept her cup near her mouth, as if drawing attention to those full lips.

"So we'll watch *Elf* tonight, and next week, we can watch some sport movie?" she offered and Vic nodded in agreement.

"That sounds—wait, next Saturday is Christmas Eve."

She winced. "Oh, yeah."

"Thursday?"

Mindy nodded. "I'd like that."

"Your friends won't be jealous if we have our own movie club, will they?" Vic asked as he picked up a cookie from the plate.

"I think they'll be okay. You know, two of them are married, so it's not as if their friends are too important to them anymore," she said in a teasing tone, but her smile twitched a bit, and he wondered if she actually felt unimportant now.

"I'm sure they don't actually think that way."

"They don't," she said reassuringly, but he wondered if that was for him or for herself. "At least they married brothers who do things together. So, they're great about letting their wives still be with their friends, especially when it comes to movie night."

Vic leaned until he nudged her with his shoulder. "Are we going to have traditions too?"

"Such as?"

He tapped his temple as if in thought and she laughed. "Sports jerseys on sports night."

"And lingerie on romance night?" She teased and then her eyes went wide. "I'm kidding." Mindy covered her mouth with her hand. "I don't know what made me say that. I'm sorry."

"I'll need a Victoria's Secret trip before movie night then. I'm all out of lingerie," Vic teased and Mindy shoved at him, but her hand lingered on his arm before she pulled back.

"I think we can just decide to order pizza from different places."

"We can start there," he agreed. "I'm not one for facial masks."

Smiling, Mindy shook her head. "Can we watch this movie now?"

"Is it scary?" Vic asked and she looked at him with a furrowed brow.

"Of course not."

"Okay. I just didn't know if we should move the plate of cookies, so if I were to jump, I wouldn't knock them over."

Mindy bit down on her lip. "We can move them."

"Oh good. I certainly didn't want to make a mess," he said, but he was thinking how he'd really like to sit closer to her.

Mindy picked up the plate of cookies and set them on the coffee table, then she closed the distance between them so that they sat next to one another, their outer thighs touching.

"Just in case you find you have a fear of large elves," she said.

"I feel better already."

CHAPTER TWELVE

WITH A SIX PACK OF MIXED CRAFT-BREWED BEERS AND A GIFT BAG in one hand, and Mindy's sweater in the other, Vic walked up the front steps of his parents' house and through the front door on Sunday.

He was the last to arrive for lunch, which was usual. It wasn't that he was late, he was right on time, but he noticed his sisters always were there a minimum of an hour earlier.

Vic wasn't sure if it was the need to settle their kids, or to help their mother, though he'd never been asked to arrive earlier to help with a meal or anything.

His mother appeared from the kitchen, though something else other than his arrival had caused her to walk his way.

She blinked as if she'd only just noticed him, and then a wide smile spread over her mouth. "Sweetheart, I didn't hear you come in."

"There's a lot going on in here," Vic noticed between mixers in the kitchen whirring, the TV was on very loud, and conversations were also at full volume.

"Your dad is in the family room feeding Isaac."

Vic nodded, and handed his mother the sweater. "Mindy sent this. She said you were interested in borrowing it."

His mother's brows drew inward as she looked at the sweater and then back up at him. "I did?"

A zing of humor ran through him. He was sure Mindy hadn't made it up, but he was also sure his mother had been making small talk with Mindy, and that was what had come out of it.

"She said you had a party coming up."

Recognition of the situation flashed in his mother's eyes. "Right. Right." She let out a long slow breath. "Listen, Amber brought someone," she said softly, mentioning his eldest sister.

"Not her husband?"

"What? Oh, no. He's here. She brought someone for you." His mother's face brightened.

Vic winced. "Why?"

"They're all worried about you. You don't get out of the house and you don't date."

"I'm doing just fine," he said, wishing he could have invited Mindy, but she had other plans.

"Be that as it may, Allison also has someone coming to meet you."

Vic swallowed hard. "So my sisters are using dad's birthday as an excuse to invite potential girlfriends for me?"

"Don't be mad."

"I'm not mad. I'm just not interested."

His mother rested her hand on his arm. "You don't know that. Wait till you meet them."

"I do know that," he said sternly, because at the moment all he could think about was the woman in the other shag carpeted house. The one whose brown eyes had specks of gold in them, whose shoulders were delicate, and fit into the palm of his hand when he'd draped his arm around them while watching a movie.

But, getting involved with the next-door neighbor only spelled disaster, so he needed to let it all go. Maybe his sisters setting him up would distract him with something other than Mindy Baldwin.

"Just be gracious, won't you. And give both women equal attention."

This was going to be a long afternoon, he thought as he followed his mother into the kitchen, where Amber jumped up from her seat and grabbed his arm.

"Come here. I want you to meet someone," she said. "This is Justine, she's a friend of mine from work."

Vic rearranged the beer and the bag in his hand so that he could shake hers from over the table. "It's nice to meet you."

"My brother is an ad exec, or ad agency owner?" she said giving him a quizzical look.

"I own my own independent agency," he said, wondering when his sisters would pay attention to those details.

"Right. He just bought our grandmother's house and is remodeling it."

Justine's eyes widened. "That sounds adventurous."

"Layers of wallpaper, it tells a story," he admitted.

Amber took the items out of his hand. "Why don't you sit down and get to know Justine." His sister gave him a tight smile, accompanied with harsh eyes.

Vic sat down at the table, but not before taking one of the beers from the six pack and popping the top off.

Justine was blonde, with beautiful blue eyes. Her cheeks had pinked when they'd been introduced. "How long do you think it'll take to finish your remodel?" she asked as she cupped both hands around her wine glass.

"At the rate I'm going, it'll take a while. Plans are usually halted when I pull up something, or find something else not up to code."

"My ex and I flipped a house before our divorce," she said, and there was a lot mixed into that sentence that Vic just didn't want to pursue. "In the end we made some money, but not enough, that's for sure."

The conversation fell flat, so Vic took a long pull from his beer, realizing very quickly the alcohol content in the specific one he'd chosen was higher than a regular beer. It went right to his head and did its job to calm him.

When the doorbell rang, Vic stood, but Allison appeared from the family room holding up a hand, and raced for the door.

A few moments later she returned with a woman, their arms looped together. But this one he recognized, and he stood when he saw her.

"Parker?" he said and the woman nodded.

"Hey, Vic," she said in a sweet tone as she moved toward him and hugged him. "Wow, you filled out nice." She gave his bicep a squeeze and he laughed.

"High school wasn't kind," he reminded her. "I didn't know you and Allison kept in touch."

She shrugged. "We see each other once in a while. She said you'd be here and I could catch up with everyone." Parker's eyes went to the woman next to him. She held out her hand. "Parker Sampson."

The flash of annoyance in Justine's eyes hit before her smile did. "Justine."

"So are you two…"

"No," Vic was quick to add. "Justine is Amber's friend from work."

Parker's smile formed slowly. "What are you drinking?"

"Craft beer. Can I get you one?"

She nodded and those soft hazel eyes were just as he'd remembered when he was that scrawny teenager. "Thanks."

Vic pulled another beer from the box, opened it, and handed it to Parker before he reclaimed his chair, and Parker took the one next to him. Interestingly enough, his sisters had disappeared, and there was an uncomfortable strain that zipped between the two women on either side of him.

When his phone buzzed in his pocket, he noticed the text was from Mindy.

What timing, he thought.

He opened the text and there was a picture of a cupcake on a plate. *This one is for you.*

His mouth twitched, wanting to smile, but he held it taut. *What color is inside?* He sent the text, feeling as if he'd asked what color her underwear was, and fully aware that the two women on both sides of him were watching.

Nope. I'm not telling you. I'll be home around seven, if you want to drop by and pick it up.

He felt the heat in his face. Surrounded by potential dates, the only woman he cared to spend time with was Mindy, but he knew his sisters weren't going to let him off the hook. *I'll see you then.*

Vic tucked his phone back into his pocket and took another long pull from his beer. More than likely he'd have scheduled dates with the two women who his sisters had brought to lunch to pine for him. But all he could think about was biting into that cupcake—or into Mindy—and that took his breath away. Then he reminded himself, yet again, that it was unwise to date the neighbor. No good could come out of that. So the decision then was either to ask out the woman he known since high school, who was slightly older, but he'd once crushed on and had taken to prom, or the divorcée who may or may not be on the rebound. But, just how desperate was he? Or more like, how desperate was his family?

CHAPTER THIRTEEN

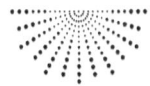

Tina squealed when she saw Mindy walking up the front step with the box of cupcakes in her hand.

"I can't wait a second longer. You're killing me with this!" Tina tapped her fingers together and joyfully squealed again.

Aaron took the box from Mindy and carried them into the kitchen of their new house as Tina enveloped her in a hug. "You're amazing, you know that, right?"

"Why am I amazing?" Mindy laughed.

"Because you've kept this secret for this long. I couldn't do it. I couldn't stay quiet."

"Well, then I won't let you be in charge of this kind of surprise if I ever get pregnant," Mindy said, and the word pregnant stuck in her throat. How was she ever supposed to even consider that when she never dated.

Her chest grew tight. Was she dating now? No, she and Vic hadn't gone out. But they'd spent the better part of the week together, and she couldn't wait to get home to give him his cupcake.

Tina disappeared into the kitchen and Ruby moved in next to Mindy.

Ruby nudged her. "You okay? You just went pale."

"I'm fine," Mindy smiled and tucked her arm into Ruby's. "You look amazing."

"Yep, I get to use all my sexy dresses for bridal showers, baby showers, and gender reveals," she scoffed. "My life is lame."

"Your life is perfect, and so is mine."

Ruby nodded. "My new roommate just moved out," she announced with a curled lip.

Lisa moved in next to them, taking Ruby's other arm in hers. "Another one? Seriously, do you sleepwalk with knives?"

Ruby shrugged. "I honestly think I'm an amazing roommate. I have no idea why these girls move in and out like they do."

Lisa bit down on her bottom lip. "Maybe you need a roommate of the opposite sex."

"As if that wouldn't get complicated," Ruby said, and Mindy thought about her friendship with her neighbor. That wasn't much different, was it?

Lisa let go of Ruby's arm and moved in front of them. "My brother needs a place. He only had short term housing while he got established at the hospital."

"You want Jason to live with me?" Ruby asked with raised brows.

"Why not? He knows you. You know him. You know he's safe and in a respectable profession, who could pay the rent, and because of his new position at the hospital, he'll never be home to get in your way. Really, I think it's a win win."

Ruby bobbed her head from side to side as if considering it. "Do you think he'd be interested?"

"We've discussed it."

Mindy nudged her. "Maybe you and I are destined to just have roommates and neighbors, but no love life. We can live with that, right?"

Ruby's lips puckered. "Oh, let's change the subject," she said raising her brows. "I want to know about the boy next door."

Lisa nodded. "Oh, yes. Do tell."

Mindy laughed. "What's to tell?"

Ruby held up a finger. "Let's see, shall we? You went MIA all week. When I invited you out, you had plans. You were eating with him. Did you say, Wednesday? And Thursday? And Saturday?"

Mindy's cheeks went hot. "I was helping him remodel."

Both Lisa and Ruby let out and exaggerated, "Oh!"

"Seriously, we tore off wallpaper and took out the carpet. There is nothing sexy about that."

Ruby turned to Lisa. "Home improvements with someone you've known was next door all of a week. Doesn't that sound cozy?"

Lisa nodded. "Almost as cozy as inviting someone to live with you a week or so after you met them," she called herself out, but there was pride in now that she and Ryan were married.

"He's a homebody," Mindy suggested. "I'm a homebody," she admitted.

"One and one is two," Ruby said. "So it's just a matter of whose home your body is in, right?"

"I'm not going to date my neighbor. That spells disaster."

Lisa nodded. "I'm not going to date my best friend's brother-in-law either—oops."

They all three laughed and walked arm in arm to where Tina and Aaron's family had gathered for the reveal.

The cupcakes had been set out on a tiered tray. Lisa moved in next to Ryan, who wrapped an arm around her and looked at Mindy. "Those look amazing. Tina's really happy with them," he said.

"I'm glad. It had to be the hardest secret to ever keep," she admitted.

Lisa elbowed her. "And you didn't tell *anyone*? Not even the good-looking neighbor you're spending all your time with?"

Mindy let out a low growl. "Not even him."

Their attention was drawn to Tina and Aaron who stood on the opposite side of the table. All of their relatives had their phones held up to record the event.

Instead of cutting open one of the cupcakes, Mindy unwrapped one, and held it up to Aaron's mouth. He took a large bite, sure to get to the center of the cupcake, and when Tina pulled it back she began to cry before she turned the cake around to show a pink center.

The group that had gathered cheered, kissed the couple, and each took a cupcake. Mindy stood back and watched everyone. When her phone buzzed in her pocket she pulled it out and looked down at the picture of Vic smiling back at her.

A girl, huh? His text read, and Mindy actually looked around the room to see if he was there.

How do you know that? I didn't give you a cupcake yet.

He sent a laughing emoji. *Check your Facebook. By the way, you look lovely today.*

Mindy swallowed hard, and scrolled through her phone to the Facebook app and opened it. Sure enough, she'd been tagged in the event that had happened only a minute ago, and there it was right on Facebook.

It must have been Aaron and Ryan's mother that had taken the video, because after the announcement, there was a scanning of the crowd, and the video landed on Mindy with the voice saying, "And Tina's friend Mindy made the cupcakes and kept the secret." Then the video ended.

Mindy replied to Vic. *Thank you,* she said since he thought she looked lovely. *How is your dad's birthday lunch?*

This time, instead of an emoji, he set a gif of Steve Carell rolling his eyes. *My sisters are on a mission. I have two women here vying for me. I now have two possible dinner dates this month. Seriously, if I wanted to date, I'd get on Tinder. Or I'd leave the house.*

Mindy read the text over and over. Why did that hurt so much, she wondered? She wasn't dating him. They were neighbors, being neighborly. But still, she had thought it was more than that.

Of course she did. She always did. That was half of her problem. She always thought that if a guy was being nice to her, or had any interest in her at all, even friendship, then they were destined to get married. When that wasn't the case, she'd be devastated, and she'd eat ice cream for a week and gain five pounds.

She and Vic had a past—a childhood. Now they were just adults that lived next door to one another in houses once owned by their grandparents. They shared some meals and some time together. Friends did that kind of thing.

Now he had two possible dates with two different women. That was okay, she kept convincing herself. He'd come over, she'd give him his cupcake, and he'd be on his way.

"What's wrong?" Ruby was next to her again, studying her. "Are you crying?"

"I'm just so happy for them," she said pointing to Tina who sobbed against Aaron.

Ruby put her arm around Mindy's shoulders. "That baby girl is going to be a princess. Be prepared for her to be joining us for movie night, masks, and toe polishing the moment she's born."

Even though the tears still threatened, Mindy put her head on Ruby's shoulder and laughed. Yes, any daughter of Tina's was going to be high maintenance.

CHAPTER FOURTEEN

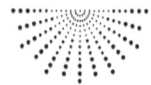

IT WAS SEVEN-THIRTY WHEN VIC RANG MINDY'S DOORBELL. IN HIS hand he carried two covered plates, compliments of his mother.

Mindy opened the door, still in the dress she'd worn to the gender reveal, which he noted was blue.

"I just got the joke," he said looking at her.

Mindy narrowed her brows. "What joke."

"You wore a blue dress knowing full well the inside of the cupcake was pink."

Her lips pursed, and she didn't seem as amused by his comments.

"I didn't actually think about it. I just picked the dress."

"Can I come in?" he finally asked, realizing that she hadn't moved to let him in.

"Yeah, sorry," she said stepping aside.

"My mom sent dinner home for us," he offered holding out the plates. "They over prepared."

"So you have dinner for tonight and dates lined up too? It was a productive day."

Her words had bite, and he wondered why. Had he crossed some line?

"What do you say we warm these up and have them?"

"I suppose." She didn't even take one of the plates, she turned and walked toward the kitchen.

Vic set the plates on the entry table, toed off his boots, and hung up his coat. Picking up the plates, he followed Mindy to the kitchen, where she sat at the island on a stool drinking a glass of wine.

"I can just leave them for you. I'm not getting the feeling that you're looking for company tonight."

Mindy watched him over the rim of her wine glass as she sipped. Was she mad? Had he said something?

Vic set the plates on the counter, still wrapped.

"Mom was grateful for the sweater loan," he said and Mindy nodded. She was still watching him over the top of his glass. "So, a girl, huh?" He brought up Tina's gender reveal.

"Yeah. That was a hard secret to keep."

"You did a good job with it. I mean you didn't even tell me, knowing I'd never see Tina to tell her."

Mindy sipped her wine again. "So how was your lunch?"

Vic pursed his lips. "There are a lot of levels as to how it all went. The meal was fantastic. My mom and sisters put on an amazing spread. I got a lot of cuddle time with my nieces and my new nephew. Dad loved his gift." He raked his fingers through his hair and then scrubbed his hands over his face. "My sisters are a bit too nosey when it comes to my life. Two of them brought guests with the intent to set me up."

Mindy finished her glass of wine and poured more. "What's under the foil?" she asked looking at the plates.

"A pot roast with potatoes and carrots. A green bean casserole and a piece of corn bread."

She licked her lips. "I suppose we could warm them."

"Do you have something to cover the plates? Film? A cover?"

Again, she watched him as she took a sip of her wine.

When she stood, she held the counter for a moment, skirted

the island, and pulled a plate cover dome out from a bottom cabinet.

Vic reached for her hand as she handed him the lid, pulling her just a little closer. "What's on your mind?" he asked, still worried that he'd done something to make her mad.

She studied him for a moment chewing her bottom lip. Then she looked down at the plates as if only to break eye contact. "Let's just say it's the holiday blues." She lifted her eyes back to his and they were sad.

Vic took the plate cover and set it down, but kept her hand in his, tugging her closer to him. "We should dance," he said pulling his phone from his pocket and scrolling through his apps.

"Dance? Geez," she huffed out, turning to move from him, but he managed his arm around her waist and pulled her to him as he started music on his phone.

At first it played some angry song from Jellyroll, and Mindy flinched. Vic laughed and shook his head. "Fat fingers," he said laughing before he managed something slower.

"You have a playlist of soft jazz?" she asked as he set his phone on the counter.

He hummed as he pulled her to him again. Vic kept his hand on her waist, and captured her other hand in his.

She moved with him for a moment before she lifted her hand to his shoulder.

They let the music surround them, and Vic kept any comments or conversations he wanted to start quiet. She just needed him close, he thought. Or, she just needed the music, maybe. Perhaps just the sway would calm her?

He didn't really know what he was doing. There was just a need to be near to her.

As they swayed, her body leaned into his. When her hand moved to the nape of his neck, and her head rested on his chest, he moved his hand from her hip to the small of her back.

She was crying. Her shoulders bobbed slightly and he could

hear her breath hitch long before he felt the dampness of her tears in the fabric of his shirt.

Vic pulled their held hands in closer, and kept swaying.

The song changed, and they continued to move.

Her breathing had calmed, and her fingers grazed the nape of Vic's neck, causing him to close his eyes.

Mindy eased her hand from his and draped it over his other shoulder, bringing their bodies to press even closer.

Inhaling the scent of her with his cheek pressed to the top of her head, Vic let his free hand slide down her back.

He'd meant to calm her, but with her pressed to him, he was anything but calm.

They were friends.

They were neighbors.

They were in unfamiliar territory, and it was all his fault for starting it.

MINDY BREATHED IN DEEPLY. THE SCENT OF VIC'S COLOGNE TOYED with her.

Why was she so out of sorts?

The man had every right to date other women.

They were friends.

They were neighbors.

They were pressed together awfully tight, and she knew how much it was affecting him, she thought as she pressed against him even more.

His hand skimmed her back, and when it reached the small of her back, where his other was, his fingertips hovered over the swell of her buttocks.

If she didn't pull back now, and go on as if this was just a normal moment between friends, she'd want more. She'd want it all.

Who was she kidding? She did want it all.

Vic was safe, right? He came from a good family. He lived in old lady chic. God, he was self-employed, and that right there said more than all the men she'd ever dated.

He was a looker—oh, so handsome. Those dark eyes that could see into her soul were burned into her memory. The sandy hair, which her fingers were tunneling up into, was soft against her skin.

They had history. They'd shared their first kiss together.

Her head swam from the three glasses of wine she'd had since she'd been home rereading his texts—the ones he where he'd said he had two possible dates.

The weight in her stomach plummeted again.

As if her own thoughts weren't enough to pull her from the beautiful moment, his phone rang with an annoying sound, interrupting the music that had them swaying.

In an instant, Vic stepped back, his hands taken off her. She had no choice but to drop her hands from his hair and step back too.

"Hey, Parker," he answered the phone and Mindy felt the heat of tears creeping up into her eyes. Parker wasn't one of his sisters. Maybe it was someone he was doing work for, she hoped. "Of course, that should work. I'm in the middle of something, can I call you later?"

She must have agreed because Vic finished the call, silenced his phone, and tucked it back into his pocket.

From the corner of her eye, she could see him rake his fingers through his hair and take in a breath. They were both unsettled.

He needed to go home. She couldn't be emotional around him anymore. She wanted to love him. She wanted to hate him. But in the end, she was just going to kiss him and sleep with him, and then all of those other things would just be confusing.

"You know, I'm really tired. Do you mind if we maybe don't

have dinner?" she said ducking into a cabinet for a container so she could pack up the cupcake.

Vic scrubbed his hand over his face. "Yeah. No problem."

He watched her as she packed up the cupcake and handed it to him.

"You're okay though?" he asked.

Mindy nodded. "Like I said—the holidays."

"I get it."

He moved to her, but she had to take a step back. She couldn't touch him, no matter how much she wanted to.

Vic stopped. "I should get the stuff to patch the wall tomorrow. I think tomorrow night I'll work on the room." Mindy wrapped her arms around herself and nodded, but she didn't engage in the conversation. "If you're free and want to come over and help?" He'd left the invitation dangling.

"I have a function at work. I'll be pretty late," she said. "In fact, I'll be all day, so I don't suppose I'll be able to meet you at the bowling alley, like we'd planned. It's just a busy season."

Nodding, Vic picked up one of the plates and the cupcake. "Well, I'll be home if you find you need company. I'll leave you a plate of food, just in case you get hungry later."

As he walked to the door, Mindy drew in a breath and let it out slowly. A moment later, she heard the door close. Oh, she could mess up a relationship that didn't even exist, she thought. She certainly was no prize for any man.

CHAPTER FIFTEEN

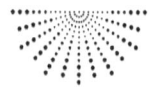

REPAIRING A DAMAGED WALL WAS NOW SOMETHING THAT VIC could put on his list of things he'd never thought he'd know how to do. What a way to spend his day. It had been house productive, but not business productive.

A quick look at his phone, he realized it was already nine o'clock. Because he couldn't help himself, he walked to the dining room and looked out the window into the stillness of the night. Mindy's house was still dark.

He'd had a restless night of sleep last night wondering what it was that he had done to upset her. Though he tried to convince himself that maybe it wasn't him, and maybe it was just the holidays as she'd said, he was taking it personally. He liked her, and he thought maybe it was more than just that friendly neighbor like. Then again, she'd always held a special place in his memory, and in his heart.

She needed some space. He'd give that to her. Hell, he had women at his disposal, he could ask what they thought went wrong. But he'd wait it out. The holidays were upon them, and everyone needed some space, he supposed.

When his phone buzzed in his hand, he looked down to see a text from Parker.

I enjoyed our coffee this morning. You are incredibly talented. I look forward to lunch next week.

He wasn't sure the text needed a response, so he didn't give one. Parker owned a small furniture store that had been in the family for generations. They'd met for coffee so he could show her his portfolio of work. They'd planned lunch the following week so they could discuss what he could do for her company.

Over coffee, Parker had admitted to not completely knowing his sister's motives for inviting her to lunch.

"I thought it was for your dad's birthday," she'd said. "I didn't know I was being set up."

Vic had laughed. "Yeah, I didn't know that was going to happen either. And they must have all been planning it."

"I don't talk to your sister too much. I know you and I went to prom together, but I guess she didn't get the memo that I don't enjoy the company of men in that way."

At that point, Vic had choked on his coffee. The woman wasn't attracted to him, and he'd never been happier to hear that.

Despite the lack of attraction, they'd had a nice morning and they'd reminisced about high school and friends they'd had in common. He promised to work up a proposal for what he could offer her in the way of advertising, and they'd made plans for next week.

So, even though his sister's intentions had missed the mark, he was still going to make out on the deal.

Justine on the other hand had texted him twice and wanted to know when they could go out. He'd yet to respond.

Vic hadn't been attracted to either of the women who had been brought to lunch, but Justine, well she didn't light any fires in him. No, the only woman that had turned his head in a very long time was Mindy, but she didn't seem to want to have much to do with him.

As he turned, he noticed the headlights coming into the cul-de-sac. It was Mindy. She pulled into her driveway, opened the garage door, parked, and quickly closed it behind her. Vic waited for the lights in the house to turn on, but none did. She was obviously trying to not draw attention to herself.

She was home safe. That's all he cared about.

Then, the front door to her house opened, and he watched as she hurried toward his house, over the frosted lawn and to his front door.

He waited for the knock or the doorbell, but nothing.

Vic hurried to the door and pulled it open. There was a grocery bag, with his mother's plate in it. He stepped over the bag and called her name, stopping her mid-yard.

"Hey," he said softly. "You could have rung."

She turned in the dark. "I didn't want to bother you. It's late."

"You're never a bother. Why don't you come in and see the wall?" he said.

He could see her tuck her hands deep into her pockets. "I don't—"

"C'mon. It'll only take a minute."

Mindy stood there for a moment before she walked toward him.

When she came into view under the porch light, he studied her.

She was still in low heels and a casual dress, not one she'd probably wear to work. Her coat was open, and he could see the font of it scooped just low enough to expose her cleavage, and that hit him right in the gut. Her hair was pulled up in a clip in the back, and small, delicate diamonds dripped from her ears. He'd seen her with her hair up before, but in that light, he noticed just how temping her neck would be to skim kisses over.

Vic cleared his throat. "You look beautiful," he said, and it carried on the cold air.

"Thank you. It was sort of a formal event."

"Come in. It's cold." He picked up the plate off the porch and followed Mindy into his house. "Can I get you something to drink?"

"No. I had my share of wine tonight."

He looked at her as he set the plate on the counter. "You were okay to drive home?"

She nodded. "Just tasting the wine. Often, you don't even swallow. And we had food," she added.

"Some coffee or tea? I was just going to make myself some."

She dragged her lip through her teeth and it stirred him up, even knowing she was going to refuse his invitation.

"I'm good. I should get home."

Vic nodded. "Come see the room. Tell me what you think."

She didn't even remove her coat, and he knew she'd leave as quickly as she could. But he just wanted a few minutes with her. Maybe after the new year, things could be different between them. Whatever it was that bothered her about the holidays, it would go away soon, right?

Vic turned on the light in the room and they both stepped inside.

"That'll make a difference," Mindy said as she walked to the wall he'd repaired and examined it. "Now you have to sand it?"

"Yeah, when it's dry I'll sand it, then I can prime and paint it. Though, I don't suppose I'll get to it until after the new year. I'm just going to have to commit to working from the dining room table for a while."

She considered him again. "You know, we have three offices where I work that they rent out. Since the company I work for downsized after the pandemic, they didn't need as many people in-house. I could get you into one of the offices until yours is finished."

Her eyes were lighter, and she finally seemed at ease around him. "Is it expensive?"

She shook her head. "Considering that you're only looking at a few weeks, really, and it's the holidays, I can't see my boss charging you too much. I'll talk to him tomorrow and call you."

The thought of being in the same building with her all day put a lightness in his chest that hadn't been there for the past few days. "I'd like that."

She nodded. "Let your mom know that dinner was excellent. I ate it very late last night."

"You're okay though. I was worried about you."

"Sure. I'm fine. Like I said, holidays."

"They're almost over," he said smiling at her. "Oh, and that cupcake was amazing. You could sell those."

She shook her head. "I'd be three hundred pounds."

"Wouldn't matter. You'd still be beautiful as hell."

Her eyes went wide and she opened her mouth as if to say something, but she didn't. Her hands went back into the pockets of her coat.

"I'd better get home and get some sleep. I'll call you tomorrow."

Vic nodded and followed her to the door. "Sweet dreams," he said as she stepped out onto the porch.

"You too."

CHAPTER SIXTEEN

Here are pictures of the offices and costs for rental, Mindy attached the photos and prices listed to Vic after she'd talked to her boss.

Next, she texted Ruby. *Yes, I can do dinner tonight. But please can we do something without karaoke?*

Vic texted back, *I love this set up. If unit D is available, I'll take it for a month.*

Ruby texted back, *You're a buzz kill. It's a good thing I love you.*

Mindy laughed and texted Vic. *All you have to do is come by and sign the agreement. I'm here until five.*

She then texted Ruby. *I'm the most fun you'll ever have. Enjoy it.*

Vic texted, *I'll head over around noon. Can you do lunch?*

Mindy gave it some thought. *Yes. There's a Greek place at the end of our building if you're up for it.*

She scrolled to Ruby's text. *I'll see you tonight*, Mindy replied.

You can always cancel if you start sleeping with the neighbor, Ruby texted back.

Mindy shook her head. She saw Vic's reply come in saying he loved Greek food as her boss passed by and she called to him. "Vic is going to sign for a month. He'll be by at lunch."

Her boss nodded and kept walking.

Mindy typed her reply to Ruby. *Girl, I'm not going to sleep with my neighbor! I'll see you tonight.*

She sent the text, put her phone down, and it buzzed again. Chuckling, she picked it back up to see what Ruby's response was.

Vic's text read, *My ego just took a hit.* And he'd added the winking emoji.

Every single part of Mindy's body went hot. *Shit! Shit! Shit!* She'd replied to Vic with that text. Didn't she know better than to text multiple people at one time? Something like this is always bound to happen.

How did she even go about explaining it?

Vic shot back another text. *I'll see you at lunch. Going into a Zoom meeting. I'll see what I can come up with to convince you otherwise about our sleeping arrangements.*

She stared down at her phone. Her mouth had gone dry. Did Vic want to sleep with her?

Mindy pressed her hand to her chest to try and stop her heart from bursting through, it hammered so hard. God, she'd led him on. Or had he led her on?

Did he think they were dating because they'd been spending so much time together? Hadn't she had to consider that herself.

Her head spun. She was going to have lunch with him before she was going to see Ruby. Really, she'd be much more comfortable if the tables were turned so that she could talk through the situation with her friend and get a hold of herself.

As it was, this was her life.

Well, she'd figure it out. She'd either ruin something that was comfortable, or she'd sleep with her neighbor. Both thoughts made her nearly sick to her stomach.

What had she gotten herself into?

. . .

MINDY'S MORNING CONTINUED TO BE CHAOTIC. DISTRIBUTORS were calling to confirm shipments. Stores were calling looking for those shipments. The warehouse lost a pallet of wine from France, and three new restaurants called looking for service.

She'd gone to the warehouse to search for the missing wine herself. If they lost that shipment, there certainly was going to be hell to pay.

Nearly an hour later, she'd found it mislabeled in a corner.

When she walked back toward her office, she pulled out her phone and realized it was already past noon.

"At least the office has a nice view," Vic's voice came from behind her.

When she turned, she saw him leaning against the doorjamb, his feet crossed at the ankles.

"I didn't realize you were here."

He scanned a look over her. "What have you been doing?"

Mindy looked down at her skirt, dirt coated it from the pallets in the warehouse. "I was looking for a pallet of wine from France."

Vic nodded slowly. "Joe, he's your boss?" Mindy nodded. "He showed me around and I signed for the space for a month. I should have my office put back together by then."

Mindy walked toward him. "You'll have to wear real clothes to the office," she teased.

He raised a brow. "How do you know I don't when I'm at home?"

Shrugging, Mindy leaned against the wall next to him. "Isn't that the whole thing about working from home? You're dressed from the waist up?"

"Do you do that?"

She grinned. "I work here. No, I don't do that."

"It would make it interesting," he said, and that heat which had attacked her earlier was back.

"Should we head to lunch?" Mindy stood and dusted off her skirt.

"If you have time."

"It's been a crazy morning. It might be a crazy afternoon too."

The corner of his mouth lifted and his eyes flashed something that kicked up her heart rate. "Hmm, maybe we can plan a crazy night," he said before turning into the office to gather his coat.

Mindy felt that heat land in her cheeks. He wasn't going to let her live that text down.

When they entered the restaurant, the man who seated them called Mindy by name and kissed her cheeks. Vic wondered just how often she ate here.

They were seated at a small table in the center of the restaurant, which was full for Tuesday's lunch rush in the small industrial area of town. There were people in casual office attire, those who wore uniforms, and a few moms having lunch with their friends while they wrangled their toddlers in highchairs.

"This is a popular place," Vic said, and Mindy lifted her head from looking at the menu.

"Good food. Reasonable prices," she confirmed.

"Kisses at the front door help boost return rates," he said grinning at her with a raised brow.

She puckered her lips. "Is that why you think I suggested this place?"

"I'm just razzing you."

She nodded slowly. "For the record, men kiss me when I walk into any restaurant."

Vic snorted out a laugh. "That is good to know." He picked up his menu. "What do you get?"

"A gyro salad."

He wrinkled up his nose. "A salad?"

"I'm going to dinner with Ruby before she leaves for Hawaii. I'm assuming there will be a few drinks and too many carbs."

"You worry about things like that?"

Mindy shrugged. "I just plan and balance."

"For the record, if you need a ride, I know I'm in your phone. Call me. I'm never too far from home."

Mindy smiled as she considered his offer. "Thank you."

Well, at least she didn't wave it off.

The server took their order and brought back an iced tea for him and a water with lemon for Mindy.

"Hydrating early too?" he asked and she grinned from behind her glass.

"Ruby can tie them on. It's better to be safe than sorry."

"Don't forget my offer."

She only nodded and continued to sip her water.

"So tell me about your job," Vic leaned his forearms on the table. "What do you do, really?"

Mindy set her glass on the table and crossed her legs, which eased her back in her seat.

"I work with vineyards and wine distributors. New vineyards pop up all the time, and I help get them to market."

"That must mean you travel a lot."

"Spring through fall, yes. I am in Italy and France at least once a year. California at least once a month. And I'll spend quite a few weeks here in Colorado at the local wineries."

"It's a good thing you'll have me to watch over your house."

Her eyes went soft. "Can I trust you?"

Vic took a breath and leaned in closer. "Oh, yeah. You can trust me with anything."

He'd meant it to sound as deep as it had. He wanted her to know that her fit from the other night hadn't detoured him. No, it wasn't smart to get involved with the neighbor, but after her misdirected text that morning, he wasn't caring much about that at all. They were adults. If it went off the rails, they could fix it. But if it didn't go off the rails...

The server set their plates in front of them and Vic quickly realized he'd be having leftovers for dinner.

"Is this the size of their regular portions?"

Mindy looked over the table at his platter and smiled. "That's their lunch portion."

"No wonder this place is packed. You could eat for days with this."

She nodded. "Sometimes that's why I come. Especially if Joe is footing the bill."

"Nice boss."

"Only the best." She smiled warmly before forking a piece of lettuce and eating it.

Vic went through the process of making his gyro from his platter of meat and fixings. "So, do you ever work directly with vineyards and restaurants?"

"Cut out the middle-man?"

He laughed. "Yeah, I guess."

"Just once. I dated a guy who had a startup restaurant. I got him some good direct deals."

"Restaurant took too much of his time?"

She swallowed hard. "Well between the restaurant, the head server, and his wife, there wasn't a lot of time for me," she said before loading her fork with meat and shoving it into her mouth.

That would break someone's spirit for sure. "I'm sorry to hear someone did that to you."

She shrugged. "You don't get to thirty and not have it happen to you a few times, right?"

"You shouldn't. I've never had that happen, and I've never done that to anyone either."

Mindy choked out a laugh, sipped her water, and then looked at him. "I don't believe any man who says they've never strayed, cheated, or thought about it."

He couldn't help himself. Vic reached across the table and captured her hand in his. "Believe it. I swear on our first kiss, I've never done that. Nor would I ever."

She bit down on her bottom lip, as she tended to do when she was thinking. "Well, you would be a first then," she said easing her hand back from his.

"It should be the norm." Vic readjusted himself with his napkin on his lap.

"It should be."

"I know what it means to be in a completely faithful relationship. My past relationships might not have worked out for one reason or another, but it wasn't because my head got turned in another direction."

"Completely faithful?"

"There's no other way to be." He took a bite of his gyro, then wiped his mouth as he chewed. "You deserve better than that. You let me know if you think you'd be interested in finding out what it's like."

CHAPTER SEVENTEEN

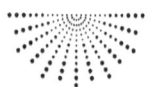

"Earth to Mindy," Ruby's voice snapped Mindy from her thoughts. "That margarita isn't going to drink itself, and it's two for one. We need to make some progress."

Mindy shook her head. Vic had already texted her to remind her that he'd pick her up. Now she wondered if he'd texted Ruby too, and that was why she wanted to drink as many two for ones as possible.

Ruby pressed her hand to her forehead, no doubt the frozen margarita gave her brain freeze. "Oh!" She winced. "Why do I do that?"

"You seem to be in a hurry to get drunk."

"I'm leaving on vacation with my mother tomorrow. I love the woman, but the traveling part is a nightmare. She gets stopped at TSA every single time. She packs as much in her carryon as she does in her suitcase, just because it might get lost. I'm not six anymore, but every time we pass a bathroom in the airport she reminds me to pee. And," she held up her margarita, "I'm not allowed to drink anything at all for three hours prior to boarding, in case there is bumpy weather and I can't get up on the plane." She took another long drink and wrinkled up her nose when it obviously froze her brain again.

"You're going to have a great time."

"Sure I am," Ruby said matter-of-factly. "Beach. Drinks. Christmas with no snow. I'll be golden. And I'll be all in, the moment we land."

Mindy laughed. Christmas would be exactly the same as it was every single year. Her sister had kids, and the gifts changed each year. But other than that, it was the same.

She'd make a dessert and a side dish to take to Christmas Eve dinner. Her father would convince her to go to midnight mass, even though she hadn't even been confirmed in the Catholic church, or followed religion in nearly twenty of her thirty years. But she knew the Catholic mass drill, as she and her sisters referred to it, so she'd go—and she'd go alone with her father, because her sister would use her children as an excuse to have to go home before Santa arrived.

Usually, Mindy would sleep at her parents' house, since mass didn't get over until early in the morning. Guilt was heavy with her parents, and Mindy fell victim to it often.

"Do you think I should get involved with the neighbor?" Mindy blurted it out and Ruby choked on her drink.

"Seriously?"

"It's a bad idea. Pretend like I didn't say anything."

Ruby set down her glass. "Like hell. I said you should hit it, and I still think you should."

Again, Mindy could feel the heat in her cheeks over something Ruby said with no filter.

"I'm not talking about just hitting it. I'm not like that."

"You should be. We all should be," Ruby admitted. "But you'll want the whole package, right?"

"Don't we all?"

Ruby shrugged. "I don't buy into it anymore. Don't get me wrong. I'm happy for Tina and Lisa, but I still don't buy into it.

Ryan and Aaron are different, like, maybe they were just raised right."

Mindy nodded and sipped her margarita. "I'm gun shy."

"You should be. When you're just one of the other women, how can you not be."

"He says he's not like that. Vic, that is," she said as if she had to clarify which neighbor she was thinking about getting involved with.

"All men are like that."

"That's what I said."

Ruby studied her. "You talked to him about it? Are you holding out on me?"

Mindy laughed. "No, I'm not holding out. It came up in conversation at lunch."

"You had lunch with him?"

"Am I supposed to tell you everything?"

"Yes," Ruby demanded. "If you were a real friend, you'd have me on speaker phone every time you spoke with a man. I mean, really, where did we go wrong?"

Mindy shook her head, smiling at her dearest friend. "I'm interested in him, but if it goes wrong—"

"You live next door."

"Right."

"And Mindy Baldwin doesn't know if she can handle it when she breaks up with the neighbor and sees another woman go into his house."

Mindy dropped her head back. "See. That's exactly who I am. Now he's working across the hall from me and—"

Ruby lurched across the table. "What the hell? Seriously, do we not talk anymore?"

Mindy leaned her arms back on the table and cupped the margarita glass in her hands. "It's too busy right now for us to finish work in his home office, so he rented one in our building for the month."

Ruby nodded slowly, taking in the information. "You're already a fucking couple," she demanded slightly louder than Mindy would have liked. "You didn't say he had to finish the remodel on his office. You said *us*. And then you got him the office across the hall from you, and you've already had lunch together. That's like a date, Mind."

"No, it—"

"It was a fucking date." The words that were being spat in her direction from Ruby were already slurring.

"Tone it down," she threatened.

"Are you afraid he's going to hear me?"

"If you get much drunker he will when I have to have him come get us."

That lit in Ruby's eyes, and the idea had been born. Mindy knew what she'd done. She'd unleashed the beast, and she was going to pay for it.

Ruby signaled the server. "We need two more margaritas, top shelf," she winked at the man.

Mindy took her phone from her purse and brought up Vic's number. *Ruby is already halfway to drunk, and she's ordering me more. Will you please give us a ride in an hour?*

She set her phone on the table.

Ruby took a chip from the basket. "Hit it, Mind. Hit it good."

With fire in her cheeks, Mindy picked up her phone when it buzzed. *I thought you'd never ask. Tell me where you are. I'll stay in contact and I'll be there in an hour.*

Maybe, just maybe, he wasn't like other men. But Mindy just couldn't believe that. The only thing she knew for sure was that she was going to make a move. Not because Ruby thought she should—okay, maybe because Ruby thought so, but because she needed to live a little bit, right? It would be her own Christmas present, she supposed. Then again, would it be weird to have sex with someone she'd kissed when she was ten?

The thought almost disgusted her. But then she considered how attracted she was to Vic. Maybe she could get over it.

Then what if Ruby was right and Mindy couldn't handle it when Vic brought other women home when things didn't work out between them?

She sipped her margarita and made a plan in her head to seduce him.

Then, she made a plan to start packing. By Valentine's day, she'd have to sell her house and move.

CHAPTER EIGHTEEN

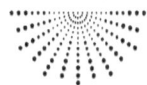

Vic paced around his house for the hour that Mindy had asked for. She'd given him the address to where they were dining, and she'd texted him throughout their dinner—and called him on accident one time.

He wasn't sure what it was that Ruby was trying to convey to Mindy, but he was sure she was giving her sex pointers by the sounds she'd been making and Mindy's giggling.

The texts that had come in as he picked up his keys and headed out had been drastically different than the ones from earlier in the evening. They were misspelled, had a lot of emojis, and then stopped making sense at all.

He laughed as he drove to the restaurant. If the two of them didn't get kicked out, he'd be surprised. On the other hand, he thought Mindy deserved a night to let down her hair.

Vic remembered her as an uptight girl. She was always a bit too serious and too much of a rule follower. But that was also some of her charm.

When he pulled up to the restaurant Mindy and Ruby were seated on a bench outside. He looked at the temperature reading on his dashboard and it read twenty degrees.

Pulling up to the curb, he put the car in park, and hurried out to help them into the car.

"It's freezing out here," he scolded. "Why didn't you wait for me inside?"

Mindy was helping Ruby to her feet. "She was getting a little loud, so I thought this was best."

Vic opened the back door and Mindy eased Ruby into the seat. She helped with her seatbelt, and then closed the door.

As she turned, Vic caught her in his arms, pulling her in toward him. "How are you feeling?"

Her hands pressed to his chest and she licked her lips as she gazed at his mouth, and then traveled her eyes to his. "I'm glad you're here."

He smiled down at her. "You're grinning at me."

"Am I?"

"Enjoyed your margaritas?"

"Immensely."

He kissed the top of her head and opened the door for her. "Let's get you home and to bed."

"That's the plan," she said under her breath, but he heard it. Oh, he heard it.

MINDY DIRECTED VIC TO RUBY'S HOUSE, AND TOGETHER THEY helped Ruby into the house while she told them just how much she loved them. A few times Mindy noticed Ruby leaning into Vic and whispering, loudly, that she thought Mindy and Vic would be a cute couple.

"I'll take her to bed," she said then covered her mouth and giggled. "I mean I'll put her to bed. Will you wait?" Mindy asked.

"I'm at your disposal," he said.

Mindy rested her hand on his arm, giving it a slight squeeze, and held there for a moment to steady herself. "Thanks."

He nodded and Mindy kept her arm around Ruby's waist and helped her to her bedroom.

"He loves you," Ruby said, loudly, and Mindy shushed her.

"You need to go to bed."

"My mother is picking me up at noon. Will you call me?"

Mindy eased Ruby onto the bed and she immediately fell back onto the bed giggling at some joke that must have been running through her head.

Knowing the room well enough, Mindy found Ruby's pajamas and did what she could to get her into them. Though Mindy's balance was a bit off, and her head a little fuzzy, she was sure she wasn't as drunk as Ruby was.

By the time she had Ruby tucked into bed, already snoring, it had been at least a half hour.

Mindy closed the bedroom door and saw Vic sitting on the couch scrolling through his phone.

"She's sleeping," she whispered.

Vic stood and tucked his phone in his pocket. "Does she live alone?"

Mindy laughed at his question as he walked toward her. "Yes. No. She always loses roommates."

"Always?"

"It seems to be her lot in life. Lisa's brother might move in."

Vic reached for Mindy's hand, linking their fingers. "Do you think she'll be okay? Should we stay?"

His hand was warm wrapped around hers, and his thumb brushed over her knuckles spreading goosebumps over her skin.

"She'll be okay. She'll sleep all night," Mindy assured him. "She'll be okay," she repeated.

His eyes moved over her before he lifted his hand to cup her cheek. "How are you feeling?"

Mindy pressed her hand to his chest, holding his gaze.

"I'm good. A little fuzzy," she giggled.

"We should get you home. You have to work tomorrow."

Mindy wrinkled her nose. "Buzz kill."

Vic brushed his thumb over her cheek. "The nice thing is, I'll drive you to work, and you can nap in the car on the way."

"I suppose this working across the hall will have its perks."

"I think so," he admitted.

Before they left, Mindy left a Gatorade and a glass of water next to Ruby's bed. Not that Ruby would have noticed, she was already snoring loudly.

The drive home was quiet, and that could have been in part because Mindy had fallen asleep, and would startle awake when Vic would come to stops.

But when his hand took hers and gave it a squeeze, Mindy's eyes flew open, and she realized they were parked in her driveway.

"We're home, sweetheart," Vic's voice said softly. "Close your eyes. I'm going to open my door and the dome lights are going to come on."

Mindy did as he instructed, and kept them closed until Vic had opened her door.

"Find your key," he said.

Mindy opened one eye and squinted at him. "We can go through the garage."

Vic took her hands and steadied her as she stepped out. The sleep and the car ride home must have shaken the margaritas in her, because she hadn't felt as drunk when she'd helped Ruby into the house as she did now.

She swayed into Vic as his arm wrapped around her waist.

"Can you punch in the code to your garage?" he asked.

"Six. Six. Three. Four," she called out the string of numbers.

"Are you sure you want me to know that?"

Mindy nodded. "You're safe."

He chuckled at that as he punched in the numbers and the door went up.

They walked through the garage, and for a moment Mindy

wondered why her car wasn't there. Then she remembered she'd left it at the restaurant. God, now she had to go get her car. This was only one of the many reasons she didn't drink more than a glass or two of wine on a normal basis.

"One more secret code," Vic said as they reached the door to the house.

Mindy looked up into his eyes, a halo of light behind him shadowed his face.

She'd had a plan. There was supposed to be seduction and sex. But as the world swayed, she wondered how she was supposed to carry out the plan.

Vic's hands gripped her waist as he pulled her close to him. "Were you drinking at Ruby's?" he laughed. "You seem to be more drunk."

She let her head tip back. "It simmered long enough."

"If you open your door, I'll carry you to bed."

Mindy felt the smile that parted her lips, and her eyes drifted over Vic's handsome face. "One. Six. Eight. Two," she called out the numbers, but Vic didn't move to punch them in.

"You're beautiful," he said looking down into her eyes.

"I'm intoxicated."

"You're still beautiful."

Mindy dragged her bottom lip through her teeth. "Are you really going to carry me to bed?"

His mouth curled up at the corners. "Yes."

"What are you going to do to me when you get me there?"

His brows rose at that, and she thought she'd misread the entirety of their conversation.

Reaching around her, Vic punched in the code to the door and pushed it open when the light turned green. Before it could automatically close, he scooped her legs out from under her, and Mindy wrapped her arms tightly around his neck as he fireman-carried her to the threshold.

"Push the button to close the garage door," he said as they slipped through the doorway. "Where's your bedroom?"

"End of the hall," Mindy managed as she nuzzled her nose into the crook of Vic's neck and inhaled. The musky scent of him intoxicated her further.

This was it, she thought, letting her head rest against his shoulder. He would put her on the bed, take off her clothes, and thus start her lurid affair with the neighbor.

It was the craziest thing she'd ever contemplated, and her nerve endings—all of them—buzzed in her head.

Caution thrown to the wind. Romance be damned. Mindy Baldwin was going to sleep with the boy next door.

CHAPTER NINETEEN

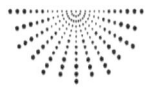

OLD LADY CHIC LIVED AND BREATHED IN HER BEDROOM. THE spirals of the white four poster bed matched the dresser, the nightstands, and the footlocker at the end of the bed.

The drapes had flowers on them, but in the room, lit only by the hall light, Vic couldn't make out what kind of flowers.

In all, the room made him nauseous, which was why, in his own house, his bedroom was the first room he'd changed.

Any fantasies that Vic might have had with Mindy, since receiving her text message by accident, had been snuffed out by walking into the room and laying her on the bed. Mindy turned on the lamp on the nightstand, and he noticed that the flowers on the drapes were sunflowers.

"Do you have Gatorade in your fridge too?" he asked and she nodded. "I'm going to get you some while you change."

As he turned, Mindy reached for him. "Don't you want to take my clothes off for me?"

He didn't know her well, but he knew her well enough that he expected her cheeks to pink when she said something so forward. The fact that they didn't told him she was more drunk that he'd originally thought.

"Let me get you that Gatorade."

Vic left her in the dated bedroom and walked out to the kitchen.

As he put his hand on the door to the refrigerator, he noticed Mindy had a photo taped to the front of the stainless steel.

For Auntie Mindy. A baby for you to spoil, was written on the ultrasound picture.

Vic noted the name at the top as Blair, T. and he knew that it was Tina's baby. It brought a smile to his lips as he opened the refrigerator door and found the produce drawer full of Gatorades.

That friendship she had with the other three women which she cherished was enviable. He didn't have anything quite like that in his life. He was close to his sisters. But after the other night, he was reconsidering that. Perhaps he was too close to his sisters when they'd both tried to set him up as they had in the ambush, and his other sister hadn't come to his rescue.

Chuckling, he pulled out a bottle from the produce drawer, closed the drawer, and then shut the door to the refrigerator with his hip.

Mindy was asleep, in her clothes, when Vic returned. She'd placed her head on the pillow, and pulled up her comforter, slightly. He laughed to himself. What a sight she was.

Setting the Gatorade on the nightstand, he switched off the lamp, and turned for the door.

"Don't go," her voice softly broke through the silence.

"I thought you were asleep."

"I am," she said, reaching her hand out for him. "Stay just a little while."

He looked around the room, but there wasn't a chair or anywhere for him to sit. "You're in your bed."

"I know," she whispered. "Lay next to me."

The misdirected text that she'd sent his way zipped through

his mind. They'd been flirty, and maybe inwardly each planned for this. But she was in no state to have him in bed with her.

Well, she didn't say anything more than she wanted him to lay with her.

Okay, his mother raised a gentleman. His grandmother would haunt him for the rest of his life if he disrespected *Little Mindy next door*.

Vic toed off his shoes and crawled from the foot of the bed to the empty space next to her.

Without rolling to face him, Mindy scooted back until he was spooning her.

Gently, Vic draped his arm over her waist and she lay still against him. Only a few moments later, her breath was heavy with sleep, and anything that could have happened had been avoided.

Vic closed his eyes and pressed his forehead to the back of her head. He breathed her in and it settled him. There was no doubt they'd share a bed, soon. But for now, she was letting him be her rock, and Vic found he wanted that position in her life more than he thought he could have. Whatever was happening between them, it was the real thing. Perhaps that kiss all those years ago, so innocent and pure, was magic.

It was just past four o'clock in the morning when Mindy looked at her phone. Her head was surprisingly clear, and ache free. She rolled over to see Vic laying with her, but the other side of the bed was empty. Maybe she'd been dreaming and he hadn't been there at all.

Placing her feet on the floor, she monitored her steadiness before she stood and walked to the bathroom.

She was still in her clothes. Her plans to seduce the next-door neighbor hadn't even come close to fruition. Was that because of her, or him, she couldn't remember.

After she'd used the bathroom, and rinsed with mouthwash, Mindy started toward the kitchen to make a cup of coffee. She'd worry about rehydrating after she was fully awake.

As soon as she turned the corner, she stopped and let the breath hold in her lungs. In the stillness of the morning, moonlight still cascading through the windows, Vic slept on her couch. The afghan that her grandmother had made was wrapped around him.

He'd stayed.

How come she wanted to cry? It wasn't sad. It was gentlemanly that he didn't stay in her bed, but instead stayed on the couch, fully dressed. Which romance did he walk out of, she wondered? God, not one would come to mind—how was that even possible?

Vic stirred, and a moment later he sat up, aware of her but not startled.

"Are you okay?" his voice, filled with sleep, broke the silence.

"Yeah," Mindy whispered. "I got up to go to the bathroom and thought I'd make some coffee."

"What time is it?"

"After four."

He chuckled. "You wake up this early?"

Mindy shook her head and took a step toward the couch. "No. Never," she laughed. "You stayed."

"You asked me to."

"You're on the couch."

Rubbing his neck, as if he were working out a kink, he moaned. "I didn't feel right sleeping in your bed, not under the circumstances."

Gentleman right to the core, she thought again. Then it hit her. Westley from *The Princess Bride*. Her heart nearly burst when she thought of Vic being her noble, gentleman hero. Sure, he hadn't saved her life. But saving her dignity, that stood for something nowadays.

"If you're doing okay, I'll head home for a little bit," Vic said standing, folding the afghan, and draping it back over the couch.

"You don't have to go," Mindy said quickly.

In the shadows, Vic moved to her, pulling her into him in what she would consider a friendly hug. "What time do you need to be to work?"

"Eight-thirty."

He kissed the top of her head and it resonated down her spine until it reached her toes. "I'll pick you up at eight. Maybe you should forgo the coffee, and get a few more hours of sleep. How do you feel?"

"I'm all good."

"Glad to hear that. I'll see you in a bit." He gave her one more squeeze with his arms wrapped around her, then he headed for the door where he must have set his shoes when he'd left her bedroom. Shrugging on his coat, he cast one more sweet glance her way before he disappeared out into the morning twilight.

Plopping onto the couch, Mindy rested her head back. It was going to hurt when whatever this was with Vic ended, and it would, but until then, it would be so worth it.

CHAPTER TWENTY

At eight, Mindy opened the front door to see Vic walking up her front steps with two travel mugs of coffee. Then she noticed his car was still parked in her driveway, and Mr. Smith was standing in his front window watching with great interest.

"Good morning, sweetheart," he said, and she knew she'd flashed him a look of panic when his pace slowed. "What's wrong?"

"Just get in here." Vic stepped through the door and Mindy shut it behind him. "Your car is in my driveway."

He nodded. "It sure is. I technically slept here last night. But, that's where I parked when I carried you inside."

"Yeah, well Mr. Smith is watching us. Your car is in my driveway, and you're bringing me coffee."

Vic winced. "And then we're both going to get into my car and drive away. We've really gotten ourselves into a pickle." The wince dissolved into a smile.

"You think this is funny?"

He shrugged a shoulder as if he were blowing off the worry that this was causing her. "I think the old man has nothing better to do than to watch us at all hours."

Mindy crinkled up her nose. "All hours?"

Vic nodded. "I'm pretty sure he saw me walk to my house bright and early this morning."

"Shit."

He handed her one of the travel mugs. "Do you really care what people say? It's none of their business, and we've done nothing inappropriate."

Only in her head, she thought.

"People know my mother in this neighborhood. People know yours."

"Right again." He sipped from his travel mug, his eyes coolly on her. "And what a travesty it would be if my mother heard that I was spending time with you, the girl who watches rom coms with friends, while wearing facial masks, and who lends out sweaters with blinking-nosed reindeer on them."

"I'm serious."

"You shouldn't be." He moved in close to her, but he didn't touch her. "Mindy, we're thirty. We were kissing in Mr. Smith's treehouse when we were ten. Don't you suppose anyone who has known us all this time is thinking *it's about time those two crazy kids got together?*"

She swallowed hard and gripped the travel mug with both hands because she was shaking. "We're not together," she stated the obvious—the obvious to her, anyway.

Vic closed the distance between them now, coming close enough that Mindy had to lower the travel mug to her side and hold it in one hand.

"Aren't we?" he asked now standing so close that his coffee breath, hinted with mint from his toothpaste, was warm on her skin.

"But we haven't—"

"Haven't what?" Vic took the mug from her hand. He turned to the entry table and set both of their mugs down before turning back to her and lifting his hands to her face. "What haven't we done?"

Every part of her trembled and her brain scrambled. "We... well, we haven't..." She couldn't make herself say anything. The words, they were just gone.

Vic's fingers slipped into her hair and then down to the nape of her neck.

Instinct had her grabbing the front of his nicely pressed shirt and wrinkling it between her fingers.

"What haven't we done, Mindy?" he asked, again his fingers now kneading the back of her neck as his mouth moved over her jaw.

"We need to go."

"Do we?"

"I mean, well, don't we?" she swallowed hard and her eyes had closed. He'd fired up every nerve ending in her body, and her knees were going weak.

"What haven't we done that keeps us from being together?"

Mindy's eyes fluttered open, but her vision wasn't clear. Was he teasing her? Was he baiting her?

"Vic..." his name was but a whisper.

"C'mon, tell me we're not together."

"You want us to be together?"

Vic eased back and raised a brow. Those dark eyes lightened as if she were questioning his motives and it had pulled him from his seduction, but it was fleeting. As he scanned a look over her face, his eyes went dark again. His tongue moved over his lips, and Mindy's gaze landed on them.

With his finger under her chin, Vic drew her gaze back to his eyes. "I want to be together."

"With me?"

The corner of his mouth curled up into a sexy grin. "Sometimes you do find your soulmate when you're ten, and you want them to yourself so you can kiss them anytime you want."

Her heart hammered in her chest as he summarized *Sweet Home Alabama.* He did know the movie better than he'd pretended to. God, Ruby had been right!

Mindy pressed her thighs together tight to balance herself. Heat had pooled like liquid lava deep in her belly. Victor Hayes wanted her.

Composure was lost. Those overstimulated nerve endings fired all at once, and Mindy lunged at Vic.

SHE'D KNOCKED HIM OFF BALANCE, AND VIC'S FIRST REACTION WAS to wrap his arms around her waist and fall back against the door with her as Mindy's mouth came to his, hot and heavy.

His lips parted under hers, and he took what she offered. Oh, this wasn't the sweet peck of legend from when they played house, this was a full on, toes curled in your shoes, breath heavy, land on the floor in a heap of bodies kind of kiss that was going to make them late for work.

Mindy kissed him as if she'd been starved for it for years.

Her hands fisted in his shirt, and his slid over the soft curve of her ass.

Certainly everything that was going on with him from the waist down was evident since they were pushed together.

"Are we together now?" he managed as she hooked a leg around him, and he slid his hand from her ass down the length of her thigh.

"Yes," Mindy managed before her mouth clamped down on his again.

His phone buzzed in his pocket. "Fuck," he murmured against her mouth.

She eased back only an inch. "Can it wait?"

"I'm supposed to have a conference call in twenty. That's my reminder."

Her body trembled against his as she lowered her leg and found her footing. "We should go."

Before she could step back, Vic caught her and pulled her in. "We're together," he said firmly, but hoped it didn't sound possessive.

"My mother is going to flip."

"So is Mr. Smith, but I just don't care. I really like you, and this," he motioned to them standing against the front door, "This is only an appetizer."

Mindy bit down on her kiss-swollen bottom lip. "I'm not good at—this," she admitted, motioning between them as he had.

"You're going to be just fine at this, because I'm the other part of it. Don't give up on me before we even get started." Vic pressed one more kiss to her lips. "At least no one can see my wrinkled shirt on a Zoom meeting," he teased and color filled her cheeks.

This was going to be the longest work day of his life, he thought as they gathered their travel mugs, slipped on their coats, and Mindy collected her bags before they walked out to his car, which waited for them in her driveway.

CHAPTER TWENTY-ONE

THE MOMENT THEY'D BACKED INTO THE CUL-DE-SAC, VIC HAD laced their fingers together on the center console and leaned over to kiss her gently. When he'd eased back, Mindy noticed that he'd looked in Mr. Smith's direction.

"He needs something to live for," Vic had said as they drove out of the neighborhood.

Vic's thumb brushed over Mindy's knuckles and she let her gaze fall on the sights out the window as they drove through the familiar streets, and this morning, the melting snow glimmered brighter. The holiday decor on the light poles was festive, as well as the decorations in the storefront windows, and Mindy's looming schedule for the day didn't even cross her mind as they pulled into the parking lot.

"I'll take you to get your car at lunchtime," Vic said, breaking the silence they'd ridden in. "I have to get inside and get to my meeting."

Mindy opened her door and stepped out into the parking lot as Vic did the same. "So this would have been your morning? Only you would have had coffee calmly in your own kitchen, sauntered to your office, and taken your call in your pajama pants?"

He moved in next to her, his arm around her waist. "I would have watched you leave, coffee in my hand, at the window—stalking you just like Mr. Smith does. Yes, I would have sauntered to my office, fully dressed, pants included. However, I might have had slippers on."

As they reached the building, Mindy turned to look at him. "You would watch me leave?"

"For the record, from the moment I moved in, I watched the neighborhood come to life. It was just something I found joy in. And, when I found out it was you that lived next door, it was more interesting."

"Why?"

"We had a history. I was curious as to who was coming and going with you. I figured you had a husband and a couple kids. Then one day, opportunity offered me the reason to show up at your door—and you had a house full of people."

She winced at the memory. "I'm lucky you still want to be around me after seeing me like that."

Vic reached for her hand, gave it a squeeze, and then let it go as he opened the door for her. "It made me want to see more of you," he admitted.

ONE DAY IN A REAL OFFICE, AND VIC WAS SOLD. SURE, WORKING from home had a million advantages, but the office had a view of the Rocky Mountain front range, there were people that passed by his door every so often and waved, even though they didn't know who he was, and the coffee was always brewed in the breakroom.

The best part, of course, was that Mindy's office was just down the hall, and he'd caught sight of her multiple times.

She was no nonsense when she was at work. She'd passed by

his door without even looking in, usually with her phone pressed to her ear. At times, he wondered if she'd even remembered that he was there.

Admittedly, Vic had been more productive before lunch than he'd been in three weeks. Had he been missing out on workplace mentality? Maybe when he got the office renovated, he'd put a spare bed in there instead.

Laughing as he sat at his desk, he shook his head. No. Spare rooms led to spare people in your house. That wasn't what he wanted. He'd put his office back together, there would always be a need for that. And of course, he'd only been in an office building for four hours, it was much too early to decide that this was how he wanted to run his business going forward.

"Can you get away to go get my car?" Mindy's voice pulled him from the view he'd been enjoying outside his window.

"Hey," he said, turning his chair so that he could look at her. "I'm good to go when you're ready."

"I'm ready."

Vic stood, grabbed his keys from the top of his desk, and pulled his coat from the coat stand by the door. "You're a busy woman. It's been interesting to watch you work."

Her mouth turned into a large grin. "Have you gotten any work done, or are you just watching me?"

He laughed. "I've been more productive in the past four hours than I've been in weeks. The view outside my window is spectacular, and so is the view from my door," he said slipping his arm around her waist.

"I guess I'm not too personable when I'm working."

"You're focused," he said as they walked from the building and to his car. "What time will you leave tonight?"

Mindy tucked a strand of hair behind her ear. "I won't be home until late. One of the vineyards is having a holiday dinner."

Vic tucked his hand into Mindy's, their fingers linking

together. "I suppose it's going to be a busy week, isn't it? I have a similar event tomorrow at a client's restaurant."

When they reached his car, he pulled open her door.

"What are your plans for New Year?" she asked, turning toward him.

"I don't have any."

Mindy ran her tongue over her bottom lip. "Usually I would spend the night watching rom coms with my friends, but Ruby will still be in Hawaii, and the other two will want to spend the evening with their husbands."

"Sounds like that leaves you all alone."

She tipped her head to look up at him, and he found that he was instantly lost in those dark eyes.

"That's what I was thinking." She lifted her hands to his chest. "Unless, you'd like to join me?"

Vic looped his arms around her. "Rom coms alone with you?"

She nodded, biting her bottom lip as she fluttered those long eye lashes at him.

Vic dipped his head to gently press a kiss to her lips. "I can't think of anything else I'd rather do on New Year's."

"Nothing else?" she said playfully.

Vic groaned and gripped his fingers into her waist. "I've been thinking about something else an awful lot lately."

He watched her throat work as she swallowed hard. Surely, the pink in her cheeks wasn't from only the cold now.

"It appears we have plans then," she said.

"It sure does." He pressed his fingers deeper into her hips. "It's been a very long time since I've kissed someone at midnight on New Year's Eve."

Her eyes flashed something that could have been taken as disbelief, maybe.

"I've never kissed anyone on New Year's Eve," she admitted.

Perhaps his face flashed disbelief too. "Never?"

"I told you. I'm no good at relationship stuff."

He smiled. "You're wrong. Look at the relationship you have with Lisa, Tina, and Ruby. That's important."

"That's different."

"No, it's not. Like I said, that's important. But if I get to be your first real kiss on New Year's Eve, I'd better make it worth it."

She lifted her arms around his neck. "From what I experienced this morning, I'm very much looking forward to that midnight kiss."

So was he.

CHAPTER TWENTY-TWO

I⊤ WAS AFTER ELEVEN-THIRTY WHEN MINDY PULLED INTO HER garage and the door went down behind her. Vic waited for lights to go on in the house, but there were none.

He was desperate to text her and tell her goodnight, but maybe since no lights went on, she was headed straight to bed.

The movement in Mr. Smith's window drew Vic's attention away from Mindy's house. Shaking his head, he wondered what the man thought with him and Mindy going in between their houses as they'd been doing. Surely the cul-de-sac had been quiet over the years. Were they creating a buzz with their friendship?

Friendship, he let out a snort. They'd changed that specification that morning, hadn't they? No wonder the neighbors were lurking in their windows to see what was going on.

His phone chimed on the kitchen counter. Vic walked toward the kitchen, picked up his phone, and smiled as he saw the rubber duck meme Mindy had sent him, which he set as her profile picture.

I'm home safe and sound. Thanks for watching for me, Mindy texted with a winking emoji. *Goodnight.*

Vic laughed. So, she'd seen him lurking in the window.

Mr. Smith and I were equally as anxious to have you home it appears, Vic replied.

I feel loved. She added a heart. *I'll see you at the office tomorrow. Goodnight.*

Goodnight, he replied, but desperately wanted to invite her over, or hoped to get an invite.

No, he couldn't rush this. Mindy wasn't the kind of girl to rush, no matter how hot and heavy their morning had started. If he didn't want to scare her away, Vic was going to have to move purposefully, and be patient.

She needed validation that he was the kind of guy he'd promised to be—not like her lying, cheating ex. The kind of guy who was honest and upstanding. The kind of guy that knew how important she was, and that she was the only one. He'd have to be vetted by the friends. He'd have to give concession to her family and be willing to come second. This wasn't going to be like any other relationship he'd ever had. This one had been brewing for decades, he thought amorously. Maybe, just maybe, he'd actually found his soulmate at ten like they'd alluded to in *Sweet Home Alabama*. Romance tropes be damned.

MINDY WASN'T IN HER OFFICE THE NEXT MORNING, AND VIC hadn't seen her when he finally left for lunch. There had been no calls or texts.

Was he expecting too much? Obviously.

The night before, he'd sanded down the areas on the wall that he needed to repair, between walks to the window to check on Mindy's return status, but he wasn't sure when he'd get to repairing them. Suddenly he wasn't in a huge hurry to finish the renovation on the room. Though, with his house in the state it was in, he wasn't too productive with anything else in his life with the mess that surrounded him, and he was much too focused on Mindy.

Had that been the reason for his success up until now? He didn't think about women or dating, so everything he had went into his business. Now, Mindy seemed to take up more space in his mind than his work or the creative aspect to it.

Surely, this was something he was going to have to pay some mind to.

It was after one when Mindy finally poked her head through his door after knocking. "Hey," she said softly, letting herself into his office and closing the door behind her.

Vic stood and moved to her without a word. He couldn't stand to not touch her, so he wrapped his arms around her and pulled her to him. Mindy's arms looped around his neck before he brought his mouth down to hers.

"This has been a very long morning," he muttered the words against her throat and felt the moan she'd let out vibrate in her throat. "Tell me you weren't avoiding me all day because you knew I couldn't keep my hands off you."

Mindy's fingers tunneled up into his hair as he feathered kisses over her neck.

"I've been so busy," her words were airy as she breathed beneath him. "I only have a few minutes before I'm off again."

His mouth found hers, his tongue slipping through her lips to explore her. She tasted like a mix of wine and coffee, and it was a stark reminder of her job and the need to get back to it.

Vic eased back only slightly, his fingers gripping her. "Where are you off to?"

"Evergreen."

He felt his entire body deflate. "I'll be gone by the time you get back. I have that dinner tonight."

Mindy nodded as her hands slipped from behind his neck, over his shoulders, and down to where his hands gripped her. She interlocked their fingers, watching as she did so before she lifted her eyes back to his. "Maybe next week we can watch a sports movie," she teased.

He'd forgotten their plan. Vic smiled. "I can't wait for New Year's," he said, and wondered if it was just him the had huge expectations for that night.

"Neither can I," she said, but her voice was low, husky. Yeah, she was planning on that night too. "I have to go. I'll see you in the morning."

He didn't want to let go, but if he didn't, she'd stop walking into his office at all.

MINDY PICKED LISA UP A FEW HOURS LATER AND THEY HEADED TO Evergreen.

"Why am I going with you and not the guy next door?" Lisa asked as she checked her makeup in the mirror on the back of the visor.

"Because we already had plans to do this, and his name is Vic, by the way."

"I know his name. It's not what Ruby calls him, but…"

Mindy turned her head toward Lisa. "What does she call him?"

Lisa laughed as she closed the cover to the mirror and pushed up the visor. "I don't know if you can turn that kind of red," she said and Mindy shook her head.

"That woman," she said, laughing.

"We should all be more like her. We shouldn't care about all the little things."

"Oh, she cares about them," Mindy said. "She just has a fuck-it attitude."

When she said that, Lisa laughed again. "I love when you say the f-word. It makes the cloud hanging over all our heads go away for a moment."

"That's silly."

"No, it just means you let down your walls for a moment."

Mindy gripped the steering wheel. "What walls?"

"The ones you stand behind. The ones that keep you from stepping over that line and doing crazy shit."

"Are you saying I'm no fun?"

"No, I'm saying you're a rule follower. You want everything to be calm with no fuss."

There was an ache in Mindy's chest hearing Lisa talk like that. "No fuss? I fuss plenty."

"You do, because you want everything just so for everyone else." Lisa turned in her seat. "Look at your house."

"What about my house?"

Lisa's hands came up in defense. "Ruby's right. You're keeping that house as a shrine. You're too afraid to change anything because it would remove your grandmother, and maybe upset your mother and the rest of your family."

"My house is just fine."

"Then keep it as it is. But it's fucking creepy sometimes. Just saying."

Mindy stiffened. "I guess you shouldn't come over then."

Lisa shook her head. "Pull your head out of your ass. I don't have any problems with you or your house—mostly. And Ruby calls him the ride next door, by the way, and she's not referring to him picking the two of you up after drinking too much."

"We haven't done anything."

"And that wall seems to be there again," Lisa argued.

"You think I'm not making moves?"

"I don't know. Why don't you tell me?"

Mindy looked at Lisa, and back to the road. Then once again to Lisa, and back to the road.

"I'll have you know that after Ruby and I drank the other night, I had all intentions of seducing him."

"No shit?"

"No shit," Mindy repeated. "And yesterday morning," she

cleared her throat. "We, I think, decided that we're a thing."

There was an enormous smile gracing Lisa's face. "A *thing*?"

"Yes, a *thing*."

"And that's your way of saying Vic from next door, the ride next door, is your boyfriend?"

Mindy shifted in her seat as she watched cars pass by her while she stayed in the slower lane. "I guess. Yes," she decided. "That's exactly what it means."

"So in a week, you got your ten-year-old boyfriend back?"

"And you think I have my head up my ass? Check yours."

"Oh, mine is fine," Lisa said. "I'm just catching up. This is what happens when no one talks to you for a week. So let's just recount; you're not banging the guy next door," Lisa said holding up a finger as Mindy went to argue. "Ruby's words, not mine."

Mindy let out a growl.

Lisa took a breath to continue. "But you want to bang the neighbor next door, and you even planned it, but yes, I know, you haven't. And now he's your boyfriend and I'm the only one that knows it."

There was an enormous amount of pride in Lisa's voice as she settled back in her seat.

"I like him."

"Yeah you do," Lisa agreed.

Mindy laughed and shook her head. "Okay, I want to bang him."

Now Lisa laughed with a snort. "Oh, yeah you do!"

"You're a pain in my ass," Mindy said, watching for her exit.

"I'm the girl who moved in with her forbidden lover," Lisa said with immense pride. "Don't you forget it."

As they laughed, Mindy turned off at her exit, feeling blessed to have friends that could bring out every emotion in her. Some of it hit too close to home though, she thought. Maybe she needed to break down that wall Lisa talked about. Then again, with Vic, maybe that was exactly what she was doing.

CHAPTER TWENTY-THREE

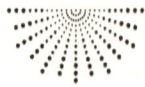

IT WAS PAST NINE O'CLOCK WHEN VIC PULLED INTO HIS DRIVEWAY and opened his garage. As he pulled in, he noticed the headlights coming down the street. Mindy was just getting home too.

He parked in the garage, climbed out of the car, and walked out to the driveway to find Mindy already walking toward him, her garage door closing behind her.

"Hey," he said watching her walk across the small yard that separated their houses.

Without a word, she folded right into his arms, lifted up on her toes, and kissed him thoroughly, warming him throughout.

Mr. Smith must be getting an eye full, Vic thought. He lifted Mindy off her feet, walked her into the garage, and then broke free only long enough to open his car door and push the button to close the garage.

She was pressed against him as soon as he turned back to her. Her chilled hands pulled his shirt from his pants, and he shuddered as she trailed cold fingers against his skin.

He'd been dreaming about her touch all day, he just hadn't expected that this was how it was going to happen.

Vic moved to push her up against the car. "Wait, we need to

get inside. The car is wet."

"I don't care," she mumbled against his lips. "I just don't care."

Fuck! His entire body reacted to that, and the brushing of her fingertips over his nipples. Seriously? A week into whatever this was with him and Mindy, and they were going to have sex pressed up against his wet car in the garage? This was a side to her he didn't think he'd get to see—the reckless, needy Mindy.

She worked her way out of her coat and tossed it aside, away from the wet car. She was in a dress that fit her curves and plunged at the neckline. Vic gripped her hips and started a trail of kisses that moved from her ear, over her jaw, down her throat, and to the swells of her breasts. Mindy's breath was heavy as she worked the buttons on his shirt and he gathered her dress in his hands so that he could—

"Wait! Shit! Wait!" Mindy said beneath him before her hands came to his chest. "Shit! Shit!"

Vic let go of her dress and took a step back. "I'm sorry. God, I'm so—"

"Shit!" Mindy moved from him and picked up her coat. "Open the door."

"Okay," Vic opened the car door and pushed the button to the garage door, opening it. "Mindy, what's—"

As soon as she could sprint out, she did.

Vic watched as she ran back to her house, punched in the code for her garage, and disappeared inside.

As the door to the garage went down, lights inside the house turned on one by one, a drastic change from nights he'd watched her return home and no lights came on.

There was a sinking feeling that landed in the pit of his stomach. He needed to remember that Mindy wasn't someone he could just ravage in the garage. Vic knew he had to handle her differently. He raked his fingers through his hair, closed the garage, and walked into his lonely, quiet house. He'd give her some space.

~

ARE YOU STILL UP? MINDY STOOD ON VIC'S FRONT STEP AN HOUR later, her stomach pinching, a headache throbbing, and humiliation swimming in her veins.

Yeah. Are you okay?

Mindy's cold fingers moved over the screen on her phone. *I'm at your front door.*

She waited and only a few seconds later he pulled open the door, meeting her in a pair of shorts. No shirt.

Mindy sucked in a breath and took in the sight of him, fresh from his bed. "I woke you."

"You got me out of bed. I wasn't sleeping," he said reaching for her and pulling her into the house, but not against him. "Are you okay? You scared the shit out of me."

Already she felt the heat rising in her cheeks. It was normal. This was perfectly normal. They had established themselves as a couple, and this was going to happen—again and again and again.

Another pain pinched in her stomach and she winced.

"You don't look so well," he said.

"Trust me, I'm fine." She handed him the paper bag she held in her hand, which she'd rolled up tightly. "I feel so stupid. But this is for you to put in your bathroom."

His brows drew inward. "My bathroom," he said skeptically as he moved to open the bag, but Mindy grabbed his hands to stop him.

"Remember what you don't have in your bathroom?" She watched his face, but it wasn't processing. "Things for women who stay here."

"Women don't stay here."

"I know," she said on a laugh because her nerves were all mixed up with his confusion. "Let's just say, someday I might. So put them in the back of your drawer and forget about them."

He watched her for another moment and then his eyes went

wide. "Oh," he finally managed, and then scanned a look over her. "Oh," he said again.

"Yeah, oh. Shitty timing," Mindy said, the heat burning through her now.

"Okay, then. This I can handle," he said, moving in to pull her to him. "I was so afraid I'd crossed a line touching you like that in the garage."

Mindy shook her head. "No. God, no. I was rather enjoying it."

"So was I," he admitted before pressing a warm kiss to her lips.

"Anyway, I wanted you to know everything was okay. And this very real-life thing happened."

"Never be embarrassed by it," he said. "I grew up with sisters and a mother who made sure I was very appreciative of what a woman's body did in order to do all the other things that was expected of it."

Mindy laughed. "I'm sure you've had your fill of PMS in your life."

"I'm stronger for it," he teased.

"I'm going to go home and decompress," Mindy said. "And, I don't work tomorrow," she added as she turned to open the door. "Day before Christmas Eve and all."

Vic nodded. "No need for me to go in either," he admitted.

"Breakfast?"

"I'd love to."

Mindy chewed on her lip and then smiled up at him. "Denver Biscuit Company?"

"I could certainly go for that."

She stepped in, rose up on her toes, and lingered a kiss on his lips making sure to not touch his bare skin. She just wasn't sure she could handle that at the moment.

"Goodnight," she said as she slipped out the door.

"Goodnight."

CHAPTER TWENTY-FOUR

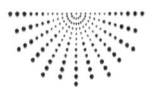

THE SMELLS THAT CAME FROM THE KITCHEN OF PIES BAKING stirred all the feels inside of Mindy. Her mother always put out a spread, and it culminated in a buffet of pies.

Cherry was Mindy's favorite, but since she was already bloated from her damn period, and the need to eat sweets was overwhelming, she was claiming a piece of cherry, a piece of apple, and taking home some of that pecan pie she knew was on the counter.

"There's my baby girl," her father's voice boomed as she walked into the house. He stood from his chair and crossed to her, enveloping her in his arms as she kept her grip on the bags of gifts in her hands.

"Hey, Daddy," she said, breathing in the comforting scent of her father. He smoked a pipe, or at least lit it often because he'd always enjoyed the smell. Mindy enjoyed it too when it mixed with his cologne.

"I napped so I can eat and make it to mass," he said without asking if she wanted to go, but she knew better. It wasn't that he wasn't inviting her, it was that he was expecting her to go with him.

"It sounds like you have a good plan."

"Make sure you get some coffee. You look tired. Father Murphy won't want you falling asleep," he said as he moved back to his recliner to sit.

And there it was. Midnight mass was on her agenda.

Mindy put her bags under the Christmas tree in the family room, but pulled out the ornament she'd brought her mother, and walked to the kitchen.

On the kitchen counter was another Christmas tree, decorated with miniature cooking elements.

"Hello, sweetheart," her mother said, jutting out her chin so that Mindy would kiss her cheek while she pulled a pie from the oven.

"Hey, Mama." Mindy moved to avoid her mother's path to the counter. "I brought you something."

Her mother set down the pie, pulled off the mitts, and reached for the small bag Mindy held out to her. Though her mother knew it was an ornament, it was always a surprise as to what it was.

Putting her hand into the bag, her mother pulled out the miniature wine bottle and glass. "Oh, this is perfect," she said examining it. "From a winery?"

Mindy nodded. "A new one in France. I brought it back from my last trip."

"I love it. Will you put it on the tree for me?"

Mindy took the ornament and walked toward the tabletop tree in the family room, which her mother decorated with items that were tributes to her daughters' careers.

Every year Mindy brought her an ornament that had something to do with wine. Her sister Carrie was a preschool teacher, so the tree boasted alcohol and educational items, and brought some humor to those who would visit.

The basement door opened and her sister and her family walked up the steps.

"Ne-ne," Mindy's niece ran to her and Mindy scooped her up.

"How's my girl?" Mindy asked as she planted a noisy kiss to the two-year-old's cheek.

"Santa come?"

"Not yet. You have to be asleep for him to come."

Her niece wiggled out of her arms and ran after the old poodle that had poked his head out from behind the couch.

"Carolyn, be gentle with the dog," Carrie called after her daughter as her husband Blake handed her their son, and then nudged Mindy as he passed by her. "Did you come alone?" she asked.

"Did you expect me to bring someone with me?"

Carrie shrugged as she ran her hand over Bo's head which rested against her shoulder. "Lisa is married now, huh?"

"Yep. Not only is she married, but she and Tina will be spending a lot of family time together since they're sisters-in-law now. Oh, and her brother moved back from England."

Carrie's brows knit. "Brother?"

"Her foster brother from the family she lived with the longest when she was a teenager."

Her sister made an O with her mouth. "Mom caught wind that you might be seeing someone," she whispered as Mindy rubbed her nephew's small back.

"Caught wind?"

"Mrs. Cartwright always calls her, you know?"

Mindy nodded. She'd been very aware of Mr. Smith's spying, but Mrs. Cartwright must have just been more stealthy in her gathering of information.

"And who am I seeing?"

Carrie raised her brows. "Little Vic Hayes."

Mindy laughed. Hadn't *Little Vic* called her *Little Mindy* when referring to her? "He's a grown man now."

Carrie leaned in. "God, give me details. My nipples hurt from breastfeeding. I have hemorrhoids from pregnancy. I haven't slept since before I was pregnant with Carolyn. I want to know what it's like to be single and have the attention of a new man."

Mindy wasn't sure if she was supposed to laugh or to cry for her sister. Carrie wasn't making motherhood appealing at all. Mindy wondered if Tina knew what was coming.

"We've been spending time together," Mindy admitted. "He's a nice guy."

"Nice guy, huh?" Carrie scanned a look over her. "You guys used to make out."

Mindy snorted out a laugh. "Make out? We kissed one time when we were playing house. We were ten."

"That's not how I heard it."

"And who did you hear that from?"

"Curt Smith."

Mindy shook her head. "Well, he was always a tall tale teller."

"You were kissing boys in his back yard."

"Yes, and I wasn't kissing Curt. I'm assuming that's why it was such a big deal."

Carrie nodded. "Here, take him," she said, handing Bo over to Mindy. "I have to pee before he wakes up again and wants to nurse."

Mindy curled the baby into her arm and walked to the couch in the family room to sit down. She let his tiny hand curl around her finger. She wasn't in a hurry to have a baby, but she wasn't getting any younger either.

Pulling her phone from her pocket, she managed a selfie of herself and Bo before Carolyn noticed her and had to get into the picture too. Mindy laughed and managed to keep Bo safe while Carolyn crawled up next to her. She snapped the picture and Carolyn hurried off.

With her free hand, she opened her text messages and pulled up Vic's text thread. She attached the picture and used the dictation to text him. "Merry Christmas," she said and watched as the text came up on the screen.

Carrie came back from the bathroom, checked on Mindy and went to the kitchen, obviously hoping for just a few moments before Bo woke up again and needed her.

As he stirred in Mindy's arms, she shouldered him and rubbed his back. When her phone dinged again, she slid her finger over it.

That has to be the best Christmas picture ever, he replied.

The peace and quiet lasted all of ten more minutes before Bo woke up in need of his mother. And because she knew the attention in the house had shifted, Carolyn took that moment to need Carrie too. Mindy watched in awe as her brother-in-law Blake moved in to distract Carolyn so that Carrie could nurse in peace.

It seemed like a lot of orchestration to keep the little family happy. But Mindy watched with admiration, wondering if the same scene was ever in her future.

Her phone buzzed and she smiled down at the text from Vic.

I told you I'm their favorite uncle. The picture attached was of Vic with two infants, one in each arm, a toddler hanging from his neck, and two young boys sat next to him. The smile on Vic's face was wide, and it came across that he loved the kids who surrounded him.

Mindy lifted her eyes to her sister who rocked Bo as he nursed. A peace surrounded them as Carrie brushed her hand over her son's head.

Looking back down at the picture of Vic surrounded by his nieces and nephews, Mindy thought maybe she could see herself with a family in the near future.

CHAPTER TWENTY-FIVE

"Liv, are you joining us out here?" Vic's father called to his mother who still flitted around in the kitchen.

"I'm coming," she called back as she appeared with a basket of rolls and set them on the table in front of Vic. He nabbed one from the top and his mother grinned at him. Then he took another, handing it to Brian, his eldest nephew of five-years-old.

Brian grinned up at him and it warmed his heart. His sisters had sure filled the table over the years, and he would never have believed anyone who would have told him how much he'd actually love every one of the kids that had joined their family.

He thought of the picture he'd sent to Mindy, and the one she'd sent him first. They were in the same place in their lives. The last of their families to get married and have kids.

As he helped his nephew fill his plate, his mind buzzed with the feelings that just thinking about Mindy stirred in him. Was he desperate to catch up with his sisters in the marriage department? Was that why he was so intrigued with Mindy? Was she just convenient? No, that wasn't how he felt at all.

"So how is Corinne?" his mother asked before she called Vic by name to get his attention. "How is Corinne?"

Vic looked around the table. "Who is Corinne?" he asked wondering why his mother was asking him about someone he didn't know.

She laughed. "Mindy's mother," she said, and he realized he had no idea what her parents' names were.

"I don't know," he admitted.

"I thought you were spending a lot of time with her. With Mindy that is."

"I am, but I haven't talked to her about her mother." Nor had he recalled Mindy's mother's name.

Amber leaned in to look around her husband and daughter who sat between them. "Who is Mindy?"

"She lives in Catherine Sanders' old house. She's her granddaughter," his mother explained.

"You spend time with her?" his sister asked.

"Yes," he replied, not quite ready to say they were seeing one another, or feeling each other up in the garage.

"Justine mentioned that she's called you multiple times and you haven't responded," Amber drilled.

"I've been busy. Besides, I'm not looking to date."

Allison handed her daughter a bite sized piece of dinner roll, breaking more pieces onto the tray of the highchair. "You went out with Parker," she said as if she'd won the contest she and Amber seemed to be having.

Amber hammered a fist onto the table. "You went out with Parker but you won't call Justine?"

His youngest sister Angie let out a laugh. "You two are ridiculous. He's sleeping with the neighbor," she said and all eyes turned to look at her as she rubbed her pregnant belly and her husband distracted their daughter.

Then all eyes turned to Vic. "What?"

Allison aimed her fork in his direction. "You're sleeping with your neighbor but you went out with Parker?"

His mother shook her head. "Vic…" she said his name just as he had when he was little and had done something out of character that disappointed her.

"I haven't done anything."

He noticed his father's lips tighten as if he wanted to laugh, but wasn't about to.

"So what about Parker?" Allison asked again.

Vic grinned as he scooped up a forkful of mashed potatoes. "I thought you and Parker were good friends," he said.

"We are. We were," she corrected. "You took her to prom."

"When I was a junior and she was a senior. That was more than a decade ago."

"But you guys went out," she said again.

"We met for coffee, and then we're going to meet up to discuss advertising for her family's furniture store."

"I brought her to you to date."

Vic ate the potatoes. "I didn't ask you to."

His mother slapped his arm. "Don't talk with your mouth full."

Vic swallowed his food. "I didn't ask you to set me up."

"But she's a wonderful girl."

He shook his head. "She is, but you should get to know your friend better."

"Why?"

"She's more apt to date you," he said. "She's not much for dating men."

Allison's eyes went wide. "Who told you that?"

Vic laughed. "She did."

And that seemed to be the end of the conversation until dinner was over. In fact, they waited until gifts had been opened, and dessert was served before his sisters and his mother cornered him in the kitchen.

Allison started it. "You're saying that Parker is gay?"

Vic rinsed the plates in the sink, handing them to Angie, who loaded them into the dishwasher.

"I'm saying that she said you and her don't keep in touch much, and that you didn't get the memo that she doesn't enjoy the company of men."

Allison rested her hip against the counter. "I had no idea."

"Maybe you shouldn't try to set me up then," he countered.

Amber covered a leftover container of desserts she was taking home. "And what about Justine?"

Vic shook his head. "You do realize I didn't ask you all to set me up with people?"

"Still, you told her you'd call her."

"Well, I'm not going to," he admitted. "Sorry."

"Why?" Amber continued, and he wondered what he owed the woman.

Angie took the last plate from Vic and put it into the dishwasher. "I'm telling you all, he's not interested because he's already involved with the neighbor."

Vic stared at his sister whose smile was sly as if she had some kind of insider information.

His mother snapped her kitchen towel at him. "You're not really involved with Corinne's daughter are you?"

Looking around the kitchen, he took in the four sets of matching eyes that stared back at him.

"I find her very interesting," Vic said, wanting to desperately escape this family inquisition he was facing.

Angie laughed again. "Curt Smith says you sleep at her house and park in her driveway. Oh, and that you make out," she whispered the last part.

Vic's mother snapped the towel at him again. "Victor!" she used his full name and he kept his eyes steely on Angie.

"You talk to Curt Smith?"

"He happens to work for one of our vendors," she said. "I talk to him every so often."

Yeah, well he must have beelined right to her to tell her what his father had seen.

The four sets of eyes stayed focused on him, before his mother used his full name again as if she were demanding an explanation.

"Yes, I parked in her driveway the other night because I'd picked her and her friend up at a restaurant when they'd had too much to drink." His mother looked shocked, but Angie's mouth had turned upward and she grinned at him.

Vic leaned against the counter. "I took her home."

"And?" Angie pried.

He ran his tongue over his teeth. "I stayed the night. On the couch," he emphasized. Then, he looked directly at his mother. "And, yes, we're seeing each other, but as in we just started seeing one another and it's not serious yet."

Angie let out a loud laugh. "As in he's going to sleep with her. He just hasn't yet."

Finally, his mother snapped her towel at Angie who yelped and jumped back. Then his mother shook her head at him, not quite as disappointed as he thought she'd be.

"Vic, you can't just make a move on Mrs. Sanders' granddaughter," his mother said in that motherly tone that made him feel small.

"I'm not just making moves on her, Mom. We understand the issues, but we're interested in each other."

Angie rested her hands on her enlarged belly, wincing at what Vic assumed was the baby kicking. "It's not like any of this is new," she said, grinning at Vic and then tilting her head toward their mother. "They've been making out in the cul-de-sac since they were kids."

His mother's eyes went wide and Vic shook his head at his sister. When the other two laughed, he realized they were still trying to ruin his life. Two of them by setting him up with random women, the other by ratting him out. Not much had changed from childhood. His sisters were out to get him and he was still kissing the girl who spent her summers on their grandmothers' cul-de-sac.

CHAPTER TWENTY-SIX

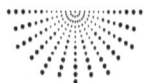

ARE YOU HOME? MINDY READ THE TEXT, SHIFTED A LOOK AT HER father who was driving them to church, and decided she had to answer the text.

Headed to church with Dad. And though it was always tradition, it pained her now to add, *I'll be staying at their house tonight.*

A few moments later Vic texted back. *I'll redirect Santa your way. Merry Christmas. I'll see you tomorrow.*

Mindy grinned down at her phone, sending only a heart emoji before turning her phone over in her lap.

"Was that your mother?" her father asked.

"No." Mindy said she looked out the window, into the darkness of the city as they passed through it.

"Your mom says you're seeing someone," he said, and Mindy couldn't help but laugh, drawing her father's attention away from the road for a brief moment.

"When did she tell you that? I didn't tell her anything."

Her father's lips pursed. "Carrie told her you're seeing the neighbor boy."

Mindy's smile widened. *Neighbor boy.*

Her father shifted a look in her direction again. "Well?"

"Fine. Yes, I'm seeing Vic Hayes. He lives in his grandmother's house."

She watched as her father's face contorted with what she assumed was concern. "Victoria Hanson's grandson?"

"Yes."

His face crinkled up. "Liv's kid?"

"You know Liv?"

His fingers tightened around the steering wheel. "Yeah. I only lived three blocks away. We all knew each other back then. I knew the Smith boys and the Cartwrights. Most of the time, everyone would find themselves in the cul-de-sac because it was a good place to run."

Mindy smiled, thinking about what it must have been like when her mother lived there. She hadn't even considered that her mother and Vic's mother would have grown up together.

"Mr. Smith is the neighborhood watch, I guess you could say," Mindy laughed. "He's always at the window watching what's going on."

Her dad nodded. "His wife was always that way, even when we were all younger. You knew that if you did something wrong, Mrs. Smith would be calling your parents."

"Really?"

"Oh, yeah. What did they have, eight kids? They had some my age, and some your age," he recollected.

"I only knew Curtis and Brian."

Her father nodded. "That's right. Once the older kids started moving out, she got pregnant again. Into her forties. And, they knew having a kid that much younger than their siblings would be hard, so they had two so they were together."

Mindy let out a hum. "I guess that makes sense."

"It does, except then your parents are the same age as everyone else's grandparents. Mr. Smith has to be in his eighties now."

Mindy nodded. "I haven't actually seen him outside of his house much in the past three years that I've lived there."

"I think his kids keep an eye on him. Especially since Mrs. Smith died."

"I see cars come and go from his house a lot." She considered the Smith family more. "Curt and Brian were ornery."

Her father laughed. "The entire Smith clan was ornery."

They shared a laugh over that.

"So, Mom and Liv, were they good friends?"

Her father shifted in his seat. "When they were little they were good friends. They drifted apart in high school."

"I suppose that happens," Mindy said, thinking about friends she hadn't reconnected with since high school. "It's funny to me to think that they hung out together. I wonder if she's said anything to Vic."

As they drove down the street, Mindy watched her father stare out the front window, passing by the church.

"Where are you going? You passed the church."

Her father snapped up his head and looked around, obviously distracted. "Oh. Crap. I'll turn around."

"What's on your mind?"

"Nothing. I'm fine."

He turned at the next street, went around the block, and they parked at the church.

Mindy walked with him into the church, her arm looped through his. Something about strolling down memory lane seemed to have jostled him. In his own time, she supposed, he'd tell her what altered his mood.

ASIDE FROM ONE TEXT EARLY THAT MORNING, MINDY HADN'T heard from Vic until she pulled into her driveway on Christmas afternoon. Before she'd even put her car in park in her garage, he was standing in her driveway.

Smiling, Mindy stepped out of her car and Vic moved to her. "Merry Christmas," he said as he wrapped his arms around her waist and Mindy raised hers to loop around his neck. "I feel as if I haven't seen you in a week."

"Family time will do that to you," she joked, pressing her forehead to his. "You win in the nieces and nephew department."

"One more on the way. Alice is having another, but she never finds out what she's having. I don't know how she handles our sisters badgering her about that. Except that she's such a stubborn ass, she finds some joy in being defiant."

Mindy lifted her head and looked out toward the street. "It appears that Mr. Smith isn't our only spy," she informed him and he laughed.

"You don't say?"

"Mrs. Cartwright called my mother on us."

That caused him to laugh harder. "Well, Curt Smith does business with one of my sisters. Looks like we were outed by everyone."

"Embracing in the garage with the door open like this doesn't help us much."

"I didn't think we were hiding this."

Mindy sighed. "You're right. Let 'em watch," she said as she rose on her toes and opened her mouth to his.

VIC INHALED THE KISS, THE TASTE OF HER, THE FEEL OF THE MOAN that moved through her. His hands moved over her bottom as she slid her hands over his chest and around his back.

"The need to finish what we started the other night keeps occupying my mind," he admitted as he ran his lips over her throat as she tipped her head back. "Maybe I shouldn't have said that. That makes me sound like some stalker."

"For the record," her throat worked under his lips, "I've been thinking about it too. Soon."

His mind went back to the other night in his garage and the reason it ended the way it did. He could be patient. After all, he cared about Mindy, and this wasn't going to be any casual hookup for either of them.

Vic eased back, but kept her in his embrace. "I brought home leftovers. Interested in dinner?"

"Let me get changed and unload my car."

Vic looked in the backseat. "Gift haul?"

Mindy nodded. "Admittedly, my favorite gift was from my niece. She's almost two."

"What did she get you?"

"A framed butterfly picture made from her handprints."

"Now those are the kinds of gifts no man could ever compete with." Vic cupped her face in his hands. "Remind me to show you my gallery of artwork from the talented offspring of my siblings."

When Mindy laughed, and her head tilted back, Vic's mind went right back to wanting to spend hours running his lips over the delicate skin of her throat.

"I look forward to touring that gallery." Now she moved from him and opened the back door to her car. "Help me carry this all inside?"

CHAPTER TWENTY-SEVEN

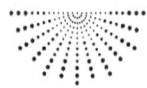

MARIACHI MUSIC FILLED THE RESTAURANT ON TUESDAY NIGHT AS Mindy navigated her way around the band to find her friends in the corner booth all the way in the back.

"I'm sorry I'm late. I was making travel plans," she said as she shrugged off her coat and slid it into the booth next to Lisa.

"Where are you going?" Lisa asked, lifting her margarita to her lips.

"Napa Valley."

Tina shook her head. "She rolls those kinds of words off her tongue as if they aren't a big deal. *I'm off to France. I'm headed to Napa Valley. Naples is beautiful this time of year.*"

Mindy sipped the margarita that was on the table waiting for her. "Some of us have curated a life of exotic travel," she grinned from behind her glass.

Lisa nudged her slightly. "Are you taking Vic with you?"

Mindy shook her head. "No. It's a quick trip."

Lisa raised her brow. "Seriously? I thought exotic travel was supposed to be the glory of your job."

"It is. I've just never asked to take someone with me."

"You've taken me," Lisa said and Mindy nodded slowly.

"Sure, to Palisade where we could drive and you could room with me." Mindy laughed. "We'll get there, I suppose."

Tina sipped her Shirley Temple drink. "Where is he tonight?"

"He was going to have dinner with his mother."

"That's nice. They're close?"

"I suppose." She hadn't really thought about them being any closer than she was with her family. "He has more sisters and they have more kids than my sister does. Otherwise, I guess our families are the same. His parents are married. Mine are married." She thought about the talk she'd had with her dad about it. "Our moms were friends when they were young, my dad said. But they grew apart in high school. But my dad talked about running the cul-de-sac when he was younger. All the kids in the area ended up over there."

Tina grinned. "It's funny to think of our parents as kids. I mean you hear stories, but you and Vic, you live in the houses they grew up in."

Yeah, Mindy thought. And didn't she live in it in pristine condition?

Lisa picked up a chip from the basket on the table. "I guess if this works out for you guys, you won't have to go through the weirdness of your parents meeting."

Mindy considered that. "That's true. But, when I talked to my dad about Vic's mom and my mom, he was weird about it. I'm wondering if they didn't get along."

Tina's eyes went wide. "Oh, maybe it will be awkward."

VIC LOOKED UP FROM HIS MENU AS HIS MOTHER WALKED TOWARD the table. He stood as she leaned in and kissed him on the cheek.

"Hello, darling," she said handing him a canvas grocery bag.

"This is that sweater of Mindy's. I thought you could give it back to her for me."

"Sure," Vic said as his mom shrugged out of her coat, and Vic took it and draped it over the open seat at the table. Then he held her chair as she sat down, before returning to his chair

"I wasn't sure if she'd be here with you," his mother said as she picked up her menu.

"She had dinner plans with a few of her girlfriends."

"That's nice that they're all so close."

"It's enviable for sure," he said as he picked up his menu.

They were silent for a few minutes studying their menus. They ordered when the server came to the table. As she walked away, Vic's mother folded her hands atop the table and smiled at him.

"Your sisters were a little ruthless on you at Christmas," she teased.

"Oh, you think that was different than any other time?" he laughed as he picked up his water and took a sip.

"They love you."

"I know. I'm a stronger person for their love," he teased and his mother laughed.

"You're a smart ass," she laughed as the server delivered her a glass of wine and Vic a beer. "Though Angie and her mouth..." His mother rolled her eyes.

"It's part of her charm."

"I'm not sure where she got that charm. Maybe from your father's side," she said sipping her wine.

"Maybe. And my quiet, loveable, studious side came from?"

"Well, from me, of course."

"Of course." He toasted her with his beer before taking a sip.

"How serious are you with Corinne's daughter?" She asked quickly, her voice flat as she lifted her glass to her lips to sip.

Vic swallowed and lowered his beer. "We're seeing each other, getting to know one another."

"She seemed like a nice girl."

"The nicest," he confirmed.

"I know I was being nice to her when I dropped off the keys. Maybe I gave you all the wrong idea as if I were setting you up to get me that sweater."

Vic chewed his bottom lip. "It did seem like a ploy. But it was just nice chit chat?"

"Yes."

"And you don't want me seeing her?"

"Oh, I didn't say that."

"I'm getting some serious mixed signals."

She sipped her wine again. "Her mother is okay with you dating?"

"Well, as we're not teenagers, we didn't ask." Vic leaned in on his forearms, his beer bottle between his palms. "What's going on?"

His mother studied her wine before setting it on the table. "I haven't talked to Corinne since we were sixteen."

"So you grew apart?"

"She's not a fan of me, I'm afraid."

Vic shrugged. "Not everyone can like you. And that was a long time ago. Everyone grows up."

His mother's mouth contorted and she kept her gaze to the table. "Vic, I hurt her when we were in high school."

"I remember being sixteen. I know what it is to have made a stupid comment or done something that made someone mad. I'm sure that…"

"I got caught with her boyfriend," she interrupted, her face turning a bright red and caught in a stunned look as if she hadn't meant to make that admission.

"Well, I didn't expect that."

His mother pinched the bridge of her nose. "So, yeah, it was a bit more than saying something stupid in front of someone."

Vic swallowed hard. "I'm sure she'd understand you spending time with—"

"God, Victor, don't make me explain it all to you." She lifted her manicured fingers to her lips, obviously embarrassed by her admission, then she picked up her wine and took a long sip.

Vic pulled from his beer trying to understand what was happening with his mother. His relationship with the neighbor seemed to have stirred her up in a way he'd never quite seen her. And *caught with her boyfriend* seemed to hold a lot of anguish. Had his mother just admitted to sleeping with Mindy's mother's boyfriend in high school?

Vic pulled from his beer again, only this time it burned in his chest on its way down. Never in his life had he considered that his mother, or father, had had lives before one another. That was a child's right to think they were totally innocent to the ways of the world—especially as teenagers.

And hadn't his mother ridden his sisters about the way they dressed, or spoke to boys? It was a bit too much to take in.

The phrase burned through him again. *I got caught with her boyfriend. Don't make me explain it all to you.*

"That was a long time ago," Vic said, his voice uneven because he was completely uncomfortable with the conversation they were having. "You would have been teenagers."

His mother finished her wine and her cheeks grew even more red. "I just don't want that to ruin anything for you. Besides, you live next door. If things go wrong…"

"They're not going to go wrong."

"But if they do…"

"We know," he said, very aware of the consequences of getting involved with the next-door neighbor. "But it's new and I don't want to put all of these exceptions on it before it becomes something. I like her, Mom. Whatever happened nearly forty years ago isn't going to affect my relationship."

His mother shrugged, then nodded, and finished her wine.

Vic wondered just how devastated Mindy's mom had been over what happened with his mother to have it be such an emotional block so many years later.

Now the question was, did he bring it up with Mindy, or did he just let it go. He didn't want anything to stall what they were building, especially something that didn't have anything to do with them personally.

CHAPTER TWENTY-EIGHT

YOU'RE NOT IN YOUR OFFICE, VIC SENT THE TEXT MESSAGE WHEN Mindy hadn't arrived at work.

I'm at the airport. Didn't I tell you I had to fly out today? She included an emoji with wide eyes.

I don't think we discussed it, he added, wondering when it would matter to share those kinds of details. Was that for months from now, when their relationship was more established, or should they discuss that kind of stuff now?

His phone rang in his hand.

"I'm so sorry," her voice was soft on the other end.

"You don't have to be sorry."

"Yes I do. That was inconsiderate. I'm headed to Napa Valley. I'll only be gone a few days. I'll be home Saturday morning very early."

A smile was tugging at the corners of his mouth. They had unspoken plans for Saturday, didn't they? New Year's Eve was bound to be epic.

"What would you like to do on Saturday? Do you want me to make dinner reservations somewhere? I have a few clients that have offered invites. Or we could just stay home and I'll make you dinner."

She hummed. "I'd like to stay in. I don't want to be anywhere else."

Vic liked the sound of that. "Movie marathon? We could start with a rom com, move to a sports movie, and end with a New Year's Eve movie."

"A New Year's Eve movie is going to be rom com," she said, but he wasn't sure if that was a threat.

"I don't think so. I'll do some research."

"You're not going to win this."

"Is it a contest?"

"Totally."

"Game on, Baldwin."

"Game on."

SATURDAY MORNING, THE DOORBELL RANG AT EIGHT O'CLOCK. VIC blinked open his eyes.

Seriously?

He pulled on a T-shirt and trudged to the door. When he pulled it open, there was no one there, but on the front step was a donut on a dainty china plate. Beneath it was a paper napkin. When he picked up the plate, he noticed there was writing on the napkin.

Happy New Year's Eve. This way we can have breakfast together. I'll be over around noon. XOXO Mindy

The smile on his lips was wide and he stepped back inside. The simple gesture made his insides warm. It was stupid to be as worked up over a woman he barely knew, but he was. Was it their past? Was it just her? Vic wasn't sure what the pull was, but he couldn't help himself. When he thought of her, he was stupid happy.

Vic had a spread set out for binging movies all day long. There were snacks planned for different parts of the day. He wasn't sure what movie Mindy was bringing, but he'd added themed snacks for the movies he'd chosen.

He'd also cleaned his bedroom, changed the sheets, put a dimmer switch on the lights, and fretted about what was to happen after midnight more than he should have. Where was the spontaneity in assuming that the midnight kiss was going to land them in bed?

This was what women complained about, wasn't it? Men only thought this way, and here he was totally guilty of it.

He'd let it all play out. If that's where they ended up, that was fine. If they took it nice and slow, he was in it for the long haul.

WITH HER HEART HAMMERING IN HER CHEST, AND A LUMP IN HER throat, Mindy rang the doorbell. Armed with the movie *New Year's Eve*, a bottle of wine she'd picked up on her trip, words of encouragement from all of her friends running in her head, and a sexy bra and panty set on under her sweat pants and sweat shirt, she was ready to make the night an epic one with the next door neighbor.

When Vic opened the door, his eyes flashed as if he knew what she was wearing under her clothes. That was impossible, but it made her skin heat.

He hadn't shaved all week, and she found that sexy as hell too.

"Hi," his voice growled in a low husky tone.

"Hi," hers met that growl of need.

In one step, they were at each other. His hands came to her face, pulling her into a kiss that warmed her even more. Mindy fought to hold on to the items in her hands as she pressed herself against him.

Vic's fingers brushed her cheeks as his tongue swept through her mouth.

Mindy pulled back, set the items in her hands on the floor, and moved into him again, and he hoisted her to his hips and held on.

"I missed you," she breathed out the words as he moved, and her back hit the wall and their lips pressed together.

"Back 'atcha," he managed, before his mouth took possession of hers again.

Mindy's fingers traveled up into his hair as Vic kept her flush to the wall. All of this was supposed to wait until midnight, wasn't it? God, what did she care? She wanted it now, and it was more than obvious that he did too.

Vic pressed against her, balancing her between him and the wall. One hand splayed against her back, under her coat. His other hand brushed up under her sweatshirt and across the flesh of her stomach.

Her skin pebbled under his touch as his fingers brushed under her bra, touching the sensitive skin under her breast.

Mindy let her head fall back and Vic's lips trailed down her throat, before he cupped his hands under her ass and carried her to the couch.

Lowering her beneath him, Vic began to peel away her coat as she kicked off her shoes.

As he looked down at her, Mindy sucked in a breath. "Touch me," she pleaded, needing his hands on her.

Vic's eyes grew darker with the need they shared. With his knee pressed between her thighs, he lifted the sweatshirt over Mindy's head, and eased back scanning a look over her appreciatively.

"Oh, Mindy."

Swallowing hard, she took his hand in hers, and guided it to her breast.

He blinked hard as his thumb brushed over her swollen nipple through the thin fabric. "I can't wait until midnight if we keep this up," his voice was low and filled with need as he cupped her breast in his hand.

"I don't want to wait."

PATIENCE. CALM. GENTLENESS. VIC REPEATED THE WORDS TO himself as he touched Mindy and she moved beneath him. His body didn't want to heed his subtle warnings that repeated in his head. His body wanted them naked and joined, but his heart kept him from taking and not enjoying.

"You're beautiful," he said as Mindy moved her hands under his shirt, causing his heart to race even faster. "Tell me you're sure. Tell me that you want this."

She lifted under him, her fingers moving to his back, and her nails digging into his flesh.

"Yes. Yes," she repeated as she looked him in the eye. "I want this."

Vic drew in a breath and watched as Mindy pulled her bottom lip through her teeth. The sweetness was gone. Beneath him lay a woman with needs that matched his. But as her fingers drew up his back, he knew the feelings moving through him were more than just the promise of sex.

He loved her.

He took another breath to say the words, but stopped. Now wasn't the time. Shit, yesterday was the time to say them, but now, here they were ready to commit, but he didn't want her to think that was the reason he'd use the words.

Vic slipped his fingers under the waistband of her sweatpants and yanked them from her hips. Mindy laughed as she fell back against the couch, but then it was only the inhalation of her breath that filled his ears as he looked down at the matching bra and panty set. Her eyes went dark when he looked into them.

She'd been waiting for him to see her splayed out before him like she was, like a present to unwrap, he considered.

He discarded her sweatpants, scanning a look over her from her dark eyes, over the lace of the bra. Mindy's body was soft and curvy, and Vic couldn't help but trail his finger between the valley of her breasts and over her soft skin, stopping at the top of her panties.

When Mindy inhaled, he locked his gaze on her.

"You're beautiful," he said, his voice hazed with the need that drummed through him.

Vic stepped back and reached his hand out to her.

She licked her lips and it made his body temperature climb.

Mindy took his hand and stood with him. Their movie night was just going to have to wait.

He scooped her legs up and her arms wrapped around his neck as he carried her to his bedroom. A present wrapped so nicely should be appreciated. Until he touched, kissed, and tasted every inch of her, he wasn't going to leave the bedroom. He was going to take the final few hours of the year to please her and make sure she'd never want to leave.

CHAPTER TWENTY-NINE

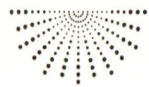

THE ROOM WAS DARK WHEN MINDY ROLLED OFF VIC AND LAY panting next to him. Her bra was the only item of clothing she had on, and it was pushed down and she was fully exposed.

With one arm over her forehead and a hand pressed to her stomach, she fought for air. "I don't know which of us were more pent up. We've been at this for hours," she laughed.

Vic tucked his hands under his head and chuckled. "It's not pent up. It's attraction. I can't get enough of you," he said before he rolled to his side, sliding his hand over hers that rested on her stomach. "This is going to sound really gross, but I didn't think I'd be able to perform in this room."

Mindy laughed again. "What the hell does that mean?"

"I mean, this was my grandparents' bedroom. My mother was probably conceived in this room."

"Oh-my-god!" Mindy sat up, taking the sheet with her to cover herself. "Did you seriously just have to bring that up?"

"It's not like they're here."

"But, ew."

Vic laughed again, pulling the sheet from her and rolling on top of her. "Do you see why I changed this room first?"

Mindy gazed up at him in the shadows. "You've never had sex in this room?"

Pushing damp hair from her face, he shook his head. "No. You're the first woman I've ever had in my house. The first one who will ever stay the night."

"Those are the kinds of words that will have me pouncing on you again."

Vic raised his brows. "You're ready to go again?"

Mindy let out a defeated breath. "No," she laughed on a sigh. "I need food."

As if on cue, Vic's stomach growled. "I guess I do too." But he didn't move. With an arm propped up on each side of her, he looked down at her as if he were drinking her in and had something else to say, but then recalculated his thoughts. "I'm so glad I locked myself out of the house that night."

Mindy smiled. "So am I."

WITHOUT MUCH PERSUASION, VIC CONVINCED HER TO PUT HER clothes back on, sans the fancy underwear. Knowing that at any moment he could slip his hand under the fabric of that sweatshirt and touch her, that had him thinking the new year was going to be filled with wondrous possibilities.

The work Vic had put into having themed snacks was over when it had become a buffet. They'd decided against ordering pizza, and he was sure it was so that they could get back into the bedroom without having to wait for the delivery, but neither of them had actually said it.

Vic leaned his hip against the counter, picked up a cube of cheese from the plate, and popped it in his mouth. He ran his free hand up Mindy's arm, and then tucked a loose strand of hair behind her ear.

"What movie did you bring?" he asked.

"*New Year's Eve*," she said as she put a grape between her lips and pulled it into her mouth with her tongue.

Vic moaned before picking up another cube of cheese. "Appropriate."

"Which movie did you pick?"

"*The Sandlot.*"

Mindy laughed. "Rom com."

"Sports movie."

"Squints and the lifeguard."

"Fuck," he sighed as he moved to pin Mindy to the counter with his body.

Her hands moved to his chest, a leg now instinctively wrapping around him.

"I guess every movie is a romance," Vic conceded to their suddenly unimportant competition as he skimmed his lips over Mindy's jaw

"I told you," she said on a heavy breath as she let her head fall back. He trailed his kisses down her throat before the sound of her phone chiming had her wincing. "I expect that's going to happen for the next few hours."

"Everyone is checking up on you?"

She puckered her lips. "Everyone knows where I am."

"So they want the gossip?"

The smile that spread her lips only made him want to carry her back to bed.

"I'm no kiss and tell girl," she promised.

"I'm no prude. My feelings won't be hurt."

Tucking her fingers up into his hair, she nipped his lips with a kiss. "Why don't we take a break and watch a movie?"

Vic gripped her waist, pressing his forehead to hers. "You'll stay all night?"

"I'll stay all night."

"The neighbors are going to talk."

She grinned. "The neighbors are already talking. We're scandalous."

Vic groaned. "It's so worth it."

They stood there, foreheads pressed together, his fingers kneading the skin above the band of her sweatpants.

Mindy lifted her hands to his cheeks. "This is more than just sex for me. I want you to know that."

"Isn't that what the man is supposed to say?"

"It's what I need to say. I really care for you and what we're building."

Vic let out a slow breath. It wasn't an admission of love, and he didn't expect it. But still, it wasn't the time to tell her how he felt. He needed to take it slow. The last thing he wanted was to scare her away. He wasn't sure how it would work, or what the end game was, but he had an idea of what he wanted.

Vic was surrounded by loving and happy couples. Wanting that for himself was as obvious to him as the feelings he had for Mindy.

Patience, calm, and gentleness, he reminded himself. If he took his time, she'd be his forever.

Mindy's phone chimed again, and she eased back.

"Maybe I will tell them exactly what we're doing. Then they'll know just how much they're interrupting us."

Vic laughed. "I've changed my mind. I'm ordering pizza, and we're watching *The Sandlot* first," he said and she agreed with a nod as she moved to pick up her phone.

He didn't move. He watched and appreciated her in his space. She belonged there, he thought. Not just in his grandparents' house, but in his life. It didn't matter where they landed, he just knew he wanted them to land together.

Suddenly the ache to have what his sisters had was nearly paralyzing.

Maybe he should talk to them.

This was a brand new feeling.

Was it normal?

When Mindy laughed as she returned the texts that kept coming in, he decided it was perfectly normal. He'd just never been in love before, and now he was. If he was smart, he'd cherish the feeling and keep it close. He'd been raised in a house full of love, and he had to assume his parents felt that same rush as he was feeling now.

He picked up his phone to order the pizza and noticed he too had a text.

Happy New Year! I hope we can get together soon. I'd really like to get to know you better.

Vic bit down and scrolled to the app to order pizza. He was going to have to have a serious discussion with his sister about her friend.

CHAPTER THIRTY

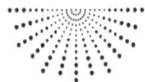

In all the times he'd watched *The Sandlot* Vic had never noticed just how centered the story was around Squints' love of Wendy Peffercorn. Okay, not the whole movie, but the moment she first came on screen, the smile that had taken over Mindy's mouth had made him want to kiss her. Instead, he just watched.

She loved plots and twists to plots, and she absolutely loved the promise of romance. Because they'd spent most of the day focused on one another, they only watched *The Sandlot* and *New Year's Eve.* But he'd watch every rom com there was with her if it meant getting to sit close to her while she absorbed the possibility of love happening around her.

As the movie ended, Vic watched as she rubbed her eyes, much like a child fighting sleep.

"Should we turn the TV channel to watch the ball drop?" he asked.

"Yeah," she said moving from her position curled up next to him to begin picking up the items that surrounded them.

Even the domestic side to her turned him on. He had to tell her he loved her. If he didn't, he thought he might explode.

Mindy gathered the cups and plates and walked them back to

the kitchen. Vic rolled down the top to the chip bag and followed her.

She moved about his kitchen as if she'd spent most of her life there. Watching her wash dishes and put away leftovers in the refrigerator was stirring him up more than the matching bra and panty set she'd shown up in.

Mindy dipped her hands into the soapy water and picked up a plate just as Vic reached for her arm and turned her toward him.

Her eyes went wide, and soap dripped on the floor as she looked up at him.

He cupped her face and pulled her mouth to his so he could taste her in that moment.

"I'm getting soap all over your floor," she said, laughing as he held her in place.

"I love you." The words tumbled out as if they had to escape on their own. "I love you," he repeated.

Mindy let out a steady breath, now not worried about the water or soap dripping from her hands or the plate.

"Vic," she said his name, but he stopped her from saying anything else by kissing her again.

Blindly, she managed the plate back into the sink as Vic moved her against the counter and began to lift the sweatshirt off her.

Her skin was bare underneath, and his hands skimmed her sides before cupping her breasts.

Mindy mimicked his maneuvers, pulling his sweatshirt over his head and running her wet hands up his chest.

Vic clawed at the band to her pants and managed them down, right in the kitchen before he pulled away. "Don't move," he said backing out of the kitchen. "I mean it. Don't even dry your hands."

He ran to the bedroom for a condom and was back a moment later, taking Mindy's hand and tugging her toward the couch.

There were no more words. As the crowd on TV began to

count down their celebration to the new year, the one filled with hope and promise, Vic kicked out of his pants, slid on the condom, and he and Mindy made love on the couch as the ball dropped and the new year was ushered in.

VIC MADE HER PANCAKES IN HIS BOXERS, AND MINDY WATCHED every move he made from over the rim of her coffee mug as she leaned against the counter in one of his T-shirts.

She'd never been so consumed by a man before, but this one…

"I didn't ask, did you want chocolate chips in your pancakes?" Vic asked and Mindy laughed at his very serious tone.

"Is that a normal ingredient for you?"

"Sometimes, and always a staple in the pantry."

She grinned as she sipped her coffee. "I take my pancakes any way you make them. In fact, I'm not sure I'll even be able to taste them."

Vic lifted a brow. "Why?"

"Because I'm not focused on them," she said, setting her mug on the counter and moving in behind him, wrapping her arms around him. "I'm focused on you standing in the kitchen in your boxers."

Vic flipped the two pancakes in the pan. "You're going to make me burn your breakfast."

"It would so be worth it," she hummed in his ear before she stepped back. "But I've worked up quite an appetite, so I'll let you finish them."

Mindy picked back up her coffee mug, positioned herself against the counter again, and admired the man.

It had been a long time since she'd awoken in the arms of another person, and she'd realized that she'd given up on the thought of it happening again. But Victor Hayes was making her rethink everything.

Was this what Lisa had felt when she'd met Ryan? Mindy had thought that relationship had moved very swiftly. They met. They went out. They slept together. He moved in. And that had all been in the first few weeks.

Mindy and Vic had known each other nearly their whole lives, minus their teenage years through their twenties.

And he'd said he loved her.

Mindy swallowed down her coffee hard.

She hadn't said it back. He'd stopped her from saying it, when she thought about it. Maybe he hadn't meant it, and the words had just rushed out.

Then again, maybe he did mean it and what did that mean that he didn't want to hear the words back?

Mindy was drawn out of her thoughts when her phone rang, and the tone signified it was her mother. She winced as she put down her coffee and moved toward the couch where she'd left her phone the night before.

"Hey, Mom. Happy New Year."

"Happy New Year, sweetheart. What are you up to this morning?" her mother asked and Mindy grimaced when she looked toward Vic.

"Having breakfast with a friend."

He laughed and Mindy shrugged. What else was she supposed to say?

"Your father wanted to have everyone over for dinner tonight. I know it's short notice, but…"

Her mother left the question hanging, waiting for an answer.

Normally it would be a no brainer to answer her mother and make plans, but it wasn't just her she was making plans for now, was it?

"What time?" She asked, her eyes still on Vic.

"Six," Mindy's mother said, and Mindy mouthed the invite to Vic, who nodded.

"I'll be bringing a guest." She didn't ask, she put it out there.

"Oh. Okay then. That'll be fine," her mother's words shook as she agreed and then paused. "One of the girls?" her mother finally asked. "We haven't seen Ruby in quite a while."

Mindy walked back to the kitchen where Vic moved the pan to a cool area of the stove and turned off the burner. He eased up next to her, lifting the hem of the T-shirt she wore and touching the skin of her hip.

"No, not one of the girls."

"Oh," her mother said again. "I assume you mean Victoria Hanson's grandson?"

"Yes."

Again, her mother paused. "It'll be nice to meet him—again," she added.

"We'll see you tonight. I love you, Mom."

"I love you too, sweetheart," her mother ended the call and Mindy set her phone on the counter.

"Dinner with the folks, huh?" Vic's hand rose under her shirt, just beneath her breast.

"I hope you don't mind. I didn't even ask if—"

"I don't mind," he said, wrapping his arms around her and pulling her in. "It kind of makes us super official, huh?"

That and him telling her he loved her last night, she thought. "I guess it does."

"Well, then let's get to eating these pancakes." He brushed his lips over her jaw and down her neck. "Because I'd like to nibble on you just a bit more before I face your family," he said as he lifted Mindy from her feet and set her on the counter, pressing himself between her thighs and kissing her so thoroughly that she forgot just how anxious her mother sounded when Mindy mentioned who she was bringing to dinner.

CHAPTER THIRTY-ONE

NOT MUCH HAD BEEN SAID ON THEIR DRIVE TO MINDY'S PARENTS' house. They'd stopped to pick up a six-pack of beer, since Mindy said that her mother had plenty of wine. They held hands in the car, and Vic watched as Mindy chewed the nails on her other hand.

"What's bothering you?" he finally asked.

"Sorry," she said, lowering her hand. "My parents have just been acting strange since I told them that we'd been spending time together. Maybe I just assume they've been acting strange," she admitted. "I mean the last man I brought around did a real job on me. Maybe they're just being protective."

Vic nodded, running his thumb over the knuckles of the hand he was holding. But he wondered if her parents were reacting to the falling out their mothers must have once had. Hadn't his mother confessed to having gotten caught with Mindy's mother's boyfriend? Seriously, that was decades ago, and who didn't make stupid mistakes as a teenager? God, if he thought back—no, he didn't want to do that.

The point was, something that far in the past shouldn't be

harbored any longer. And Vic wasn't the man Mindy'd once been involved with. He loved her, and he'd told her so. He wasn't in for a casual relationship with the next-door neighbor. He was in too deep for that. Mindy had rocked his world and taken him under. He was in it for the long haul, no matter where that led.

Maybe they would live side by side for years, enjoying one another's company. Or maybe, he'd finally have what his sister's had. He saw the allure in that now. Love. Commitment. Family.

Vic pulled the car to the curb in front of the house that Mindy directed him to.

"Nice place. You grew up here?" he asked.

"Yeah. I guess that's funny, huh? We have a past together, and yet it doesn't include our lives beyond the cul-de-sac our grandmothers lived on."

"You're right. Our memories are cemented in the neighborhood where we live now." He lifted her hand to his lips and pressed a kiss to her fingers. "Are you okay? You seem nervous."

"I am. I want them to love you."

"If they don't, it's okay too," he said smiling. "Though, I don't chew with my mouth open or burp after I drink."

Mindy finally laughed. "I'm not worried about that. I want them to know I'm okay. I don't bring men around, and I think we're all just nervous about that."

"I hope I'm not just any man," he said and Mindy's eyes went wide.

"You're not. You're very important to me."

"Good. I don't plan to go anywhere."

She nodded, looked down at their joined hands, and back up at him. "Did you mean it when you said you loved me?"

Vic nodded. "I did. It was quick and probably unacceptable, but I meant it."

"It wasn't unacceptable." She licked her lips. "Unexpected."

"It was supposed to be. And I didn't say it just because we'd had sex. I said it—"

"I love you too," she interrupted him.

Vic let out a slow breath. "You do?"

"I do. And yes, it is quick, but everything inside of me tells me that it's right. I don't know what to expect, but I know that wherever I go from here, I want you to be a part of it. Even if we live in old lady chic next to one another for the rest of our lives."

Now he laughed. "We'll have to discuss that someday. Though my days of old lady chic are coming to an end," he promised. "I'm going to finish that office next week and then move on to the family room."

Mindy bit down on her lip. "And maybe it's time I started disassembling the shrine I live in."

"Only if you're ready."

"I think I'm ready."

Vic leaned in to press a kiss to her lips. "Then I'll be there to help you. Though I'm quite sure Ruby would love to help you demo."

Mindy laughed loudly. "I will guarantee it."

MINDY HAD GONE HOME AFTER DINNER, AND VIC FOUND HIMSELF wandering around his own home as if he were a stranger.

Her family had been cordial to them. Her sister Carrie was easy to reminisce with. Her daughter Carolyn loved having Mindy around, and when Mindy held her nephew Bo, Vic realized just how much he wanted things to work out between them. For the first time in his life, he could see himself as a family man.

But there was a buzzing tension in the air, and when Mindy chose to go home for the night, he knew she'd felt it. Seriously, was it all because his mother had caused trauma to her mother when they were teenagers?

As far as he was concerned they'd all have to figure it out. He wasn't going to give up on what he was building with Mindy, just because his mother's morals as a sixteen-year-old girl were a bit out of whack.

Making another loop through his house, nursing the beer he'd been drinking since he'd returned home, he noticed a car pull up into Mindy's driveway. Only a few minutes later two more cars arrived.

Vic stood at the front window and watched as her friends emerged from the cars and headed to the front door.

Had she had plans she'd forgotten to tell him about, or had she called in reinforcements to deal with the tension? Seeing her friends slip through the front door, he was sure that was what it was.

Vic's phone buzzed in his hand.

Listen, your silence is sending the signal that maybe you'd rather not go out. I get that, but Amber made it seem as if you were going to call me. Maybe instead of the silent treatment, we could just meet for a drink. What do you say to Tom's at nine?

Vic wondered why the silent treatment didn't work. He also wondered if Amber was behind Justine's continued assault on his phone.

Fine, he was the kind of man to usually face things head on. He'd meet her, tell her he wasn't interested, and ask her to move on. He'd do it face to face.

Then he'd call his sister and give her a piece of his mind. Vic hadn't asked to be set up on dates.

Setting his beer on the counter, Vic picked up his keys, and shrugged on his coat. Between his mother's angst with Mindy's mother and his sister's friend, Vic felt as if he were dealing with high schoolers all over again. This was ridiculous.

When he walked into the garage and lifted the door, he looked at Mindy's driveway. Perhaps Mindy was feeling the same thing. Was that why the girls were there for her? Was she in need of finding calm after her family dinner?

It wasn't his imagination, and he knew it. Her parents were harboring some feelings against him. He and Mindy would work it out. He loved her, and he wasn't going to let whatever it was ruin what they'd just started.

CHAPTER THIRTY-TWO

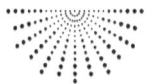

Ruby handed Mindy a glass of iced tea, then plopped down next to her on the couch.

Tina rubbed her stomach and looked toward Ruby. "You know it's totally unfair of you to prance around here with a tan while the rest of us are pasty white and warmth-deprived."

The curl of Ruby's lips was devious. "If you all weren't falling in love, getting married and knocked up, we could have all gone together. But no, I'm the only sensible person among us," she said.

Mindy sipped her drink. "I don't remember getting an invite."

"You wouldn't have left your family for Hawaii during the holidays," Ruby observed. "You're too old fashioned."

Mindy waited for the comment that would land on her shrine of a house, but it never came.

Lisa tucked her feet up under her on the chair. "So what's going on? You sounded pretty desperate when you called," she directed the question in Mindy's direction and then all eyes were on Mindy.

"I slept with him," she said and waited for the gasps, the cheers, the taunts, but there weren't any.

"Of course you did," Ruby finally said. "And, by just looking at him, I've had a few orgasms, so I'm going to guess it was good."

Mindy felt her cheeks flush with heat. "I'm not going to go into detail."

"Not yet, but you'll get there." Ruby gave Mindy's knee a squeeze. "But what happened? In all honesty, you shouldn't want to see us much if you're in the throes of a new romance."

Mindy looked around the room at her friends. Ruby was right. And maybe it wasn't the best call to have made when she was feeling anxious. It put a bad light on something Mindy didn't even understand. Surely Vic noticed the girls pulling up too. She was making a mess of the situation, which wasn't a situation, she reminded herself.

"I don't really have a lot of information, but I don't think my mom and Vic's mom get along," she said, running her finger down the side of her glass.

Ruby shrugged. "It's not their love affair. Who cares?"

"I care," Mindy said. "On Christmas my dad was all weirded out when he found out I was seeing Vic. He mentioned that my mom and his mom were friends until high school, but they grew apart."

Tina readjusted in her seat. "She came into your house and talked to you on movie night," she reminded her. "She didn't seem put out by you."

"I wasn't a threat to her."

"You're a threat?"

Mindy shrugged. "I mean I wasn't sleeping with her son yet."

Ruby's lips curled into a wide smile. "God, I'm going to get those details. These two are tight lipped, but he rocked your world, I can sense it."

They all shared a laugh, and Mindy realized that was exactly what she'd needed. These women could make everything fall into place.

Ruby was right. It wasn't anyone's business but hers and Vic's, and they loved each other. Or they'd said it, at least.

She sipped her tea.

No, she'd meant it when she said it. She did love him.

No matter the ancient battle their mothers had had, it didn't have anything to do with her and Vic. They were all grownups now, their mothers would have to work it out.

VIC WALKED INTO TOM'S AND LOOKED AROUND. HE WASN'T GOING to stay more than a few minutes.

"Vic Hayes?" a man's voice called out and Vic turned to see Curt Smith sitting on a bar stool, a beer between his hands.

"Hey, Curt," Vic said.

"Never seen you here before."

"Yeah, I've never been here," Vic said looking around.

"Can I buy you a drink?"

Vic shook his head. "No. I'm good, thanks. I'm just here to meet someone for a hot second," he admitted.

Curt nodded. "Dad says you and the girl in Mrs. Sanders' house have something going on, huh? That one is Mindy, right?"

Vic fisted his hand to his side. He understood Mindy's hesitation about Curt Smith. He still had a jerk quality to him.

"Vic," Justine's voice broke the stillness between him and Curt.

"Hey," Vic stepped back as Justine nearly lunged at him. "I was looking for you."

Justine looked at Curt and then nudged him. "Hey, Curt. I didn't realize you and Vic knew each other."

"Yeah, we grew up together. You know each other?" Curt asked scanning a look between Vic and Justine.

"My sister introduced us," Vic was quick to say and then

turned his attention to her. "Do you have a moment to step outside and talk?"

"Aren't you staying for a drink?" Justine asked.

"No. I just want to talk."

She blinked hard. "Oh. We could just grab a booth and—"

"No. I'm not staying," he confirmed.

Justine exchanged another look with Curt before she nodded. "Okay."

"See ya round, Curt," Vic said as he turned to walk out of the bar, Justine following behind.

Vic paced a full circle before Justine made it through the door and was standing in front of him.

"It's kinda busy here tonight being New Year and all. We could go—"

"I didn't come here to be with you," he interrupted her. "Listen, I don't know what my sister was thinking when she decided to set us up, but I'm not interested."

She blinked hard and her mouth opened in an O, but she didn't say anything, so Vic continued.

"I'm sure you're a great gal, but I'm seeing someone else."

Justine blinked hard again. "You didn't even give us a chance."

And wasn't he glad he hadn't? There should have been an *Oh, I didn't know. I'm so sorry to have kept texting,* or *Thanks for letting me know. I hope you'll be happy.* But this was one of those desperate kinds of women that Vic stayed clear from, and now he'd wished he'd only blocked her number—which he was going to do immediately.

"I wanted to let you know where things stood, in person." Vic turned, and walked toward his car. He couldn't believe that the woman was actually calling after him. At least she wasn't following him.

His sister owed him big time now, he thought as he opened his car door and slid in behind the steering wheel. What a nightmare.

CHAPTER THIRTY-THREE

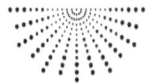

THEY BACKED OUT OF THEIR DRIVEWAYS AT THE SAME TIME ON Monday morning, and Vic wondered where Mindy was going. She didn't work on Mondays.

She gave him a wave and pulled out into the street. But where she'd usually turn right to go to work, she'd turned left.

Vic sat at the stop sign for a moment gathering his thoughts. He missed her, and it had only been a few hours since they'd been together. Maybe it was time for them to have a long discussion about what they were feeling. Had they both said they loved the other one because of feelings associated with sex?

No, Vic didn't believe that.

But there was some uncomfortableness that had been brought on by her parents at dinner. They needed to resolve that. It was obvious that their mothers' falling out as teenagers was going to put some tension into the new relationship they were forging, but it didn't have to be that way forever. But they'd have to work on it, and that was what relationships were, right? Two people opening up communication so that even the petty things didn't destroy what was being built.

At the office, Vic dove into his work. He wanted to meet with

Parker that week and go over his proposal for her family's store. The resort in Castle Rock had some new items they wanted him to work on as well.

Vic was used to diving into his work, and in all honesty, having an outside office made him more productive, but whenever someone would pass by his door and he could see them through the small, frosted window, he thought of Mindy and wished she'd walk in.

Mindy sat at her mother's kitchen table, a mug of coffee between her hands.

"It's nice to have you here this morning," her mother said as she sat down at the kitchen table with her own mug of coffee. "I've missed our Mondays."

Mindy nodded picking up her coffee and taking a sip. "I'm going shopping with Lisa later. She's got something in mind for her next video, so we're going to an antique store."

"Her video last week with the lemon chicken was fantastic. Daddy really liked it."

"I'll let her know," Mindy said smiling. "Lisa will appreciate that."

"And Tina, how is she feeling?"

"She's good. She's excited to have her baby girl."

Her mother sipped her coffee and smiled over the rim of her mug. "Having daughters was the most wonderful gift in my life. She's going to enjoy being a mother."

"I know she will."

"And what about Ruby?"

Mindy laughed. "Her roommate moved out so Lisa's brother is going to move in."

"Lisa's brother? Her foster brother?"

"Yep. He moved home to work at a hospital. He's a doctor."

"Isn't that nice?" her mother said taking another sip of her coffee. "Did you see that there is a new antique store in Golden?" Her mother circled the conversation back to Mindy's plans for later that day.

"I'll have to mention that to Lisa. We're going to start at the antique store and then head to the home improvement store to pick out paint colors," Mindy said and watched as her mother lifted her eyes to her and lowered her mug.

"Paint colors? You're painting?"

"Yep. I'm ready to make the house my home. I'm going to start with the bedrooms."

Her mother pursed her lips, then bit down on the bottom one before hiding again behind her coffee mug. "The house is very nice the way it is," she finally said sipping her coffee.

"It's dated and it's mine. I should make it reflect who I am," Mindy said.

"You're Catherine's granddaughter."

"That shouldn't be reflected in the decor of my house."

Her mother set her mug on the table and ran her finger over the rim. "Is this all because your neighbor is fixing up his house?"

Mindy shook her head. "My neighbor? Vic? Vic whom I brought for dinner? Vic whom I'm dating?"

"You don't need to get snippy with me about it," her mother scolded.

"I'm not understanding your issues with me painting the walls in my own house, or the man that I'm seeing."

"I didn't say there was a problem with you painting."

Mindy waited for the continuation of the comment to be about Vic, but her mother stopped.

"Then I'm going to start cleaning out the house and changing things."

Her mother bit her lip again and nodded hesitantly.

Mindy reached across the table and took her mother's hands in hers. "Now what is your problem with Vic?"

Blinking hard, her mother kept her eyes averted. "I didn't say there was a problem."

"Are you kidding me? You and dad were so weird around him when he was here. I think you should be happy for me."

"I'm happy for you."

"I don't think you are."

Her mother pushed her chair back and stood. "It's just a big step for you. Maybe you should think about—"

"Big step? I'm thirty-years-old. I'm perfectly capable of being part of a relationship. Hell, my sister is married and has kids. Why aren't you happy for me?"

Her mother paced the kitchen. "He's Liv's son," she blurted out the words and Mindy watched as she picked up the kitchen towel, folded it, and then hung it over the edge of the sink as if to occupy herself.

"He is Liv's son. What does that have to do with anything?"

"I'm just saying, maybe it's not going to work out. I mean you live next door to him."

"I don't think that's what you're saying at all," Mindy argued and stood to walk to her mother. "What's going on? You and Dad are very strange about my relationship with Vic."

"I just want you happy, Mindy. I want someone to take care of you and treat you nice."

"He does treat me nice, and I can take care of myself."

Her mother nodded. "I just think that there is someone else for you. Don't get too attached."

"Does this have to do with you and his mom having some falling out?"

Her mother's eyes went wide. "Who told you that?"

"Dad said that you two grew apart in high school, but really that was a long time ago."

Mindy watched as her mother's cheeks reddened and her lips flattened into a straight line. "Your father told you that?"

"Yes."

"I don't want to talk about this," her mother said moving to the small Christmas tree on the kitchen counter, where she began pulling ornaments off the branches and setting them in a pile.

"Maybe we should."

"Maybe you should just leave it alone, Mindy," her mother snapped out the words.

When Mindy's phone buzzed in her pocket, she pulled it out to see the text from Lisa. "I have to go."

"Okay."

"I wish you'd talk to me. I'm happy with Vic." Her mother only nodded. "I want you to be happy for me too," she said.

"I'll see you soon, sweetheart," her mother said, continuing to take the ornaments off the tree.

Mindy moved in and kissed her mother on the cheek, but she didn't say another word.

CHAPTER THIRTY-FOUR

LISA PICKED UP A SERVING SET, STUDIED IT, AND SET IT BACK before turning to pick up another and do the same. On any given day, Mindy would be searching the shelves for unique items too, but today, she just wasn't finding joy in it.

"I can't decide if I want the ornate silver one, or maybe just go with a nice china set," Lisa picked up a china plate with rosebuds on it.

"What are you making again?"

Lisa lifted a brow. "Scones and tea."

"Right. Didn't you do that already?"

"New recipes and I'm blending a tea of my own."

Mindy nodded, absentmindedly running her finger over a dish on the shelf.

"You're a million miles away. Really, you didn't have to come with me," Lisa said with a bite.

Mindy tucked her hair behind her ear and pointed to the china. "Get this one," she said and Lisa nodded. "I love Vic," she blurted out the words as Lisa began to pick up the other pieces to the dish set and gingerly set them into the cart.

"I know you do. And, I'm not as crass as Ruby, but I'd love those sexy details too when you're ready."

"One margarita too many and I'm sure I'll spill them," she admitted. "But my mom isn't too happy about my relationship."

"You said your mom and Vic's had a falling out?" Lisa asked as she began to push the cart down another aisle.

"Yeah, but my mom won't talk about it. Just something about him being Liv's son."

"What does Vic say about it?"

Mindy shrugged. "I haven't actually talked to him about it yet."

Lisa stopped in front of stemware and looked at her. "And in normal Mindy style, you had us over last night instead of sleeping at his place. And you haven't talked to him today."

Wincing, Mindy nodded. "We waved this morning as we pulled out of our driveways."

Lisa leaned her arm on the cart and steadied her eyes on Mindy. "Whatever happened between your mothers isn't your fight. Don't let them ruin what you're building."

"I feel like it's all going to upset her—my mom." Mindy rubbed her fingers over her lips. "She freaked out that I want to start fixing up the house, and she freaked out over Vic too."

"You're going to start fixing up the house?"

Mindy nodded. "I want to start with the bedrooms. It's time to move my grandmother out and me in."

Lisa grinned at her. "You're serious?"

"Yes."

"I don't think Tina should be part of it, just because of the baby and all, but Ruby would give anything to help you."

"She'd do it out of spite."

"Would it matter?" Lisa laughed. "The point is, it's beyond time that you made the house your own." She reached for Mindy's hands and gave them a squeeze. "And I think you should still keep banging the neighbor."

Mindy groaned. "Why are you all so crass?"

"Because it gets a reaction out of you. Besides, I can tell that you really do like him. It's in how you look when you talk about him."

"I do really like him. I love him."

"Then don't let these little things get in the way."

Mindy let out a groan. "Our mothers hating each other isn't a little thing."

"It's not your thing."

She supposed Lisa was right. And with that, she began to miss Vic terribly.

Pulling her phone from her purse, and following Lisa down another aisle, she texted Vic. *Can I make you dinner tonight? My house? Six?*

Before they'd even made it to the end of that aisle, Vic texted back. *I'll be there. I miss you today*, he added and Mindy felt her chest squeeze.

I'm missing you too.

WHEN MINDY OPENED THE FRONT DOOR, VIC MOVED IN, WRAPPING his arms around her and sweeping her up into a kiss that had heat covering her body.

Even when her feet were on the ground again, her head still spun as his mouth opened to hers and his tongue moved with hers.

It wouldn't take much for her to forget all about dinner and walk him to the bedroom, but then the thought of the bedroom stilled her and she eased back, still wrapped in his arms.

"Do you like tacos?" she asked.

"Who doesn't like tacos?"

Mindy lifted a brow. "That doesn't answer my question."

Vic chuckled. "Yes. I like tacos."

Mindy draped her arms around his neck. "Good, because I have tacos and beer. I also have paint swatches and I'd like some help picking out colors."

"You're ready to paint?"

"I'm ready to do a lot of things, no matter what my mother thinks."

Vic nodded slowly. "She's not ready for you to remodel?"

Mindy let her gaze fall to Vic's lips and then back up to his eyes. "She's not open to a lot of things at this moment, and I'm trying to figure that out, and not let it mess with my head."

Again, he nodded slowly. "Anything I can do?"

Mindy smiled up at him, enjoying the feel of his arms wrapped around her and the heat of his body pressed to hers. She wanted this—this relationship they were building. No matter the state of her house or their mothers' problems with one another, she wanted this man in her life—forever.

"Just don't give up on me."

Vic's brows drew in. "I'm not giving up on you. Why would you say that?"

Mindy shook her head, keeping the smile on her mouth to lighten the mood. "I'm just saying that dependable Mindy, the one who lives in a sanctuary to her grandmother and never— ever— dates men is changing. Not everyone is on board, but I'd really like you to be."

Vic lifted his hands to her cheeks and cupped her face. His eyes locked on hers, and she knew what she'd said had upset him.

"I don't know what this is all about, but I'm not going anywhere. I happen to be in love with this Mindy, and it doesn't matter what color you paint the rooms in this house, or if you live here at all. And as for this guy you're interested in," he grinned, "I think you need to give him a chance. He's into you."

Mindy let out a little laugh. "Our mothers don't seem to like one another."

His eyes flashed acknowledgement in her statement and then

returned to their warmth. "Water under the bridge," he said. "This isn't their love affair, Mindy. It's ours."

She settled against him again, and his hands dropped to her waist. "Thank you."

"I love you."

"I love you, too. I just want them to be okay with us."

"As soon as we totally understand what happened, maybe we can work on that. And, to be honest, I don't think it's us they have the problem with. With us together, they'll have to face each other. And that's what they have a problem with."

"Holding a grudge that long is stupid," Mindy said on a slightly strained laugh.

"I guess it was important."

"I wish I knew what it was," she said, and again his eyes flashed, but this time she saw knowledge in them.

Mindy eased back to look up at Vic.

"You know what their falling out was about, don't you?"

Vic lifted his hands to her shoulders and caressed. "Remember teenagers are stupid."

"I wouldn't relive those years for anything. What happened?"

Vic winced and his lips puckered. "I'm hesitant to tell you, because it appears that my mother is the party at fault for the fight. Although, mind you, I don't have all the details."

Mindy felt as if she were reading a secret diary. She pulled Vic in closer. "I don't judge. Your mother has obviously raised you right. You don't cheat. You don't lie. You love your nieces and nephews, and your sisters."

He cocked his head to the side and wrinkled up his nose. "They're currently on my shit list."

"You still love them."

"I do."

Mindy pressed her lips together. "So what did your mother do to piss my mother off so much that I'm getting heat for this relationship I'm in?"

Vic ran his tongue over his teeth. "It appears that my mother got caught with your mother's boyfriend. And when I say got caught, she really made it sound as if they got caught in a compromising situation."

Vic felt Mindy go stiff in his arms. She blinked hard and then the blood drained from her face.

"Are you okay? This has nothing to do with us, remember?" Vic said, worried that this news had changed her feelings for him. "This was nearly forty years ago. Teenagers are stupid, remember?"

The look on her face of sheer devastation had rocked him, and it had nothing to do with him as a person. However, after everything she'd said about her last boyfriend, now he worried that his mother's indiscretion reflected directly on him.

Mindy pulled back from him, her hand went to her mouth and she paced a circle in front of him.

"Mindy, I'm sorry. I'm sure my mother is sorry too. I'm embarrassed for her. But—"

She lifted her eyes to his and they were filled with tears, ready to spill.

"This is why he was acting so weird on Christmas." She hiccupped. "He didn't say anything except that they'd had a falling out."

Vic reached for her hand and she snapped it back before he could take hold. "Who? What are you talking about?"

Her lips trembled now and she pressed her fingers to them. "My parents have been together since they were fourteen. My dad was my mother's high school boyfriend."

Now sickness swirled in his belly. "Oh, no."

Mindy nodded.

Vic ran his hand over his face. "Why does this feel so vile?"

"It is vile."

"This has nothing to do with us," he reminded her, but even he was completely grossed out by the news they'd just happened upon.

"No, it doesn't. It's fine. It's fine," she repeated.

Silence fell between them for a long moment.

"Tacos." Mindy lifted her eyes to his again. "I have tacos."

"And beer. You said you had beer."

"I do."

"We're going to need to drink that. All of it."

"I have tequila too."

Vic nodded. "We need it all."

Mindy nodded in agreement and turned to the kitchen, not reaching back for him.

CHAPTER THIRTY-FIVE

VIC SAT AT HIS DESK, IN THE OFFICE ACROSS THE HALL FROM Mindy, tapping his pen to his forehead. Since Monday night, things had been awkward between him and Mindy. They'd gone all of Tuesday hardly speaking, and certainly not doing anything else.

Wednesday morning, she'd been in the office nearly two hours before he got there. Was it her? Was it him?

Things had been awkward between him and everyone, he reconsidered. Vic just wasn't dealing with their shared information well.

We can all manage drinks when you're done with work, the text message from his sister Angie confirmed. *Are we celebrating or drinking away troubles?*

He chuckled. *You're pregnant. You're not drinking.*

She sent the middle finger emoji. *I can make sure we all cancel too.*

She'd do just that, he thought. *I just need my sisters. That's all.*

You slept with her and broke up, didn't you?

Vic blew out a breath. No, they hadn't broken up, they were

BERNADETTE MARIE

just taking time to process something that neither of them could wrap their heads around. *We didn't break up.*

This time his sister sent a gif of Jim Carrey doing some hip thrust and he laughed. At least his sister could keep him calm.

AT FIVE-THIRTY, VIC WALKED INTO THE SPORTS BAR WHERE ANGIE had told him to meet them. He quickly found his sisters in the bar at a table. Amber was nursing Isaac, Allison was having a beer, and Angie sat rubbing her stomach. What a sight, he considered, as he walked toward them.

"Why didn't you just pick a coffee house or something. The three of you look completely out of place," Vic said as he made his way around the table, kissing each of his sisters on the cheek, and Isaac on the top of the head.

"You're an asshole, you know that?" Angie shot back. "Besides, Amber with her boob out in public gets guys to look at us."

Vic pinched the bridge of his nose as he sat down. The thought that Angie and Ruby could be great friends humored him. He knew his reaction to the things his sister said were just like Mindy's when she told him about the things Ruby would say.

Amber adjusted herself when Isaac let go of her, and she handed the baby to Vic, who wondered why him when there were two other mothers at the table who could have helped her. But, he'd been around it long enough. He rested his nephew on his shoulder and gently patted his back until Isaac let out the burp that they were looking for. Then, he cradled the infant in his arms and sat with him.

"What did you want to talk to us about?" Amber asked, taking Allison's beer and having a sip. "And why didn't you want Mom or Dad here? Did we miss an anniversary or something?"

Vic shook his head, now glad that he had the baby in his arms. "I need to know how to handle something."

Allison raised an eyebrow. "Did you already knock your next-door neighbor girlfriend up?"

His other two sisters laughed as he shook his head. "No."

"Too bad. That would have been funny," Angie laughed.

"Your sense of humor worries me," Vic said, readjusting the baby and putting him back on his shoulder. "I found out something that I can't get out of my head. It's going to cause a bit of a problem between me and my next-door neighbor girlfriend," he said.

Angie sipped her iced tea. "Spill it."

Vic thought about what he was going to tell them, and even thinking about it made him wince. The only way he was going to get through this was to spill it, and spill it fast.

"Mom and Mindy's mom don't get along," he said.

Three sets of eyes settled on him, and Angie shrugged. "So what?"

"It's awkward to date someone and for your mother to dislike their family."

"Mom will get over it."

He loved his sister's optimism. "I don't know. It appears our mother is the one that caused the rift. Well, half of it," he corrected.

"Are you freaking going to talk in code all night? What the hell did Mom do?" Angie waved the server over to fill her tea.

Vic waited until the server was clear from the table. "She told me herself that she got caught with Mindy's mom's boyfriend in high school."

"Caught?" Amber asked. "What is *caught*?"

Vic swallowed hard and took a breath to answer when Allison looked at Amber. "Probably making out or going on a date."

Okay, that proved that no one wanted to hear what he had to say.

"Right?" she looked to Vic for confirmation.

"To be honest, I took it that it was a little more involved."

No surprise that it was Angie who laughed, nearly spitting out her drink. "God, how was I born to such wusses? Mom got caught fucking the neighbor's boyfriend in high school? Do you think she's some pristine virgin?"

Vic and his other sisters sat there with their mouths open. Yep, Angie and Ruby would be quite a pair.

Allison shook her head and crinkled her nose. "I don't want to think about Mom doing anything like that."

"You have kids," Angie said. "You know how the system works, right?"

Amber shifted a glance between their sisters and then to Vic. "Mom really slept with the neighbor's boyfriend?" Her words dripped with disgust.

"That's the way we understand it. Though, she didn't exactly use those words. But she got caught—that's what that means, right?"

Amber shook her head. "Do you know the lecture I got when she caught me making out with Eddie Kiffin?"

Again, Angie let out a loud laugh. "Because she was so worried about the two of you, I had me a fine 'ole time in high school. I'm going to guess, my kids are going to have a conversation like this too some day," she said unapologetically.

Vic bit down hard. "Okay, well, moving on. The thing is that Mindy's mom and dad dated from the time they were fourteen."

Now his sisters' eyes all went wide, but it was Angie's mouth that curled up into a wide smile. "Mom slept with your girlfriend's dad?"

"Ew," Allison shot out.

"Please say she's wrong," Amber begged.

"I don't think she's wrong," Vic admitted.

Allison shook her hands as if she'd touched something gross. "Why did you have to share this with all of us. Now we all have trauma."

"Because I need to know how to handle this. Mindy and I are weirded out about it."

"You should be," Amber agreed. "Maybe you just need to break up."

"I'm not breaking up with her. I love her."

The wide eyes of his sisters softened.

Amber nudged him. "You love her?"

"I do."

"That's very sweet," she said with tears pooling in her eyes. "It's hormones. Don't give me shit for crying."

Vic chuckled as he rubbed his nephew's back. "We don't want our families to hate each other, but this is a big deal. I mean, Mom slept with Mindy's dad—maybe."

"The more you say it, the grosser it gets," Allison pleaded.

"I have to talk to Mom, don't I?"

Angie shook her head. "You're all so stupid." She sipped her tea again. "Shit. I have to pee." She stood from her chair and looked Vic in the eye. "What you need to do is do what you've been doing. Keep screwing the neighbor and loving her, if that's what you really feel. Let Mom and Mindy's dad deal with their emotions about what they did. Obviously, everything worked out. So, what's the big deal? Just because Mom is your mother, it doesn't mean she had to be some pure and amazingly perfect person. None of us are. Dad probably has a skeleton or two in his closet too." She shuffled her feet as if she were trying to buy herself a few more moments. "If you lose out on a great thing because of this, then you and Mindy are stupid," she said. Then, she hurried off to the bathroom.

Vic let out a long, heavy breath, and continued to rub his nephew's back.

He was glad he'd called his sisters. And, wasn't it always Angie, with her less than subtle ways, that brought understanding and calm to an otherwise crazy situation?

CHAPTER THIRTY-SIX

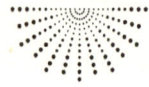

Mindy climbed into Vic's car on Saturday night, leaned over the console, and kissed him gently. "Thanks for driving," she said as she eased back into her seat.

"Anytime. You look beautiful."

Mindy laughed. "You haven't even seen me. I have on a big coat."

"I just know you look beautiful." He took her hand once she'd settled into the car and fastened her seatbelt. Interlacing their fingers together, Vic felt as if he were holding on for dear life. "We're going to Ruby's?"

"Yeah. Turn right at the stop sign," she said.

"This isn't movie night is it? You seem over dressed for that."

She smiled. "No. That's next weekend. Lisa's brother will be there tonight. They've been talking about him moving in with Ruby. I think she just wants to have everyone together casually to feel it out."

Vic turned at the stop sign and continued down the street. "I thought them moving in together was a done deal."

"I think so. I thought so," she corrected. "His job seems to take up a lot of his time, so he hasn't been around too much for Ruby to get to know him."

"I thought they already knew each other."

Mindy shook her head. "Left at the light," she instructed. "Jason didn't come around until, well, right before Lisa got married. And, like I said, he's not around much."

"So she's always known her roommates well? Ruby that is?"

"No, that's why this is humorous. Ruby gets new roommates all the time. And, then they move out. Ruby has been in my life for more than a decade. She's not that hard to be around. I have no idea why people move in and out."

Mindy directed him through a few more turns, their hands still joined. "When do you want to start painting?" he asked, trying to ease them into conversation.

"We should finish your room first," she suggested. "You'll want to get back to work."

Vic shrugged. "I kind of like working in the office."

Mindy turned her head and watched him. "You do?"

"I do. I think working from home can be overrated."

"Oh, I leave town on Tuesday," she blurted out the warning as if it had only crossed her mind.

Now Vic turned his head to look at her, before focusing back on the road. "You didn't mention that before."

"I forget that someone would care."

He gave her hand a squeeze. "Where are you going this time?" he asked, understanding that this thing between them was new. He hadn't told her everything he'd been up to either, had he?

"Napa Valley again."

"Short trip?"

"Tuesday through Friday."

There was a tightness in his chest when he thought of her being gone for most of the week. That was what happened when there was love, right? When you loved someone, you wanted them around all the time, and when they had to be away it just wasn't right.

"I'd be happy to drive you out to the airport and pick you back up," he offered.

"Really?"

He chuckled. "Of course."

Mindy fell silent for a moment and worried her lip. "Have you talked to your mom?"

"Just small talk, if you will. She wants to have lunch on Wednesday."

"With just you?"

Vic shrugged. "She just mentioned lunch."

Mindy huffed out a breath. "I asked my dad to go out to lunch on Saturday."

"Before movie night?"

She ran her hands down her thighs and made fists. "At least I'll have lots of support after I ask him all the questions I have. I want some answers. Do you see why I don't trust that any man won't cheat? Ex-boyfriends do it, dads do it."

He flinched at her words, and he knew she'd seen him do it.

Vic put the car in park and turned in his seat to face her. "Remember whatever happened between all of them, it has nothing to do with us."

Mindy pursed her lips. "Of course it does. How can I trust anything if I can't trust my own father? If it didn't have anything to do with us, we wouldn't be so awkward around each other."

So, she felt it too.

"I know my mom loves my dad and the indiscretions of a teenager didn't cause problems in my life until recently."

Mindy nodded. "My parents' marriage has always been enviable."

"We just need to move past the shock of it all, that's all this is —shock. Our parents are normal. Our parents had a past. Our parents were stupid—stupid teenagers."

That warranted the tiniest chuckle from her.

Vic tucked a lose strand of hair behind her ear and held her gaze. "And I swear, I would never, ever, be unfaithful to you. I will always be honest and upfront with you about anything that's bothering me."

She batted her eyes as if there were tears that threatened to rise. "I would never, ever, be unfaithful to you either. I don't believe in it."

Vic smiled. "Then I think we can agree that we're okay here. As icky as the past may be," he said laughing and she did too, "we aren't our parents. And, our parents turned out okay."

"You're right. But I still want answers. I—we deserve answers."

"We'll get them."

Mindy leaned in, placing both of her hands on his cheeks. "I love you."

"I love you too. Let's go hang out with your friends, and then go back to my place. I've missed waking up with you."

"I like the sound of that."

With Lisa's help, Ruby had put out a spread for dinner. Mindy sat back with her hands on her full stomach.

"You girls outdid yourself. This was wonderful," she said.

Ruby lifted her wine glass toward Lisa. "She's the queen of dinner parties. Honestly, I warmed it up and opened the wine."

Lisa's cheeks pinked. "You gals are sweet. I made a video of the prep, and posted it as bonus content." She was smiling wide as she took Ryan's hand. "I received the highest number of views I've ever had."

Tina rubbed her swollen belly. "That's exciting."

"It is. It means—"

"It means she's hotter than anything out there," Ryan said,

lifting Lisa's fingers to his lips and placing a kiss on them. "I'll be able to quit my job soon and just be her assistant."

Lisa laughed and nudged him. "That's the plan."

Jason shook his head. "When I met you, you were shy," he directed the comment to Lisa. "I can't believe you make a living recording yourself and putting it on the internet."

Lisa reached for her brother's hand, giving it a squeeze. "Without the love and support you and your family gave me, I would never have had the strength to do it."

Vic reached for Mindy's hand under that table, lacing their fingers together. When she turned her head to look at him, there was an understanding that resonated between them. Lisa faced situations in her life that none of them would ever understand. She survived and thrived beyond anyone's expectations of her. If Lisa could overcome her upbringing as a foster child who was tossed from home to home her entire life, then Mindy and Vic could take the love they had for one another and push away their feelings of betrayal caused by their parents—which they both knew had nothing to do with them.

Vic smiled and mouthed the words *I love you.*

Mindy leaned into him, resting her head on his shoulder. They were going to be okay, and Mindy was excited for what was to come for them.

CHAPTER THIRTY-SEVEN

MINDY STEPPED INTO THE MIDDLE OF THE ROOM, PLACED HER hands on her hips, the paint brush still gripped in her hand. Blowing out a breath to move the piece of hair that had fallen over her forehead, she studied the walls, which they'd spent their entire Sunday painting.

"You did a great job repairing the wall," she complimented Vic as they looked at the paint they'd spent all day rolling onto the walls. "Even empty, this makes this room feel totally different."

"You wield a mean paint brush," Vic teased. "I've never seen edges so precise."

Mindy laughed and nudged her shoulder into his arm. "I've been known to be called a bit of a perfectionist."

"I think you're perfect."

When she turned her head he was gazing at her, and warmth filled her until she had to let out a slow breath to calm the beating of her heart.

"We should get this all cleaned up."

Vic ran his finger over her cheek and streaked it with paint. "I think we should get ourselves cleaned up." His voice dripped with that sexy tone that made Mindy's insides twist.

"That wasn't very nice," she whispered as he stepped in and closed the gap between them.

Vic licked his lips as he looked at hers. "I promise to make sure there is no paint on you anywhere," he said as he slid his finger down the dip in her shirt and between her breasts, smearing another line of paint on her.

Mindy dropped the paintbrush in her hand to the tarp below them, and raised her arms around Vic's neck.

"I think this shower is going to take a long time," she said jumping up on him and wrapping her legs around his waist.

Vic's hands came under her ass and held her in place. "A very, very long time."

THE WATER IN THE SHOWER HAD GONE COLD BEFORE VIC WAS DONE touching Mindy. As promised, he'd removed all the paint, and had inspected her skin with slow, methodical kisses as her hands tunneled in his wet hair. One thing about old lady chic, there were handles in the shower to hold on to when their knees had gone too weak to hold them up.

Barely dry, they'd landed in bed, and that was where they'd spent the rest of their Sunday. Vic wasn't sure what they were going to do with two houses, because he knew for certain, he didn't want Mindy to ever be even as far away as next door. He wanted her to share his space—always.

As she lay in his arms, her hair now wild from drying against the pillow, Vic ran a finger down her bare arm and watched her smile.

"I'm hungry," Mindy said.

"You should be," he teased.

She turned to her side and pressed against him. Just as it had all day, his body immediately reacted to her.

She dragged her bottom lip through her teeth. "One more time and then we make some dinner?"

"I'm easily persuaded," he said as Mindy rolled him to his back and straddled him.

"I see that."

VIC RUSHED INTO THE GREEK RESTAURANT AT LUNCH TIME, ON Wednesday, to find it as busy as it had been when he'd gone with Mindy. He frantically searched for his mother, since he was already twenty minutes late.

She was scrolling through her phone when he found her and hurried through the restaurant to the booth in the corner.

"I'm so sorry I'm late," he said approaching the booth.

His mother set her phone down and looked up at him as he took his coat off and tossed it into the booth before sitting.

"Busy day at the office?" she asked with a wary smile.

"Best day yet," Vic boasted. "Do you remember the account I got for the resort they're building in Castle Rock?"

"I think so," she nodded.

"Well, they're slated to open three more of them in different states, and they have reached out to contract me to exclusively to do their advertising."

His mother batted away tears that arose every time he or his siblings shared good news. She reached for his hand across the table and gave it a squeeze. "That's wonderful news. I'm so proud of you, son."

"Thank you," Vic smiled before pulling his hand back and picking up the menu. "My hands are shaking."

"Are you nervous about it?"

He shook his head. "No. I'm so excited. I'm going to have to hire someone. I'm a big company now," he chuckled and his mother's smile spread wider.

"This is wonderful news." His mother eased her back against the booth. "Perhaps you could hire Mindy."

Vic lifted his eyes from his menu. "She has a great job. I don't see advertising being something she'd want to give that all up for."

"She sells wine," his mother said blandly.

"She creates relationships," he corrected. "She gets to know the wineries and she knows her buyers. Not to mention, her wine knowledge is extensive."

His mother nodded. "Where is she now? You didn't invite her to lunch?"

Vic set the menu down. "She's in Napa Valley. She travels a lot."

His mother's mouth opened into an O before she folded her hands in her lap. "That sounds nice."

A moment later their waiter arrived and took their order. Then, Vic decided, it was game on. His mother already seemed out of sorts, so he assumed the high he was on was going to dip rather quickly.

"Thanks for the lunch invite," he said, trying to calm the tension he already felt.

"I thought it would be good to talk."

"Sure. About what?"

She shook her head and then picked up her napkin and draped it in her lap as if she needed something to do with her hands.

"There's a lot of tension between us over you dating Corinne's daughter."

"There shouldn't be. I love her. I love you. You should be happy for me."

"You love her?" his mother raised the question.

"I do. I can see a future for us."

She nodded. "I am happy for you. I guess it just brings back a lot of hurtful memories."

Vic picked up the glass of water that was on the table and sipped. "I don't mean to hurt you."

"You didn't hurt me. I did that to myself." She drew in a breath as if facing what had happened was helpful to her. "I should have dealt with this forty years ago."

Because he still wasn't steady about the truth, Vic set the glass down. "What happened?"

His mother's lip trembled and he saw her eyes well with tears. "I always thought that when we became an adult all of the things that happened to us in our youth would go away."

"You always told us to think about everything we did so it would never come back at us."

She chuckled. "All parents say that." His mother picked up her water, took a sip, and set her glass down. "Part of being a parent is never talking about the missteps in our own youth."

Vic reached for his mother's hand. "I had detention three times." Her eyes went wide and he smiled. "I skipped biology and got caught off campus at the Dairy Queen. Then I got caught cheating on a test."

That caused his mother to take in a loud breath.

"I think I would have known if you had detention," she said.

Vic shook his head. "The third one I got caught smoking on campus."

"Victor!"

"I wasn't perfect either," he laughed. "I just knew the right people so you never got called."

His mother pursed her lips, studied him, and eased back. "Corinne and I were best friends," she began wiping at her eyes. "She was so pretty, funny, and everyone loved her."

"I've only been around her once. She was very nice."

A line formed between his mother's brows. "I wasn't so popular."

"I doubt that."

"Well, don't." She clasped her hands in her lap again. "Age has taught me that I was a petty and jealous person."

"You're not—"

His mother held up her hand. "I was. We all change, Victor," she said using his full name. "Corinne was a cheerleader, and I wasn't. She was a straight A student, and I wasn't. Corinne did all the amazing things, and I was always second best."

Vic's chest ached as he heard his mother recall her life. He'd never heard her talk about herself in such a negative way.

She wiped at her cheek. "She and Ben were a thing, on and off, since junior high. Our junior year in high school," she paused and drew in a breath, "I moved in on Ben when I knew they were going through a difficult time."

"So they broke up?" Vic felt a bit of hope in the story.

"For a little bit."

"So no foul."

She shook her head. "Ben and I dated a bit. Nothing, and I mean nothing big." She sipped her water. "They got back together, and I was so jealous, I made my move."

This was the confession. This was the moment his mother was going to come clean, and Vic wasn't sure he wanted to know the rest.

"I knew Corinne was at some cheer thing, and my parents were out of town, so I had a party."

Vic noticed his knee bounced, and he willed it to stop. He didn't want to hear any of this. "Ben was on the tennis team, and so were a few of my friends. So I convinced them all to come over. We drank and smoked some weed," she said, and Vic felt the tips of his ears grow warm. *Weed? Did she say weed?*

His mother arranged her silverware on the table. "We turned down the lights and danced to music, and there were couples making out. I was drunk, Ben was drunk, and we started to make out too."

Vic was sure he was going to be sick before his lunch ever arrived. He wasn't sure if it was because his mother was about to tell him what happened between her and Mindy's dad, or if it was the thought that his perfect mother hadn't been so perfect. Weed? Alcohol? Who was this woman?

This woman kept a perfectly neat house and baked brownies for bake sales. This woman sipped wine and had coffee dates with friends. This woman coddled her grandchildren and had raised four—okay three—perfectly mannered children of her own while being the president of the P.T.A.

"Anyway," she continued, "Ben and I were making out, some of the people passed out here and there, so we moved to my room. I took off my shirt because I had all intents on feeling things out," she choked on her words and coughed, never once looking at Vic. "We got on my bed, and we both passed out."

"You passed out?"

"Yep. Then at some point, the lights in the basement came on and my door flew open. There was Corrine in her cheerleader uniform. I have never heard someone scream so loudly—so violently."

Vic was on the verge of laughing, but it wasn't funny, so he reeled it in. His mother was horrified by what she'd done. Okay, he was too. But she wasn't the only party at fault—and she'd been a teenager. Wasn't that forgivable?

"You didn't sleep with Ben?" he finally asked.

His mother's eyes went wide. "You thought I did?"

"Well, yeah. It all pointed to that. Wasn't that your intent?"

"Oh, God!" She was more mortified than when she'd started the story. "I can't believe you thought—"

He held up his hand. "You told me you'd been caught with Corinne's boyfriend."

"I was, and it was a horrific moment in my life." Her eyes were wide. "Please tell me you're the only one that thought that."

Vic shook his head. "No. Mindy and I both thought it, once we figured out it was her dad." He raised his brows. "And admittedly, so do my sisters."

"Victor!" she shouted in a hushed tone. "You told your sisters?"

"I needed some therapy."

His mother wiped her brow with her napkin. "I'm going to have to go into hiding forever."

Now he did laugh. "No, you're going to have to swallow your pride, because I want to marry Mindy, and you're going to be face to face with Corrine and Ben."

CHAPTER THIRTY-EIGHT

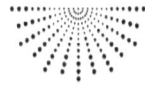

THE CROWD ON THE TRAIN FROM THE TERMINALS MOVED TOWARD the escalators. Mindy looked down at her phone at the text from Vic. *Traffic is crazy. I'll be there soon.*

She couldn't wait to be wrapped up in his arms, but if she had to wait a few minutes, then that's what she'd do.

As she cleared the top of the escalator, she watched as travelers found those who had come for them. They enveloped one another in embraces, and laughed at signs that were held up.

It was then she noticed him.

Standing among those waiting, Vic stood with an enormous grin on his face, and in his hands he held a bouquet of sharpened pencils with a bow wrapped around them.

Mindy batted her eyes to focus on him, because they'd welled with tears.

"Are you seriously standing here with a bouquet of freshly sharpened pencils?" She laughed and Vic's arms came around her and pulled her to him.

"It's not fall in New York, but..."

She laughed as he pressed his lips to hers. "How do you know that line?"

"Do you think you and your friends are the only people to have ever watched *You've Got Mail*? It's one of my mother's favorites, and it was on TV late last night, so I watched it."

"That's a rom com."

"It most certainly is," he admitted.

"There are no sports references in it."

"Sure there are. He's on a treadmill," he humored. "But it even has movie quotes from other great movies in it."

Mindy grinned. "That it does." She eased back from him slightly, her arms still draped over his shoulders. "You said traffic was bad and you'd be here soon," she reminded him.

"It was my devious plan to throw you off. I didn't want you to know I'd been standing here waiting for you, dying to see you come up that escalator."

"You missed me?"

"Like crazy," he dipped his head until their lips met. "Welcome home, my love."

Mindy sighed when he called her that. "Thank you."

"I don't have to share you until tomorrow, right?"

Pulling her bottom lip through her teeth, Mindy looked up into his dark eyes. "Right."

"This stupid airport is so far away from everything. Maybe we should just find a hotel and get a room."

Running her finger over his jaw, Mindy stepped back from him and took her bouquet of pencils. "I promise to make it worth the drive," she said, slipping her hand into his as they walked toward baggage claim.

WITH THEIR HANDS STILL CLASPED, VIC GRINNED AS MINDY TOLD him about her trip, which seemed to have been eventful. He wondered, with her enthusiasm over a new line of wine, if telling her about the discussion with his mother was worth bringing up.

Maybe it was better that it wait until Mindy asked about his lunch with his mother.

"I already have eighteen orders," she boasted with a wide grin.

Vic lifted her hand to his lips and kissed her knuckles. "That's wonderful. One more reason to celebrate."

"What about you?" she asked as she shifted in her seat to look at him. "The other night on the phone you mentioned something about that resort."

Vic laughed. He had mentioned it, and she'd cut him off at one point because another order had come in, which had been massive, and she'd screamed right into the phone.

"They want to use me exclusively for their resorts. And they're building more of them."

"Vic, that's fantastic."

He nodded. "I'll have to hire someone, or more than one someones."

Vic caught a glimpse of her grinning at him.

"I'm so proud of you."

Vic glanced at her and then back at the road. "Thank you. This is what I dreamed of when I started my company. I have to admit, I really never thought it would happen."

"You deserve it. Now that I work near you, I know how hard you work."

Running his thumb over her fingers, he wondered how she could observe his work habits, when her own work habits had her running back and forth from her office all day long on the phone or with potential clients.

"It'll be a great boost so I can finish up the house, and then decide what I want to do about it."

"Do about what?"

"The house." He took the exit off the highway. "I'd like to think this is going somewhere bigger, and maybe we'd want to combine households one day."

The smile on her face faded, and that warranted some worry on his end. "Oh." Mindy blew out a breath. "You'd give up your grandmother's house?"

Vic shrugged. "I've thought about renting it out. And maybe this is a conversation for another day," he admitted as he eased the car to a stop at a light.

"I just didn't anticipate—"

"It's okay. We'll get there."

"We're there," she said nervously and he noticed she smiled, but it shook her. "I think you're right. It's time to think about what to do with the houses."

"I love you. All I know is I want to be with you forever."

"Wow," Mindy waved her hand in front of her now damp eyes. "This isn't really a surprise. I don't know why I'm crying."

"Maybe you're happy about it?"

"So happy," she admitted as Vic eased through the intersection.

THEY STAYED AT HIS HOUSE AND ATE LEFTOVERS IN FRONT OF THE TV as they watched *The Intern*, which was one of Mindy's go-to movies. She thought about what Vic had said in the car about combining households. Was she ready for that? Could she step away from her grandmothers' house? Admittedly she'd never made it her own. Could she live with Vic and rent out her house and still live so close?

God, her mother would flip if she even mentioned it, she was sure. But again, Mindy's choices had nothing to do with her mother, and she had to remember that.

Vic answered emails on his phone and Mindy studied him. He hadn't mentioned talking to his mother. She couldn't help but wonder if it all turned out to be nothing, or if he was keeping it secret.

No, she eased in next to him, and his arm came around her shoulders.

He didn't lie. He didn't keep secrets. He didn't cheat. They'd established all of that. If he had something to say about what their parents had done in high school, he'd tell her.

CHAPTER THIRTY-NINE

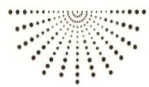

MINDY WATCHED HER FATHER WALK INTO THE SANDWICH SHOP AND wave as he walked toward her. She stood as he neared the table, and he pulled her in and hugged her.

"Hey, peanut," he said and looked down at her. "You okay? You're shaking."

Nope, she wasn't okay at all. "Just have a chill," she said and he nodded as if he were accepting her lie.

"Did you order?" he asked looking at the line at the counter.

"I did. I got us a BLT to share, but each a bag of chips and a drink."

He smiled. "Perfect."

They sat down at the small table and a moment later their sandwich was delivered. Mindy fussed over unwrapping it and setting each half on napkins. It didn't go unnoticed that her father watched her fuss.

"Have a lot on your mind?" he finally asked.

"I have a lot happening in my life," Mindy admitted. "I have a new wine line that I'm selling and it's netting big sales."

"That's wonderful."

"It is," she tried to lighten her voice and the mood. "I picked out paints to start painting the inside of the house."

Her father's nose wrinkled. "Did you tell your mother that?"

"I did. She was none too happy."

"I'm sure, but it's your house."

"It is. And Ruby reminds me all the time that I'm living in a shrine."

Her father shrugged. "I have to agree with Ruby, but I don't put all the blame on you. I think your mother sometimes forgets that it's your house now. You should be able to do anything to it."

Mindy nodded. "Vic's done some great things to his house, so I know what's possible."

She noticed her father's face tighten as she mentioned Vic's name, but it had softened just as quickly.

"How are things going with the two of you?" he asked.

"Wonderful. Perfect," she added. "I love him, Daddy."

Her father nodded. "He's a lucky man then."

She watched as her father took a bite of his half of the sandwich. She contemplated the questions she had for him, but decided the direct route was the easiest.

"Did you really cheat on Mom in high school with Liv?"

Her father's eyes went wide as he chewed his bite.

It wasn't quite how she'd wanted to ask him, but it had just come out that way.

When he was finished with his bite, her father wiped his mouth with a napkin he pulled from the dispenser on the table.

He clasped his hands together, resting them atop the table. Obviously he was contemplating his answer, and Mindy waited, though she thought if he were innocent he wouldn't have had to take so damn long to answer the question.

"Well, you've been holding on to that, haven't you?" he asked and Mindy felt her shoulders drop.

"I'm sorry, I—"

He held up his hand to stop her. "That's what you want to

know? I guess we're having this discussion." Her father opened his bottle of tea, took a sip, and recapped it.

"Dad—"

"No, let's talk about it." He pinched the bridge of his nose. "Wow, I never thought I'd talk about this after it happened."

Mindy clasped her hands in her lap. She wasn't ready for this. She thought she was, but every muscle in her body trembled, and she thought she should have just let it be water under the bridge.

"Yes, the reason your mother and Liv weren't friends in high school was because of me." He opened his tea again and sipped. Now she saw that his hands shook, and she felt terrible for putting her father through this. But she needed answers so that she could go on.

Her father drew in a breath. "Mom and I got together in junior high school. So you can imagine we were on and off over the years. You're not together from that young of an age without some issues. It so happened that during our junior year, we broke up for a bit."

Mindy felt the tension in her chest ease. They'd broken up. Still icky, but okay, she thought.

Her father twisted the top back on his bottle. "Liv and I went out a few times when Mom and I were broken up. Nothing much. To be honest, she was a little petty back then, so I didn't enjoy hanging with her all that much. But, egos get stroked when someone is into you."

"She doesn't seem like someone who is petty," Mindy admitted.

"We all change, sweetheart. I'm not the kind of man who would ever hurt my wife either. But, at sixteen, I did."

The tightness in her chest was back, and Mindy fisted her hands under the table. "You did cheat on mom?" She felt the heat rise in her cheeks now, and the trembling was back. Would it be immature to stick her fingers in her ears and run out of the restaurant?

"I got caught in a compromising situation with Liv," he admitted, and Mindy felt her throat tighten.

"You said you broke up."

"I said Liv and I went out when Mom and I broke up. But, at the time, your mother and I were very much together."

Mindy swallowed down the lump in her throat. "I really had hoped we misunderstood the situation," she said and her voice shook.

Her father narrowed his eyes as if he were scolding her without words.

"I was sixteen, Mind. I made plenty of mistakes when I was a teenager. Liv was one of them." His voice had grown harsher, and she didn't like it.

Mindy felt her cheeks grow even hotter, and she placed her hands on them. "Mom caught you?"

He ran his fingers over his brow. "Yes. Liv had a party when Mom was at some event. We all got drunk, and stoned, and well—"

"You don't have to go on," she said and kind of wished he wouldn't. *Drunk. Stoned.* She couldn't hear any more of this.

"I got caught. Your mom came in," he continued anyway.

Mindy clasped her hands again, and listened.

"Liv and I had been making out, we ended up in her bed, and passed out."

Mindy waited for more, but he'd stopped. "You passed out?"

"We did. Mom had heard I was there, and she busted in." He rubbed his hand over the back of his neck and eased back in his chair. There was a lightness to him now, and the corner of his mouth curled up into a slight smile.

Her father took another bite of his sandwich, and when he'd finished chewing, he grinned.

"Your mother lost her shit." He shook his head as he remembered it. "She screamed so loud I thought the police would come. A moment later she was standing over me pounding me with her fists. Then, she went after Liv."

This time he laughed.

"It had to be the most epic cat fight I'd ever seen. Your mother, in her cheerleader uniform, climbed up on the bed and began pulling Liv's hair. Poor Liv, she'd taken off her shirt, so she was half naked, and your mother was ripping out her hair when the rest of the people from the party crashed into the room.

"I eventually got your mother off Liv and carried her out of the house. From there, she threw rocks at my car windshield, scratched the door with her keys, and called me names I didn't even know she knew."

Mindy stared at him, horrified that either of her parents had ever acted like that. She hadn't destroyed her ex's personal property. Okay, she'd thought about it, but she'd just walked away. Was this the difference in reactions to when you were in love and when it just didn't matter that it ended?

"Why are you laughing?" Mindy asked, her hands now flat on the top of the table. "This is horrible."

"This was forty years ago, and reliving it makes it funny." He crossed his arms in front of him. "Mindy, your mother and I have been married for thirty-five years. There is no one I've ever cared more for than I do for you and your sister. But your mother is everything to me. It took me six months to get her to talk to me after that, and of course, to get your grandmother to let me back into the house. But your mother is the only woman I've ever loved."

Mindy clenched her hands. "You both were acting weird around Vic. This affects us."

Her father reached for her hands and held them in his. "It shouldn't. Yeah, it was weird to have him at dinner. He looks so much like his mother, it was a little freaky."

"That's why you were so weird?"

He shrugged. "I was weird because I knew it affected your mother too. It brought up a lot of hurt."

"You cheated on Mom," she spat out the words, still angry that his teenage self had been so stupid.

He shook his head. "Okay, so I did. I kissed another girl while I was dating your mother—in high school. I married your mother years later and had two amazing daughters. Now we have grandchildren. Mindy, I made a mistake. I'm sure that in your life you've made a mistake that would be devastating if it came back and hurt those around you." His voice wasn't full of humor now, and that hurt too.

She sat back. Did she have something in her past that would someday devastate her children?

"I'm in love with Vic," Mindy said and her father nodded.

"I know."

"You do?"

"I could tell."

"What do I do with all of this? How do I make it okay?"

Her father rose, walked around the table and pulled her up to him. He wrapped his arms around her and squeezed. "Sweetheart, if I had known when I was sixteen that my actions would devastate my daughter when she was thirty, I would have acted different. Liv was a nice enough gal. I know she married a good man and raised a wonderful family. Don't hold this against us. Your mother eventually forgave me. I need you to do that too."

"But they'll never accept this."

"They will. They are just going to have to get used to the thought that you and Vic are together. If it's long term, then honestly, I think it's a funny story that ends with me and Liv sharing the same grandkids."

CHAPTER FORTY

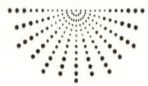

MINDY, LISA, AND RUBY SAT ON THE SOFA WITH THEIR FEET UP ON the coffee table, and Tina had disappeared to the bathroom after they had polished her toes. Their toes were bright pink, and matched as they always did after movie night. The movie was *The Princess Bride*, so Mindy had brought over *Buttercup* frosted cupcakes with gold sprinkles to add to the theme.

The sheet masks they wore were a change from masks that hardened and cracked, giving them each a moment to let their heads fall back and relax while the terrifying mask did its job.

Tina returned from the bathroom and sat in the new rocking chair that adorned her living room. "Pregnancy is all about throwing up all the time, not just in the morning, and peeing."

Mindy laughed. "My sister ended up wearing those disposable underwear when she was pregnant with Bo."

Tina let out a sob sound. "I'm too young to do that."

"It's just an option," Mindy said, keeping still so that her mask wouldn't slip.

Ruby nudged Mindy. "Are we going to get sexy details about you and the neighbor yet?"

Mindy shook her head. "You have your own imagination. I don't need to give you details."

"My imagination is quite creative," Ruby admitted. "The things I've thought about are probably well beyond your gymnastic ability."

That caused Lisa to howl out a laugh, and Mindy couldn't help but join in.

"Let's just say, I'm not lacking in affection."

Ruby threw her hands up. "Affection, my ass. Tell me he has you gripping the sheets and that you've never felt anything like it before."

Under the mask, Mindy's cheeks heated. "He has me gripping the sheets and I've never felt anything like it before," she repeated, and again they all howled in laughter, and Tina gripped her belly as she laughed.

"I miss sex like that," Tina said, tears rolling over her maskless cheeks.

Ruby groaned. "I thought pregnant sex was supposed to be something extraordinary."

"Not when you have to get up to pee all the time."

Again, they all laughed, and Mindy looked around at the women whom she cherished as much as her own sister. Even though she loved a man, they were still there filling that need that no man ever could.

Lisa sucked in a breath when her laughter subsided and turned toward Mindy. "Did you get the moms not liking one another sorted out?"

Mindy pulled the mask from her face, folded it, and set it on the table. Then she rubbed in the leftover lotion on her face.

"I suppose we did. Though we haven't gotten them together yet," she said.

Lisa followed Mindy's lead and took off her mask. "What was their fight over?"

Mindy winced and Ruby quickly caught on to that. "Oh, something big happened. Cat fight?"

"Why do you say that?" Mindy asked.

"Because I can just feel it. One of them got caught doing something, didn't they?"

"Are you psychic?"

"I'm right, huh? Okay, which one them lied, cheated, or stole something?"

Mindy stood and walked to the kitchen to retrieve her wine glass that awaited her. Before she could make it back to the living room, the other three had followed her.

"Shit," Ruby said picking up her own glass. "What did I stumble on?"

Mindy drank a long sip of wine hoping it would numb the ickiness of it all—still. "My dad got caught with Vic's mom."

"Your dad screwed his mom?" Ruby's voice grew louder.

"No. No. I didn't say that. No," Mindy countered.

Lisa shrugged. "You didn't give us anything better to go with."

Mindy finished her wine. "Okay, they made out when they were drunk as juniors. They ended up in her bed, and my mom found them."

"So they did screw?" Ruby cheered.

"No." Mindy set down her glass and pressed her fingers to her eyes. "I suppose they might have, but they didn't. They got caught, and well, now I'm living this hell because of it."

Ruby shook her head. "What hell? He makes you grip the sheets. Screw your moms if they're not happy for you. It would appear that they got over it and your mom took back your dad."

"She did. I'm still just a bit freaked out about it. Is it in us to cheat?"

Tina held up her hands. "Seriously? You're worried about him cheating on you because of this?"

Mindy shrugged. "Maybe I would cheat."

Lisa shook her head. "No. You've already been cheated on. You're just on high alert. And you're not the cheating type."

"I wouldn't have pegged my father to be either."

Ruby groaned. "Your father was a sixteen-year-old boy. They only think with their dicks."

"Gross," Mindy refilled her wine glass again.

"I'm serious. If he thought he'd get some, he'd go for it Especially if he was drunk."

"I guess it's a good thing they never got that far," Mindy said as she took another long sip of wine.

Ruby slipped her arm around Mindy's waist. "So there was a cat fight?"

"There was," Mindy laughed. "I guess my dad was quite a catch."

"So are you, honey," Ruby kissed Mindy's cheek. "And now you've been caught. We should start picking out wedding colors."

"Let's start with wall colors."

Ruby clapped her hands together. "You're fixing up your house?"

"I'm going to start. And I'm going to start with the bedrooms."

"It's about damn time."

"Well, it'll be easier to grip the sheets if everything in the room didn't belong to my grandmother."

"I'm all in," Ruby said with a howl. "Now let's get drunk and watch this silly movie."

Tina sighed. "It's not silly."

"It's totally silly," Lisa interjected.

"It's supposed to be silly," Ruby added.

Tina looked at Mindy, who felt as if she needed to side with Tina. "It's fantastically romantic. Let's go watch."

VIC PULLED UP IN FRONT OF TINA'S AROUND ELEVEN, AFTER MINDY had called him nearly incoherently to come and pick her up.

When he reached the door, Tina pulled it open and grinned at him. "She could have crashed here, but she insisted she call you."

"I don't mind," he said, stepping into the house. "I think she needed to blow off a little steam."

Tina nodded. "I know you've done this pick up thing a few times now. I feel as if it's my duty to tell you, she's not some lush. She doesn't always tie one on."

Vic smiled. "I know. I'm not judging her, or anyone."

"Good, because Rube is already passed out."

He chuckled at that, thinking of the night they took her home and Mindy put her to bed.

"Victor!" His name came from down the hall, loud and slurred.

Vic followed Tina to the living room where Mindy sat in a recliner, fresh faced, with her hair piled high on her head in a messy bun.

"Hey, baby. Are you ready to go home?"

She nodded, and somehow managed to put the footrest down on the recliner, but nearly launched herself into the coffee table before Vic grabbed her.

She looked up at him, her eyes glassy, and her cheeks pink. "I'm drunk."

Keeping the laugh inward, he grinned. "I know. That's why you called me."

Aaron stepped into the living room and wrapped his arm around Tina's shoulders. "Do you need any help?"

Vic eased Mindy to his side. "We'll be fine." He looked around the room. "Anyone else need a ride?"

"My brother just picked up Lisa," he said.

"And Ruby can sleep it off on the couch," Tina added as she rubbed her belly. "For the record, that new wine she's selling, it seems to be strong in alcohol content."

"I'll make a note of that," Vic said, realizing that Mindy had fallen asleep standing up, her head resting on his shoulder. "Hey, baby, can you walk?"

One of her eyes opened and she smiled up at him. "You make me grip the sheets," she said and Vic noticed that Tina covered her mouth and Mindy's eyes went wide when she said it.

"Do I?"

Mindy nodded heavily. "Let's do that."

"How about we get you home, and then you can tell me all about that." Though, by the surprised look on Tina's face, he was fairly sure he knew what it meant.

Vic managed Mindy to the car and buckled her in. Before he climbed in, she was already snoring in the passenger seat. She was going to hurt in the morning, he thought as he pulled away from Tina and Aaron's house.

He'd bring her back when she felt well enough to get her car.

And though he hated to think of what was coming her way in the next few hours, there was a warmth that filled him when he thought about her calling him to come and get her. That was trust, and wasn't that nearly as fulfilling as love itself? Mindy trusted him with everything.

He thought about what he'd told his mother about wanting to marry Mindy. Perhaps it was too soon to make that decision—or to include her in it.

It was something to work toward.

They could finish their houses, and then decide where they'd live. Then, perhaps with the new business coming his way from the resort contract, he could surprise her with a ring.

Vic looked at Mindy, hunched in the seat and he smiled.

She deserved to be surprised and spoiled, and that was how he knew she was the right woman for him. He'd never considered that with anyone else.

CHAPTER FORTY-ONE

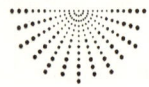

SUNLIGHT. IT BURNED MINDY'S EYES, AND SHE WINCED AND turned away.

Her head throbbed, her mouth was dry, and when she did pry her eyes open, she had to piece together where she was.

The bed next to her was empty.

She reached toward the nightstand to pick up her phone, but it wasn't there. Had she left it at Tina's?

Swinging her legs over the edge of the bed, Mindy pressed her fingers to her eyes as she sat up. This was the second time Vic had come for her. what kind of impression had she made? She wasn't used to getting drunk, but last night, it just seemed as if everyone had some steam to blow off.

Walking to the bedroom door, Mindy pulled it open and she could hear Vic's voice.

"Bowling resumes tonight," he said. "But why don't we meet for lunch this week?"

There was silence as he listened to the person on the other end of the phone.

"I can't wait to see you either," he said, then a moment later, he said goodbye and disconnected the call as he looked toward her in the hallway.

She noticed that he looked down at his phone once more before setting it on the counter and walking toward her.

"How are you feeling?" he asked, skimming her jaw with his finger.

"Like a truck ran over me."

"Tina says your new wine line has more alcohol content," he teased.

"Yeah. And Ruby poured a few shots from something Aaron had in the cupboard."

He nodded, and then grinned at her. "It's almost lunch time. Why don't I make us something."

"Lunch time?"

"You were out cold."

"I should go home. You have things to do today."

He studied her, a line forming between his brows as if in confusion. "I only have to take care of you."

"I heard that you have bowling," she said nodding toward where he'd been standing on the phone.

"I do. I'd invite you, but I'm not sure how your head will be by then. That might be a bit loud."

"Maybe," she admitted. "Besides, my dad is coming over to help take down the lights on the house. I can't have Christmas all year round."

He continued to study her, and then took a step back. "C'mon, let's get some food in you."

MINDY WATCHED VIC PULL OUT OF THE DRIVEWAY AS HER FATHER pulled down lights and she wound them around her arm. Under the circumstances, they'd decided that she shouldn't be on the ladder.

BERNADETTE MARIE

Vic waved, blew a kiss, and smiled before he drove away.

"Bowling, huh?" her father asked as she focused on Vic's car.

"Yeah," she said.

"I thought he was blowing smoke up my ass so he didn't have to help." Her father chuckled at his own joke.

"He would have helped me if—"

"Kiddo, I'm kidding," he said as he handed her another string of lights. "Every man needs something he does with the guys. Just like you have your movie nights with your girls."

Mindy nodded. She didn't much care that he bowled on Sunday nights. That was something he told her early on, though it had been on hiatus for the holidays. What seemed to be bothering her was him telling her that he didn't invite her because of her hangover. Shouldn't that have been her decision to not go? Then again, she didn't invite him to movie nights unless it was agreed upon to include the guys.

"Mindy?"

She snapped her head up at her name being called from the sidewalk. Walking toward her was Curtis Smith.

"Hey, Curtis," she called back, her voice shaking at the mere sight of him.

"This got delivered to Dad's. I told Dad I'd bring it over to you. It has your name on it," he said handing her a box. His eyes shifted to her father who climbed from the ladder. "Hello, Mr. Baldwin."

"Hi," her father said, holding his hand out to Curtis. "How's your dad?"

"He's hanging in there. He's stubborn, so I think that keeps him young," he laughed as he said it.

"That's good to hear," her father said before moving the ladder from the house and carrying it back to the garage.

"Thanks for bringing this over. I appreciate it," Mindy said.

Curtis shoved his hands into the pockets of his coat. "You bet. How have you been?"

Mindy didn't expect the friendly banter. Curtis never had much time for anything but formalities in the past when she'd dealt with him. Then again, he was a man now. Maybe manners had come with age.

"I'm doing great. And you?"

He shrugged. "Can't complain. Doesn't get me anywhere." He pulled a hand from his pocket and ran it over the back of his neck. "I'm divorced. One kid. I've been helping Dad when he needs it."

"I'm sure he appreciates that."

"Yeah. He says you and Vic have been spending time together."

Of course he said that. Hadn't the man been watching them since Vic moved in?

"We have."

"He's always been a good guy. Justine was a bit put out when he met up with her at the bar. But, hey, who wouldn't choose you over her?"

Mindy swallowed hard. Who in the hell was Justine?

"Anyway," Curtis continued. "Maybe we could catch up sometime."

Mindy stared at him before realizing what he'd said. "Right. Sure."

"I'll talk to you later," he said, lifting his hand in a small wave as he headed back to his father's house.

Mindy stood alone in the yard, the cold settling in around her.

Justine was a bit put out when he met up with her at the bar.

When had Vic met someone at a bar?

The conversation he'd been having when she'd walked out of the bedroom earlier struck her too.

Why don't we meet for lunch this week?

I can't wait to see you either.

Piecing it all together made her sick to her stomach. God,

what had she thought? They could just move from neighbors to a couple who said they loved one another in a little over a month?

She'd slept with him. She'd stayed with him.

Hadn't the entire past of his mother and her father proved to her that he came from stock that couldn't be trusted?

No. No. She looked down at the box in her hands, which Curtis had given her. She was letting her imagination get the best of her. Vic wasn't dishonest. She just wasn't understanding the situation, that was all.

He owned a business. He'd have lunch with people from time to time. Mindy was no stranger to that concept.

And Curtis hadn't said when Vic had been at the bar with that Justine person. That could have been before she and Vic began seeing each other.

Her heart rate began to settle.

Then again, hadn't his sisters set him up on dates?

She swallowed hard. Maybe he was dating them and her. Just like the last relationship she'd had, maybe she was just one of many.

Her father moved from the garage and walked toward her. "Are you just going to stand in the yard and hold that box?"

Mindy blinked hard. "No." She cleared her head. "Let me take this inside and I'll finish helping you."

CHAPTER FORTY-TWO

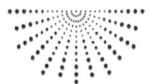

Ruby stood at the counter in her kitchen pouring hot water into the mugs she'd taken out of the cupboard. Mindy knew she was giving her a moment to reflect on everything she'd just spurted out to Ruby. This was Ruby's process.

Oh, she might be the first one to want juicy details on everyone's sex life, and the first one to say fuck-it to everyone and everything, but when one of them came at her with a dilemma, she was completely focused on helping her friends through it.

That was why Mindy showed up on her doorstep.

When Mindy's phone buzzed again, she turned it over and looked at the screen.

"Is that him?" Ruby asked as she carried the mugs to the table and set one in front of Mindy, then sat down with the other.

"Yes," Mindy said turning her phone over again so she couldn't see the screen.

Ruby opened the box of teas she had on the table. She took out a spice one for herself, and handed Mindy a packet of mint.

"Thank you," Mindy said as she tore into the bag.

"Don't you think you should have asked him a few questions

before you showed up here? I mean, your information did come from a guy you don't have anything positive to say about."

"I'm thinking it all through."

Ruby thoughtfully examined her tea bag, then let it sit in the water as she tucked her feet up under her. "You do realize you're being a jackass, right?"

"Screw you," Mindy shot back.

"Fuck you," Ruby countered. "You've been sleeping together for a few weeks and you said those stupid three words that make people lose all their senses. And now, here you are crying at my table. Maybe you should have had a few more talks before you sprinkled those words around."

"Why did I come here?"

"Because I'm the only one that's going to put you in your place, and you know it."

"You don't know anything about Vic."

"And neither do you," Ruby said. "You're all wigged out because you thought your dad screwed his mom. And you think because they screwed around when they were teenagers that Vic can't be trusted. Well, what about you?"

"What about me?"

"Maybe he went bowling so he could have this conversation with one of his friends. Maybe, he's not sure you're not seeing someone when you fly away without telling him."

Mindy took a breath to argue, but then sat back. She'd left town twice in the past month and only remembered to tell him when she was on the way out the door. Did he really think she was messing around behind his back? Was this how adults had relationships? After all, wasn't that how her last relationship went? He'd had a girlfriend and a wife—and Mindy.

When her phone buzzed again, Mindy only looked at it.

Ruby shook her head. "If you don't answer that, I will."

Mindy picked up the phone and looked at the message. *Is*

everything okay? You're not home and you haven't read any of my messages. I'm worried.

She scrolled through the rest of his messages.

I bowled a 210!

French fries from the counter are better with an entire bottle of ketchup, he'd said and sent a picture.

Did you go to bed already?

Just got home. Wanna have a sleepover?

Hey! Are you there?

Just knocked on your door. Text me when you can.

The messages continued.

I don't mean to be a pest, but I'm worried about you. I love you. Text me.

Things I have realized...I don't have your family's phone numbers or the numbers of your friends. I'm starting to freak out. Please let me know you're okay. I love you.

Ruby reached for her hand and gave it a squeeze. "It's ten o'clock. Give him something so he knows you're okay. You don't have to talk to him. After that, you can turn off you phone. But it's the decent thing to do—especially since you don't have any proof he did something wrong."

Mindy nodded, and then sent the text.

I can't talk right now. I'm fine. I'll talk to you later.

Vic reread the text from the night before. No other texts had come in, and none of his later texts had been read.

All he could do was pace around his house with his coffee mug in his hand, and wait.

He'd tried to do some work, since he couldn't sleep, but his creativity was at an all-time low. All he could do was focus his attention out the window, waiting for Mindy to pull up and park in the garage, but she'd never returned.

When the reminder on his phone chimed, he knew he had to head into the office. He had a presentation for the resort team, and he'd secured the conference room so that they could meet in person.

However, Vic wasn't sure how he was going to sell his new ideas. He hadn't had any sleep, and his mind certainly wasn't on advertising.

He packed up his things and headed to the office.

The entire drive, he wondered if he should just cancel the meeting, but he knew that would be the wrong thing to do. The team was driving up from Castle Rock. He needed to tend to his business. But, as soon as the meeting was over, he was going to find Mindy. This ghosting worried him. Had he done something wrong? Had something happened?

When he pulled into the parking lot, he turned off the engine and sat for a moment. Pulling out his phone, he scrolled through his messages again. Still, none of his had been read, and Mindy hadn't responded.

He sent her one more text.

I love you. I hope everything is okay. Please call me.

On a sigh, he slid his phone into his pocket, picked up his commuter bag from the passenger seat, and headed into the building, knowing full well the light in her office would never be turned on today. Mondays were always lonely at the office. This Monday was turning out to be even worse.

CHAPTER FORTY-THREE

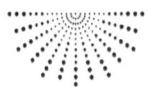

A‌VOIDING THE OFFICE ON A T‌UESDAY MORNING WASN'T AN OPTION. And that meant Mindy could no longer avoid Vic—nor did she want to.

Whatever was driving her to be mad at him was also driving her into a sadness that didn't need to exist.

Ruby had finally kicked Mindy out late Monday night. "In true Mindy style, when there's a little shakeup or drama, it's easier for you to hide than to face it. You need to grow a pair," she'd said as she led Mindy to the door

Though Ruby was hellbent on Mindy talking to Vic, she'd somehow made it into her house without him noticing, and all that did was offer her more time to drown in her thoughts.

Ruby was right, as she usually was. Mindy was running from something she didn't even understand or have confirmation on. She wasn't quite sure how to handle it either.

All she knew was she couldn't avoid Vic any longer. At the first opportunity, she was going to be straight-forward with him. She needed to know who Justine was and why he'd met her at a bar.

If he really loved her, he'd understand her pettiness.

As she let herself into her office, she replayed that in her head in reverse. If she really loved him, she'd give him an opportunity to share his side.

Dropping her bags into the chair in the corner, she realized that she deserved to be single and living among her grandmother's relics. She'd been hiding from true love for so long, she didn't even recognize it when it came along.

Maybe the barista had spiked her coffee, because standing in her office, knowing that Vic was going to walk in any second, she was filled with clarity.

Ruby had been right to shove her out of her house. Mindy was sabotaging her relationship with Vic, and for what? Over something Curtis Smith had said?

Mindy pulled her small compact out of her desk drawer and looked at herself. She was a bit of a mess, but he'd seen her look worse.

Brushing her fingers through her hair, and dabbing on a bit of lipstick, she thought she looked presentable.

Across the hall she heard his door open, and distinctly heard his voice. Any moment, he'd knock on her office door.

Tucking the items back into her desk, she moved toward the door. He hadn't knocked yet, so she opened the door.

"Thanks for breakfast," the woman's voice was soft.

"Great way to start my day," Vic said as the woman hugged him, then cupped his face with her hands.

"I have never been happier. I'll see you tomorrow."

He was smiling that smile she thought he saved for her as he watched the woman walk away.

Mindy's jaw trembled, and her eyes stung with tears.

He turned to see her standing there and his smile widened before it disappeared.

"Mindy." He said her name and was in front of her before she'd blinked. His hands were on her arms holding her there.

"God, what's wrong? Why haven't you returned my texts or my calls? What happened?"

She was keenly aware of everyone in the office now. The phones rang. Doors opened and closed. People moved about talking to one another.

She turned back into her office and he followed. She realized she hadn't moved fast enough to slam the door in his face and lock it.

When Mindy heard the click of the door shutting behind him, she picked up a pen and threw it in his direction, missing completely, but his eyes grew wide.

"What is wrong?"

How was she supposed to handle this now?

"Get out," she said sternly, keeping her voice at a reasonable level.

"Mindy, I have no idea what—"

"You've been lying to me."

He stepped closer, and she picked up another pen stopping him as she held it up and aimed it at him.

Vic held his hands up in surrender. "I have no idea what you're talking about."

"I guess having sex with someone, and saying I love you, doesn't qualify as exclusive."

He blinked hard and lowered his hands. "I still don't know what you're talking about."

Those tears that had stung her eyes now rolled down her cheeks. "I'm so fucking mad at you I could scream," she said in a forceful whisper, and every muscle in her body shook.

Vic took a step toward her, and she took a step back.

"Mindy, I don't know what you're talking about. I've never lied to you."

"Okay, you just left out everything."

He pressed his fingers to his eyes. "Could we just sit down and have a normal discussion?"

"I want you out of my office, and out of my life."

"Give me one reason."

Mindy fisted her hands. "Justine."

Again, his eyes went wide and his mouth opened. "How do you know—"

"You're a son-of-a-bitch!" Her voice was no longer soft and quiet. "No need to meet her at bars and take her out for breakfast anymore behind my back. You can do what you want whenever you want. Maybe if you screw around on her, don't do it where Curtis Smith will see you."

Vic rubbed his hand over his forehead. "You don't know what you're talking about."

"Whatever I just witnessed in the hallway was all I needed. Tell me you didn't think I'd see that?"

"There was nothing to see."

"Get out!"

For a moment Vic stood there. He'd scrubbed his hand over his face, and left it over his mouth. Perhaps he was trying to keep the vile lies inside, she thought.

He turned and reached for the knob. "Mindy, it's not what you think."

"I don't even want to hear it," she sobbed. "Go away."

Vic's face had gone pale and his eyes were sad, but he turned around and left the office.

CHAPTER FORTY-FOUR

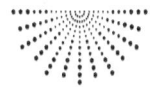

Vic raked his fingers through his hair and paced through his kitchen as his sisters watched him.

"You're making me dizzy," Angie scolded. "Sit your ass down."

Vic pressed his hands flat to the countertop, and sucked in a breath. He looked at Amber and narrowed his eyes on her. "This is your fucking fault."

Amber's eyes went wide. "My fault? I don't even know what the hell is going on with you."

"Justine is going on."

His sisters exchanged a glance and Amber sat back in her seat at the breakfast bar. "What does this have to do with Justine?"

"You brought her into my life."

He saw the flash of hurt and regret on his sister's face, and guilt punched in his gut for the way he'd delivered that.

Amber's lip twitched. "I'm so sorry."

Vic stood up and ran his hands over his hair. "No, I'm sorry. I shouldn't jump on you like that." He went back to pacing before he stopped in front of them all staring at him. "She wouldn't just go away. She kept texting and wanting to meet up. As if I'd promised her something. So one night she texted me about meeting at a bar, so I went to tell her that I was involved with someone, and she needed to leave me alone."

Amber wiped a tear from her cheek and batted her eyes. "I didn't know she'd be trouble."

"I know. It's just that when I went to the bar, Curtis Smith was there and he saw me meeting with her."

Angie shook her head, her lips pursed. "You fucking got caught meeting another woman at the bar."

Vic threw his hands in the air. "Yes, sort of."

Allison moved toward him and stood next to him. "This is about Mindy then? I mean, is that what happened? You got caught?"

Vic shrugged. "Actually, I seem to have gotten caught with Parker, but Mindy doesn't know the difference between the story Curtis told her from the friend she caught me with."

His sisters fell silent.

Vic turned toward the refrigerator and pulled out a beer. While his sisters scanned curious and sad looks over him, he opened it and took a long sip.

Angie held up a finger. "Didn't you explain who Parker was?"

"I didn't get a chance to. She was launching pens at my head."

That caused Angie to snort out a laugh. "I always did like Mindy," she said.

"Thanks for that," Vic retorted.

"You live next door to her, dumbass. Go talk to her."

"She's not there. I'd assume she's at one of her girlfriends' houses." Vic set the beer on the counter. "Yes, I got caught with Parker in a hug and she was thanking me for breakfast."

"Intimate."

"I suppose that's what it looked like. But my ad campaign for their store seems to have generated some excitement within her family, and she can't wait to get started with it. She said they have a big buyer looking at them, and she thinks this will be what sells them."

Allison shook her head. "Your ad campaign is going to get them a big buyer?"

"I get businesses in front of people. It's not always consumers that are looking."

Allison made an O shape with her mouth and nodded.

Angie hopped off the bar stool and placed her hands on her low back. "Looks like you got yourself in a huge mess."

"So give me some advice."

Three sets of eyes stared at him before Angie walked around the counter and stood next to him. "Time. It's going to take time."

"I don't want it to take time. I need to find her and make her understand."

Angie nodded. "Mindy was single when you met her, right?"

"Yes," he drew out the answer, unsure of where she could possibly be taking the conversation.

"She's always been a sweet and beautiful woman."

"Still is," he confirmed.

"So why was she single? Good catches aren't single at thirty unless she's gone through something."

Vic ran his hand over the back of his neck. "The last relationship she had, the guy ended up having another girlfriend and a wife."

Angie's eyes went wide. "Shit!"

Vic nodded. "She's gun shy."

"Sure she is. And you're a hell of a catch, so..."

Now Vic laughed. "Did you say I'm a catch? That's creepy."

"It's a fucking compliment," Angie said. "God, I have to pee again."

Vic and his sisters watched as Angie disappeared down the hall.

Allison picked up Vic's beer and took a long pull. As she set it back on the counter, she let out a satisfied sigh.

"She's right. You need some time. She'll eventually talk to you.

I mean, sooner or later you're going to get a piece of her mail that will need to be delivered to her," she said with a wink.

"I thought the thing between our parents was bad enough. It seems as if the odds are stacked against us."

Allison leaned in and kissed Vic on the cheek. "No. Every relationship goes through trust issues. There's always a point where you think it won't work. It's getting past that that makes it work."

Amber nodded. "Dave and I went to marriage counseling one month into our marriage," she admitted and Vic noticed that even Allison's eyes went wide. This was news to them both.

Allison picked up his beer again and took another sip. "I didn't know that."

"No one knows that," she admitted. "God, by then we'd been together for five years, but he went to a bachelor party, a picture got posted to social media of him with some woman hanging off him, and I lost my shit."

"Did anything happen? With him and the woman?" Allison asked, fully invested in the conversation now.

"Oh, he took her home," Amber said.

Vic leaned in. "Are you fucking kidding me? What an—"

"She was the groom's mother," Amber said holding up a hand to ward off the anger she'd created against her husband. "She'd showed up drunk to the party."

Allison shook her head. "Why was she at the bachelor party anyway?"

Amber shrugged. "To keep an eye on her husband—the groom's dad," she laughed. "Actually, it was a tight-knit family. Where the dad went, the mom went."

"If his dad was there, why did Dave take home the mom?"

"The groom was trashed. His dad was a paramedic and he took him to get him an IV."

"You can just go get an IV?"

"They do have companies that do that," Amber said. "But he

was a paramedic. They do that kind of stuff for each other all the time."

"Oh," Allison drew out the word. "But the mom didn't want an IV?"

Amber shook her head. "She wanted to get home to the cats. Dave was done being at the party, so he offered to take her."

Vic nodded slowly. "So you knew he took her home and you'd seen a picture of the two of them…"

"So I lost my shit. I was also pregnant and didn't know it, so my hormones were completely out of whack." She held out her hand so that Allison would hand her the beer. She took a sip and handed it back. "I could track his phone, so that made it worse. What I couldn't track was him getting the woman inside the house, and one of the cats getting out. He spent an hour looking for the cat before his friend and his dad got home. Then, he came home to my wrath."

Vic narrowed his eyes on his sister as Angie walked back toward them and took her seat.

"So you believed everything he said after that?"

Amber shrugged. "No, hence the reason we ended up in counseling the first month of our marriage, and by then, I knew but didn't tell him I was pregnant."

Angie leaned in on her fist and scanned a look over their sister. "You withheld that kind of information from your husband?"

"I didn't trust him."

"Don't any of you talk to the people you love?" Angie asked, rubbing her stomach.

Amber let out a breath. "The point is, we did. We worked it out. I was wrong. I was completely wrong. But it took time and conversation."

Vic picked up his half-finished beer and took a pull. "Well, I'm not married to Mindy. Counseling isn't going to help."

"Ass," Amber said. "I'm telling you to just talk to her. But give her time to process. She doesn't have all the details of what happened. She doesn't know you told Justine to kiss off, or that Parker is an old friend whom you have a history with. Nor does she know that Parker isn't interested in your *kind*."

"My *kind?*"

Amber groaned. "Men," she threw out the word. "You have to get the facts to her. If the last guy she dated had another girlfriend and a wife, then she's obviously going to be gun shy. If you love her, you won't let this go."

Vic finished the beer. "You're right."

"Of course I am."

"You were wrong about Justine," he said, smiling at his sister.

"So, I was desperate to get you hooked up with someone."

Vic shook his head. "Just for future reference, never feel the need to help me out like that again."

"If you're patient and take time to help Mindy understand, I'll never have to."

CHAPTER FORTY-FIVE

THANK GOD FOR FRANCE, MINDY THOUGHT AS SHE WATCHED THE world transform through the window on the airplane.

It hadn't been a planned trip, but when the boss said head to France to buy wine, she jumped on the next flight.

She needed the time to think anyway. A week with just her thoughts to keep her company? That should help her sort some shit out.

Mindy eased back in her seat.

She'd have a week to think things through, and maybe she could calm down enough to talk to Vic. The past few days had been miserable, and Mindy was quite sure letting her mind stew hadn't helped the situation.

Ruby had been right, and Mindy needed to let Vic tell her what happened. She couldn't hold their parents' actions against who he was, but then again, what she'd seen, heard, and knew, wasn't helping her anger dissipate either.

The flight attendant brought Mindy her drink and her dinner. As she situated everything on her tray, she considered texting Vic, but then thought better of it. She'd be back in a week. She'd talk to him then.

~

You've Got Mail, The Wedding Planner, My Best Friend's Wedding, When Harry Met Sally, it had been a binge watching nightmare Vic decided. But when he'd gotten sucked into Kathleen Kelly's battle of wits with Joe Fox, he'd kicked up his feet and absorbed all the silliness that Mindy loved so much—those beloved rom coms.

Okay, he had to admit, he'd seen all those movies, but he'd never paid attention to them in the least. They were noise in his head, but now, they were a connection to the woman he loved.

What was it that made Mindy love the Kathleen Kellys and Sally Albrights? Was it the characters themselves or the happily ever after at the end? Of course, he'd seen a few rom coms that didn't tie everything up in a nice little bow. Hadn't he sat with Allison when she was pregnant and she sobbed over *La La Land?* Okay, even he hadn't seen that coming. A romance that didn't end with happily ever after, but with contentment?

All the rom com marathon did was make him think of Mindy, who hadn't been home in a week, who hadn't texted or called, and she hadn't even been in the office. It had taken him until Thursday afternoon to learn that she was in France.

He'd picked up his phone at least fifty times to text her or call, but he'd always refrained. She'd come to him when she was ready to talk, or he'd go insane before that.

It was worth fighting for, he promised himself. He hadn't done anything wrong, and he loved Mindy more than life itself. She'd come around. He had to have faith in that.

It was almost nine o'clock, and Vic had been staring at his laptop for the better part of four hours, when he heard a car drive through the cul-de-sac.

He sat for a moment, but curiosity got the better of him. He stood from the table and moved to the window. Mindy's garage door was up and the taillights of her car were still illuminated.

Like a stalker, he watched her get out of her car, pull her suitcase from the back, and then look around as if she were watching for strangers—or him— before she walked to the mailbox.

Now he certainly couldn't help himself. Vic opened the door and stepped out onto the front porch.

"Hey," he said as she pulled the mail from the box and jumped when he spoke.

"Shit!" she said as she dropped the mail into a puddle from melted snow. "Shit!"

As she bent over to retrieve the mail, Vic moved to her.

"I'm sorry. I shouldn't have startled you like that."

"You're creeping around in the dark," she shot back.

"I was just happy to see you."

Mindy shook out an envelope. "I have to get—"

"I'd really like if you could spend just five minutes with me and talk."

He could see the whites of her eyes as they grew wide in the dark. "Fine, you have five minutes."

"Let's go—"

"Right here. Talk."

He hated this. Why couldn't they move past this. This was the classic misunderstanding in all of her god-damned movies. She should know how to overcome this, right?

Vic held up his hands. "Fine." He took a breath. "I love you."

"Nope. You don't get to start the conversation off like that. You don't get to say that when I heard a woman tell you she enjoyed breakfast while she was in your arms," her voice rose as she spoke.

"And if you're going to give me five minutes to explain that, then I'd better get those five minutes to talk," he suggested back.

Mindy pursed her lips and nodded in his direction as his cue to speak.

"Parker is who you saw me hugging."

Mindy took a breath to speak and Vic held up a finger.

"Parker is the woman Allison tried to set me up with. Parker was my crush in high school, she was a year older. We even went to prom together her senior year. Her family owns a furniture store, and because we reconnected, I was hired to do the advertising. And because of my advertising, they have bigger stores looking to buy theirs. This is all because Allison tried to set us up."

Mindy's shoulders eased, so he continued.

"We had planned for lunch, but decided on breakfast instead because she was eager to tell me about the possible sale of their company. Since you weren't much speaking to me, I didn't tell you."

Vic shoved his hands into his pockets. "Parker is a friend. And I have to admit, I'm very happy to have her back in my life—as a friend. And maybe I should add that Parker also isn't into men." Before Mindy could speak, Vic stepped closer, and she didn't move. "Now, let's talk about Justine."

"Vic—"

"Nope, I'm talking."

Mindy nodded, holding the mail to her chest. This time she did take a step back, and he let her have her space.

"Justine was the woman Amber tried to set me up with. She's someone who works with her or something. I have to admit, she gave off a weird vibe, and I didn't do a lot of listening. Once Parker showed up, I was more at ease that day. Anyway, Justine kept texting me wanting to get together. I seriously ghosted her. Then the night you called the girls over, she texted and wanted to meet at a bar. I thought the best thing to do was be honest with her and tell her I was involved with someone and she needed to leave me alone."

"You met her at a bar?" Mindy's voice rose in pitch. "You went to a bar to meet some woman?"

"I did," he admitted.

Mindy spun away from him. "Go home!"

"Not until you listen to me," he said following her up the driveway.

"Why should I?"

"Because you love me, dammit."

CHAPTER FORTY-SIX

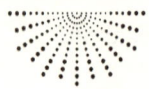

MINDY SUCKED IN A BREATH, AND THEN ANOTHER. DAMMIT, SHE did love him and all of this was stupid. But she couldn't back down. Her heart hammered in her chest because she felt betrayed.

"I can't believe you would go to a bar to meet someone. Why didn't you just block her number?" Mindy spat out the words.

"I don't know. I just don't know."

"You were still feeling out your options, weren't you?"

Vic lifted his chin. "Is that really what you think? You think I would have you in my home, in my bed, if I were feeling out the options?"

"Other men have done it."

"I'm not one of those men," he argued back. "Okay, so you and I have some issues with communication."

"You should have told me she was texting you."

"I should have."

"And that you were doing business with Parker."

"That didn't cross my mind. That one is business, and a lot of the people I work with and see on a regular basis are women."

Mindy's lip trembled when she considered that most of her time spent in her field was with men.

She chewed on her lip to keep it still. "Ruby says I'm not too forthcoming with things either. I don't remember to tell you when I'm going to go out of town."

"Because all of this is new," he reasoned and Mindy nodded.

"Our parents didn't have sex," she blurted out the other fact, and Vic actually chuckled.

"I know."

Holding the mail to her chest with one hand, Mindy threw up the other. "But you didn't tell me that. You knew last week, didn't you."

"Yes, my mother and I spoke about it."

"You should have told me."

"If you don't remember you haven't been speaking to me much since you came back in town, and then you flew off again." His voice had risen and the anger in his words rattled her.

"Maybe we're not made for this."

Vic stepped toward her. "Don't do that. Don't start dismissing this."

"I mean, maybe we're out to hurt those we love too, just like our parents did."

"We're not our parents."

"How do I know you won't decide that someone you work with isn't—"

"Mindy, don't you dare compare the adult me to my mother as a teenager. I could easily turn that back on you and you know it."

It socked her in the gut, but he was right. How were they ever going to get past that?

Before she could argue or dismiss him, they heard a noise, and they both turned toward Mr. Smith's house.

Under the glow of the porch light, they saw Mr. Smith fall down the two small steps of his front porch and to the ground.

BERNADETTE MARIE

Mindy dropped her mail and followed Vic as he ran across the dark street and up Mr. Smith's driveway.

"Call 9-1-1!" Vic shouted as he reached Mr. Smith at the bottom of the steps.

"I don't have my phone."

He pulled his from his pocket and handed it to her. "Two-One-Zero-Five," he shouted out the numbers to unlock his screen as he assessed Mr. Smith. "He's not responding."

Mindy dialed the number and watched as Vic calmly talked to the man, felt for breath, and then for a pulse.

When Vic got to his knees over him, Mindy knew it was bad. She relayed the information to the operator as Vic began compressions on Mr. Smith, and then listened for breath and checked for a pulse again. Then, he started the process over as the woman on the other end of the phone asked more and more questions Mindy just didn't have the answers for.

"His sons are Brian and Curtis," she told the woman. "I don't know how to get hold of them."

"That's fine. We'll find them. Who is there with you?"

"My boyfriend," Mindy said the words before she could even consider them. "He's doing CPR on him right now."

"The ambulance is only around the corner," the woman said and Mindy could hear the sirens.

"They're almost here."

Before the lights could be seen, a car raced down the street, screeching to a halt in front of the house. Curtis emerged, leaving the car running and the door open.

"Shit! Shit!" he screamed. "Dad! Dad!" He knelt down next to his father.

"Mindy fill him in. I'm busy here," Vic demanded as he continued CPR as the fire truck, followed by the ambulance pulled into the cul-de-sac.

Curtis' wide eyes looked up at her.

She swallowed hard. "We were standing out front and we

heard a noise. I guess he made some noise and then we saw him fall down the stairs and hurried over," she poured the words out as quickly as she could.

"He told me his chest hurt," Curtis said, grabbing his father's hand as the paramedics hurried toward the house. "He said he heard you two out front and was going to ask for help."

Mindy covered her mouth with her hand. God, had they killed him because they were standing out there arguing and didn't see him trying to get their attention?

Vic eased back as the paramedics stepped in and took over. He relayed what it was he'd done for Mr. Smith, and how they'd watched him fall. Then Curtis told them about the phone call with his father shortly before that.

Vic eased an arm around Mindy's shoulders and they stepped out of the way as the paramedics loaded Mr. Smith into the ambulance.

Curtis scrubbed his hands over his face. "I should call my brothers," he said pacing a circle. "I need to get to the hospital."

"Do you want to ride with him? I can follow in your car and leave it, and Mindy can pick me up."

Curtis drew in a breath. "Really man? That would be great. The keys are still in it," Curtis said as he hurried toward the ambulance, then turned before he climbed in. "Thank you for saving his life. I'm glad you were here."

Mindy and Vic watched the ambulance pull away with its lights on, and she realized the other neighbors had all come out of their houses to watch.

"Are you okay with picking me up at the hospital?" he asked and Mindy nodded.

"Of course."

He leaned in and pressed a kiss to her forehead. "I'll meet you there."

Vic started for Curtis' car, but Mindy reached for his hand and stopped him.

"What you did tonight was amazing," she said.

"I just knew what to do. Anyone would have."

Mindy shook her head. "I had no idea what to do, and everyone else in the neighborhood stood watching from their porches. You stepped in."

"Proof I'm not a bad guy, right?" He tugged his hand free, climbed into Curtis' car, and a moment later he drove away.

CHAPTER FORTY-SEVEN

As Mindy navigated the dark streets toward the hospital, she decided she needed a voice of reason in her head. She asked Siri to call Ruby, because for some reason Ruby seemed to say the things Mindy needed to hear—no matter how they sounded coming out of Ruby's mouth.

"Are you back from Paris?" Ruby's voice rang through the car.

"I went to France. I didn't go to Paris."

"Yeah, yeah. Do you have samples?"

Mindy laughed. "Of course."

"Good. That last stuff you brought back from Napa Valley was brutal."

"It's all brutal when you drink it all."

Ruby chuckled. "I guess you're right. But, in your honor, I've been watching *Sabrina* today. You know, it has a Paris local and the 'in love with the neighbor' twist."

"I guess you could say they were neighbors," Mindy admitted. "You've watched it all day?"

"Both versions. And I have to tell you, I would totally choose Harrison Ford over Greg Kinnear. Though, that's a hard decision to be firm on. Kinnear has some sexy quality that I just can't put my finger on," Ruby admitted.

"Okay, what about Bogart and Holden in the original?"

Ruby grunted. "Neither of them do it for me. Bogart just reminds me of my grandpa," she said on a laugh. But when the humor of the moment died down, Ruby cleared her throat. "Now, if you just got home from a trip abroad, and you're calling me, I'm going to assume you haven't talked to the sexy neighbor? Or if you did, it didn't go well?"

Mindy stopped at the red light, drew in a breath, and gripped her steering wheel. "We talked a little. I'm headed to the hospital to pick him up now."

"The hospital?" Ruby's voice screeched through the phone. "Oh, my God! What happened?"

"He's fine," Mindy assured her, realizing what she'd said would have set off alarm bells. "Mr. Smith had a heart attack or something while Vic and I were arguing in the driveway."

"That's a lot to unpack. Mr. Smith had a heart attack?"

"Yes. We ran over to help him. Vic did CPR on him."

"Mindy, shit! Tell me he's okay."

It wasn't until that moment that Mindy realized, other than Curtis thanking Vic for saving his dad's life, she didn't know if he was okay. Tears began to stream down her cheeks.

"I think so. I don't know. I'm headed to the hospital to pick up Vic. He drove Curtis' car, so Curtis could ride with his dad." She wiped tears from her cheeks.

"Do you want me to come down?"

"No. No," she said as she came to another light and stopped, wiping away tears. "I'm sorry I called. I just needed to sort everything out."

"You said you were arguing with Vic."

Mindy swallowed hard as the hospital came into view down the street. "Yeah, he came out to talk to me, and I don't think I was very nice about it."

"What did he say?"

"He explained everything."

Ruby hummed into the phone. "So he wasn't messing around?"

"He said he wasn't."

"You still don't believe him?"

"I don't know what to believe."

"Dammit, Mindy. Have some faith in the fucking world, and stop projecting your last relationship on a good guy. You're going to end up alone and miserable if you don't start to trust and be open."

And that was what Mindy knew she needed to hear. "I love you," she said to Ruby as she pulled into the parking lot of the hospital.

"I love you too. Seriously, Mind, take a chance for once. He makes you grip the sheets, remember? And he picks your ass up when you're drunk. Mishaps and misunderstandings are going to happen. And, on the bright side, your parents didn't fuck, so it's good."

"God! Will you forget that one?" Mindy laughed through her tears. "Thank you."

"Go make sure your neighbor is good, and for heaven's sake, let go a bit."

"We'll come back for you as soon as we have him stable," the nurse told Curtis, and Vic rested a hand on Curtis' shoulder.

Curtis scrubbed his hand over his face. "Fuck."

"Can I get you some coffee or some water?" Vic offered.

"If you hadn't been there—"

"We were there. They'll take care of him."

"He's in his eighties. I'm just not sure," Curtis admitted. "He's never been the same since Mom died."

"He has all of you. Have some faith."

Taking in a deep breath, Curtis nodded. "Thanks again."

"When he gets home, I'll make sure to check in on him too."

"I don't know that there'll be a going home for him. At least not without one of us being there with him. But he's stubborn enough to not want to leave the house."

"My grandmother was like that."

A smile curled up the corner of Curtis' mouth. "He liked your grandmother. He liked Mindy's grandmother." Now he laughed. "Hell, he liked Mrs. Cartwright too. But I think us kids gave him a rep, and he couldn't get anywhere with any of them."

Vic thought about what he'd learned about his mother in the past few weeks. He certainly didn't want to entertain any gossip about his grandmother.

"I'm glad to see you and Mindy together though," Curtis said. "She always was a great gal. You're a lucky man."

"I'm not sure she's convinced."

Curtis shoved his hands into his front pockets. "I was surprised when I saw you at the bar looking for Justine."

"Yeah, well, not one of my better decisions."

"How'd you get involved with her?"

"I didn't. My sister was trying to set us up. I was already involved with Mindy, and she just wouldn't stop texting."

Curtis raised a brow. "You decided to meet her in person instead of ghosting her?"

"Maybe I didn't want it coming back on my sister. I don't know. I just thought it was the decent thing to do."

Rubbing his hand across the back of his neck, Curtis nodded. "You always were a decent guy."

They both looked up when someone called Curtis' name, and Brian headed toward them.

"What the fuck?" his voice was low, and Vic knew he'd spent the drive to the hospital crying.

"They're getting him stable, then they'll come for us," Curtis said. "If Hayes hadn't been there, I don't think he'd have made it."

Brian held his hand out to Vic, and Vic took it. "We owe you. Thank you."

"No one owes me anything. I just did what I knew to do."

"We're grateful." Brian pressed his palm to his chest. "Hey, Mindy," he said, and Vic turned to see her walking toward them. She too looked as if she'd spent the drive crying.

"Any news?" she asked looking at all three of them.

"They're getting him stable. They'll come for us," Curtis said.

"Can we bring you anything?"

"I think the two of you have given us enough. Thank you for stepping in."

Vic felt Mindy slip her hand in his and link their fingers. "Call if you need anything else," he said.

A nurse called for Curtis and he nodded to her before turning back to Mindy and Vic. "I'll let you know what happens."

Curtis and Brian turned to follow the nurse as another one of their brothers hurried through the door and caught up with them.

"He's okay?" Mindy asked, and Vic studied her face, and then their joined hands.

"They're stabilizing him."

"So you saved him?"

Vic shrugged. "We bought him some time. They'll do what they can." He pulled his hand from hers. "Let's go home."

CHAPTER FORTY-EIGHT

VIC DROVE MINDY'S CAR, AND SHE SAT IN THE PASSENGER SEAT watching him. The lights of the dash illuminated the strong lines of his face against the dark.

He hadn't said another word to her.

She'd pushed too hard against him when all he'd wanted to do was clear the air. Because of past experiences, she didn't trust him—or at least she had let that be her excuse to not trust him. Then, she had to admit, she was still a bit freaked out over what she'd learned about her father and his mother. Though hadn't that been sorted out, and hadn't her father laughed about it?

Vic pulled into her driveway, pushed the button to open her garage, and parked the car. He turned off the engine, handed her the keys, and climbed from the car.

Before Mindy could get out, he'd already started down the driveway.

"Where are you going?" she called after him.

"Home," he said without turning back.

"Wait." She called after him, slamming her car door, getting her coat caught in it, and having to open it again.

Vic turned as she struggled. "I'm tired. I'll talk to you later."

"Vic," she called after him again, finally freeing herself from the car. "Wait."

Mindy hurried down the driveway and reached for him as he crossed the yard.

He stopped and turned to her, pulling back. For the first time, she was intimidated by their height difference. And in the shadows, she could see the anger in his eyes.

"What do you want?"

"I want to talk. We were talking before, and—"

"We weren't talking. I was talking. I was trying to salvage something that means the world to me and you were judging."

Mindy sucked in a breath to argue, but how could she? That was exactly what she'd been doing.

Vic scrubbed his hands over his face. "I'm tired. I'm going to bed."

He turned again and started toward his house.

"I love you," she called after him, but he didn't respond or turn around. A moment later he disappeared into his house, and she heard the door slam shut and lock.

MINDY SAT AT HER DESK, HER OFFICE DOOR OPEN, AND HER EYES focused on the door down the hall. It was nearly eleven and Vic hadn't come into the office.

She'd done it. She'd ruined the only good relationship she'd ever had.

A woman stepped into view, looked through the small window next to Vic's door, and then across the hallway at her door.

A lump formed in Mindy's throat when the woman stood just beyond the threshold and smiled at her.

"Have you seen Victor?" the woman asked, using his full name.

"No," Mindy's voice croaked. "He hasn't come in yet."

"Fucker," the woman said, leaning her shoulder against the door jamb and then resting her hands on her pregnant stomach.

Mindy's body reacted to the sight of the woman, and the fact that she'd called Vic a fucker. Then she realized she'd seen the woman before. No, not in person, but the day Vic had handed her his phone to look at the before and after pictures of his house. She'd scrolled too far, and staring up at her was the blonde that now stood in front of her.

When Vic had looked down at the picture, he'd smiled as if the woman had meant something to him.

God, she thought she might just throw up. Especially when the woman winced because the baby must have kicked her.

"Do you mind if I sit down for a moment?" The woman asked and then moved to sit in one of the chairs in front of Mindy's desk.

Not wanting to be horribly cordial, Mindy couldn't fight herself when she asked, "Can I get you anything?"

"No. He's supposed to buy me lunch and the baby is hungry," the woman laughed as she rubbed her stomach again. "Only a few more weeks. Vic's already spoiled this kid too. Fucker," she said again.

Mindy swallowed hard. This wasn't a client. This was so much more and her head throbbed now.

"Vic is involved with your baby?" Mindy managed the words, but they weren't stable. "Your picture is in his phone."

The woman lifted a brow. "I should hope it is," the woman laughed. "He takes more pictures of the kids than me, but—"

"Are you his wife?"

That caused the woman to break out in a hysterical laugh. "Oh, God! You don't know who I am, do you?" Her mouth had curled up into a wide smile and her eyes lit with humor. "He really is a fucker."

"I'm sorry. But no, I don't—"

"He hasn't brought you around yet because we were all wigged out thinking that our mom fucked your dad and all."

"God you have a mouth," Vic's voice came from the door.

Mindy looked up to see him lean against the door jamb, just as the woman had.

"Yeah, well you told me you'd be here to take me to lunch, and you weren't. The baby is hungry and kicking the shit out of me. And your girlfriend doesn't know who I am, because you never bothered to bring her around."

The corner of Vic's mouth curled up and his eyes landed on Mindy. "Mindy, this is my sister Angie, whom you've met, but it's been a hot minute and she was probably terrorizing a neighbor kid." He laughed. "Angie, this is my girlfriend, Mindy."

His eyes were still locked on hers, and the only word Mindy heard was *girlfriend.*

She stood and walked around her desk, moving to him. "You mean it?"

"Mean what?"

"That I'm your girlfriend? I mean, you walked away from me last night. You—"

"I was mad. Tired. And I had a lot on my mind." He brushed his hand over her hair, and rested it on her cheek. "Mr. Smith is going to recover, by the way."

"You saved his life."

"*We* got him help," he reminded her.

"God!" Angie groaned and managed to her feet. "You guys are disgusting. Can we go to lunch now?"

His eyes hadn't wavered from Mindy's.

"Are we okay?" she asked.

"No. We have a lot of work to do," he said, but his hand stayed on her cheek. His thumb brushing small circles on her skin. "Because if you think I'd have a knocked-up wife, you still don't trust me yet."

Her heart hammered in her chest. "I'm so sorry."

"I don't want you to be sorry. I want you to trust me."

"I do."

"Do you?"

Mindy nodded. "I don't know why—"

Angie groaned again. "Seriously, can we..." She stopped, gripped her side, and then looked down. "Fuck!"

Vic finally looked away from Mindy and to his sister, then he moved to her.

Angie's eyes had gone wide and she looked up at him. "My water just broke."

"Let's go." Vic took his sister's hands. "Why are you here if you were in labor?"

"I have three weeks left. I thought I was hungry," she countered as he moved her to the door.

"It's not your first baby. Don't you know what you're doing?"

"Fuck you. Each pregnancy is different," she said as she gripped her stomach.

Vic had one arm wrapped around Angie, and he looked back at Mindy.

"I'll call you."

Mindy nodded.

"I love you," he said as Angie gripped his arm.

"I love you too," Mindy called back after him.

CHAPTER FORTY-NINE

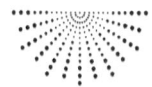

It was an impromptu Rom Com Movie Club night. Lisa had called everyone at three, and they had assembled by six.

Ryan was on a ski trip with Aaron and a couple of their childhood buddies, so Lisa had thought it fitting to have everyone over.

"*Fools Rush In?* Didn't we watch this not too long ago?" Ruby asked as she looked at the paused TV screen while painting her toes a deep blue.

"I thought the rule of the club was we could watch whatever the hostess chooses. So even if we watched it, it's fair game," Tina countered.

"Talking about rushing in," Ruby lifted her eyes to Mindy. "You and the sexy neighbor?"

Mindy fanned her freshly painted blue fingernails. "I think, maybe, we're okay. He introduced me as his girlfriend to his sister before they rushed out of the office because her water broke."

Three sets of eyes widened.

"No shit?" Ruby shouted.

"No shit."

Lisa handed Mindy a glass of wine. "You think everything is going to be okay?"

Mindy sipped from the glass that was adorned with her cherry charm.

"I do. I let fear take over. I shut down. I accused. I—"

"She Mindy'd the whole thing," Ruby interpreted.

"What the hell does that—" Mindy began and it was Tina that held up her hand.

"You sabotaged it so you wouldn't get too close," she defended.

"What the hell?" Mindy set her glass down. "I don't need to be attacked."

"We're not attacking. We're pointing it out," Tina continued. "Don't be afraid. You got a good one."

Lisa nodded in agreement. "You've had your first fights. You've accused. You've withheld. You're freaking in love, and that trumps it all."

Mindy tucked her lips between her teeth because they'd begun to tremble with the tears that were lodged in her throat.

Lisa moved in next to her, wrapped an arm around her shoulders, and kissed the top of her head. "You're worthy of a man's love. And just his love. Don't fight it."

Mindy studied the sincere smiles of her friends. "I know I did all of that. I almost ruined things."

Ruby laughed. "Yeah, but now you get to have makeup sex. God, how lucky are you? Makeup sex!"

They all laughed as Mindy's phone buzzed on the table and Vic's picture popped up on her screen.

Lisa kissed the top of her head again. "Take that."

Mindy reached for her phone and answered the call as she stood from her chair and walked toward the balcony. She pulled open the door and stepped outside.

"Hey," she said softly as she eased herself into one of the chairs that overlooked the golf course.

"I have a new nephew," Vic's voice beamed from the other end. "Chad."

"Chad?"

"Baby Chad," he repeated. "Isn't that the male version of a Karen?"

Mindy laughed. "Maybe he's a new breed," she offered.

"Maybe. I'd love for you to meet him."

A warmth spread through her chest. "I will."

"I'm headed home, but my Mom wanted me to invite you to dinner on Sunday."

"Really?"

"Yeah, she'd like to get to know the woman I'm so enamored by."

Mindy crossed her arms to ward off the January cold. "You are?"

"I never stopped," he said. "We have some things to work through, but, Mindy, I love you. I really do want to spend the rest of my life with you."

Those tears that had earlier threatened, now pooled in her eyes and threatened to freeze in place.

"You do?"

"I do," he confirmed. "When will you be home?"

"We haven't started the movie yet, but—"

"Spend time with your friends. Come over when you're done. I need to hold you all night."

"I'll be there."

"I love you," he said and the tears began to dry in Mindy's eyes.

"I love you too."

After they'd disconnected their call, she sat and looked down at her phone. *Don't mess this up, Mindy*, she said to herself. This was the one, and she knew it, and she wanted it.

Lisa opened the sliding door. "Are you okay?"

"I'm perfect," Mindy replied as she stood from the chair.

"Are you leaving?"

Mindy smiled. "I think I am."

"Good. Report back on how tightly you grip the sheets."

THE KITCHEN TABLE WAS COVERED IN AD COPY FOR THE FURNITURE store Parker's family owned. They'd asked for three different campaigns, and that alone had given Vic reason to put the ad online for an assistant.

He lifted his head when the doorbell rang, then he looked at his watch. It was only seven o'clock.

Pushing back his chair, he stood, and walked to the front door. Pulling it open, he smiled at Mindy standing on the front porch in a long winter coat and boots.

"I hope you don't mind me just coming over," she said.

"I just didn't expect you for a few hours."

Mindy nodded. "The girls said I should come now."

"I'm glad you did. Let me help you out of your coat."

Mindy took a step back. "No. I need to say something."

Vic felt the sharp pain in his chest before his stomach knotted. "Okay."

"I'm an idiot. I was hurt before and I decided that everything you did was done to hurt me too. I didn't ask questions. I didn't share information. I got totally wigged out over our parents," she said and Vic felt that knot in his stomach ease slightly. "You're the first good thing to ever happen to me. There was a reason I kissed you all those years ago in the Smiths' treehouse. Because I was comfortable with you, and the thought of playing house forever was real back then."

"Mindy—"

She held up a hand. "Don't give up on me. I'm not going to be perfect with this just because I can admit when I'm wrong—well, finally admit that I was. I'm scared. I'm worried. I'm in love with you, and that confuses everything I know about the Mindy that's been alone and independent."

"Are you telling me you want to be with me?"

Mindy nodded, biting down on her bottom lip. "Will you have me?"

"I introduced you as my girlfriend, didn't I?" Vic smiled down at her, taking one step closer to her. "I never wanted to lose you. I'll make sure that every part of my day is relayed to you. I don't ever want you to worry about what I'm doing."

She shook her head. "No. I trust you. You're going to work with a lot of women, one on one. And I'm going to travel and meet with a lot of men. I've done that for years and never thought it would be something someone would worry about."

"For the record, I didn't worry."

Mindy took a step toward him, closing the gap between them. "No, I did all the worrying."

"I love you," Vic said, lifting his hand to her cheek. "I think I've loved you since you grabbed the front of my YMCA camp shirt and laid that kiss on me."

Her cheeks deepened in color. "I guess I made a good impression."

"A lasting one for sure."

"We're okay?"

Vic lifted his other hand and cupped her face. "We're okay." Mindy stepped back and turned away. Vic watched her as she started down the hallway. "Where are you going. Do you want to take off your coat?"

Mindy stopped in the hallway, turned back to him, and toed off her boots. Then, with dark eyes of need, she unzipped her coat and let it fall to the floor.

The pain that had resonated in Vic's chest dulled and

squeezed as he looked at her in a sexy bra and matching pair of panties.

"I have been assured that makeup sex will have me gripping the sheets," she said, her voice husky.

"I'm totally willing to find out."

EPILOGUE

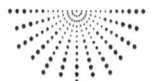

Six Months Later

Mindy watered the pots of flowers she'd planted, on the front porch. Vic's house was a bit cooler, and the flowers hadn't dried up as fast as they had on her front porch in the summers past.

She looked across the yard at the moving truck parked in the driveway of her grandmother's house.

For the past six months, Mindy and Vic had spent every spare moment fixing up the house so that it was modern. And, because Ruby had freaked Mindy out about the wiring, they'd had a professional electrician go through the house and make sure everything was up to code.

"Do we have to go help them move in?" Vic asked, walking up behind her and sliding her arms around her waist, resting his chin on her shoulder.

"Lisa said the movers are supposed to do all the work, and that's what they paid them for. But, she did say, when the truck leaves, she expects dinner, wine, and help unpacking."

"Are you okay with her and Ryan living there?"

Mindy set the watering can on the ground and turned into

Vic's arms. She looped hers around his neck and looked up at him.

He'd been playing golf instead of bowling, and his skin was sun-kissed and his hair was lighter.

"I can't think of anyone I'd rather have living there," she said, raking her fingers through his hair.

"Maybe Lisa would appreciate dinner over here. That way, there isn't another mess in her house to contend with."

"You know what I love about you?"

"Tell me."

"Aside from sheet-gripping sex," she teased, licking her lips, "you're so compassionate. You think of others first."

He nodded slowly. "Yeah. That's what I'm doing. Thinking of others."

It happened that Vic had a favor called into one of the restaurants that he worked with, and they'd offered to bring him dinner. Knowing it would feed an army, he had it delivered when he'd seen the moving truck leave the driveway of, now, Lisa and Ryan's house.

As he put out plates and looked around his house, he couldn't help but smile at the fact that Mindy was in every corner of the house he shared with her now. Their belongings had become mixed together. They'd picked out towels and sheets—together. They'd taken the paneling off the basement walls—together. But they'd opted to leave his grandfather's tinker room intact.

"Hey!" a voice called from the front door, and a moment later Curtis was standing in Vic's kitchen. "Sorry to just bust in. The door was open."

"No problem."

"Mindy said to come over and get a plate of food and one for my dad."

Vic chuckled. "Yeah. Thanks for helping them get the patio furniture set up."

"No problem. It'll be nice to have more people our age living on the cul-de-sac. I mean, if I have to live with my dad, it'd be nice to meet in the street and share a beer with people I relate to," Curtis said.

Vic nodded as he filled two of the to-go containers that came with the meal.

A half hour later, Mindy walked through the front door holding Tina's daughter on her shoulder.

"Is this how you're helping them?" Vic asked. "You stole the baby?"

"Luckily, she's just old enough that Tina welcomes these kinds of breaks. Especially when she suddenly saw potential in organizing Lisa's pantry."

Vic moved to them, running his hand gently over the baby's soft hair. "This looks good on you."

"What?"

"You holding a baby."

Mindy batted her eyes up at him. "Maybe someday."

"Most definitely someday." Vic stepped back. "They do know dinner is ready, right?"

Mindy nodded. "They're on their way."

Vic tried to hold in his grin, but it was hard, so he turned around.

MINDY SWAYED WITH THE BABY AGAINST HER AND ONLY TURNED when her friends, their husbands, and Lisa's brother walked through the front door. Seeing that the baby was asleep, they moved in quietly, forming a circle around her.

Mindy looked at each of them, grinning at their strange antics.

"Here, give her to me," Tina stepped in and reached for her baby.

"She's fine. She's sleeping," Mindy protested, but Tina shook her head.

"You can have her back in a minute."

Mindy handed over the baby. "What are you all doing? Get some dinner."

"They will in a moment," Vic said as he breached the circle and handed Mindy a glass of champagne.

She looked around and noticed Ruby and Jason passing glasses to everyone else.

"Did you have these poured already?"

Vic nodded. "You were too busy cooing over a baby to notice."

"And what are we celebrating?" she asked looking toward Lisa.

"Oh, we will celebrate our move later. It's worthy of its own celebration," Lisa said.

Mindy looked back at Vic who smiled at her, and the love she felt for the man made her warm.

"This is your celebration," Vic said tapping his glass to hers.

"Mine? What did I do?"

"It's what I hope you'll do."

Mindy narrowed her gaze on him. "What do you hope I'll do?"

She watched as he handed his glass to Ruby, then got down on one knee.

In an instant, Mindy's eyes filled with tears, her body shook, and her breath stuck in her lungs.

"Yes! Yes!" she managed the words, and Vic looked up at her, his hand in his pocket.

"Yes? I didn't ask you anything."

"Are you going to?"

He grinned up at her. "I was," he said holding out a ring to her.

"Yes!"

"Are you sure?" Vic asked now chuckling.

"Very. Oh, my God. Are you asking me to marry you?"

Vic rose and took Mindy's hand. "I was going to ask you that."

"I'll marry you. Yes. I want to marry you."

"Then I guess there's no reason for me to ask you, is there?" he said as he slipped the solitaire diamond on her finger and held her hand in his. "I hope you're that enthusiastic when we get married."

Mindy handed her glass to Jason, and jumped at Vic, wrapping her legs around his waist tightly, and crushing her mouth down on his.

Ruby cheered loud enough that the baby lifted her head and started to cry, but Mindy stayed wrapped around Vic, his mouth working against hers.

When he set her back on her feet, their friends went about making themselves plates of dinner.

"I can't believe you asked me to marry you," Mindy's voice shook as she looked at the ring, her hand pressed to his chest.

"I didn't."

She laughed. "No, I guess you didn't."

"I don't know how many rom coms I watched looking for just the right proposal, but—"

"Yours was perfect," Mindy countered.

"Will you play house with me for the rest of your life?" Vic wrapped his arms around her, pulling her tightly to him.

"You're the only one I've ever wanted to play house with. Yes, I'll play house with you forever."

"Good. Now, let's talk about those babies."

THE ROM COM MOVIE CLUB - BOOK THREE

We hope you have enjoyed *The Rom Com Movie Club - Book Two*. Here is an excerpt from *The Rom Com Movie Club - Book Three*.

THE ROM COM MOVIE CLUB - BOOK THREE

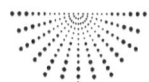

CHERRY RED NAIL POLISH, CHERRY WINE, AND PINK CHAMPAGNE facial masks. Rom Com Movie Club was in full swing. Ruby couldn't have been more disappointed that they didn't have cherry facials to go with her theme, but when did anything ever work out for her in that way? Not that it was a deal breaker for having a great time, but just for once, Ruby would like to have that perfect moment.

Sitting with her friends in her living room, *Mama Mia* paused on the TV, the four women, laughed at the expense of Tina's tales of pregnancy, childbirth, and motherhood as she nursed her daughter.

"I have a list for all of you," Tina said. "Things no one mentioned to me—at all."

Mindy, newly engaged to her next door neighbor, stared at Tina with wide eyes. "Never, in my entire life, have I heard someone say you might poop when you give birth."

"That's what I'm telling you," Tina confirmed through gritted teeth in a hushed tone, as to not stir her daughter who suckled at her breast. "There are these little things that people keep secret. They want you to think this is glorious, and it is not."

Lisa wiggled her cherry red polished toes. "You're making me think that if Ryan and I want to have babies, maybe I should adopt."

Ruby nodded in agreement. "Thank God I'm single."

Tina blew out an annoyed breath. "First of all," she directed the comment toward Lisa, "you'd better be thinking about a baby, and soon. I'm not carrying this alone. Their mother wants a house full of grandkids and that's up to you and me now."

Lisa wrinkled her nose, her mask cracking. "I reconsider my marriage to your brother-in-law," she said and that warranted a laugh.

"You'll be a good mom," Ruby said, playing with the ruby slipper charm on her wine glass.

"You think so?" Lisa asked.

"You'll take your childhood as the example of what not to do. You'll be attentive and loving. I mean, you're already ahead of the game. You're married to an amazing man who understands love and commitment. You'll be okay."

Lisa batted her eyes, as if tears had begun to sting them. "Thank you," she said, and Ruby knew it would be true.

Lisa had been brought up in foster care. The first family to really take her in and love her hadn't happened until she was twelve, and they moved to England when she was sixteen, having to leave her behind before they could officially adopt her. But the impact they had on Lisa in those few short years changed her life. Ruby knew that Lisa would take those lessons to heart, and create a wonderful life for her own children.

Just as Lisa started in on some story about the foster family that had loved her so dearly, the front door opened, and her foster brother, and Ruby's roommate, Jason, walked through.

Dressed in scrubs, his hospital ID clipped to his pocket, he stopped and looked around the room. His face was unshaven, eyes dark with lack of sleep, but he smiled when he saw them all.

He'd moved in with Ruby a few months after he'd returned to America to work in a local hospital. So far, he'd only been there a few months, and he'd lasted longer than some of her other roommates.

She still wasn't sure what made all the others just up and leave, but he seemed to be stable enough to stick around.

Ruby didn't see much of Jason at all, since he was a doctor and worked crazy shifts. She thought it was a shame he wasn't around more. With all of her friends being other wise in committed relationships, she spent more nights alone than she'd have liked. But when he was around, they cooked dinner together, took walks around the lake not far from their place, and watched her beloved rom coms together.

He hadn't lived in America since he was a pre-teen. If he were around more, maybe she could show him around and they could see the town together.

To his credit, looking at the four women with pink masks on their face, and Tina with her boob out, he didn't look all that surprised.

"Movie night," he said matter-of-factly. "I forgot that was tonight."

Ruby stood, walking on her heels to keep her toes from touching. "I thought you were working a twenty-four."

Jason scanned a look over her, smiled, then nodded. "I got lucky. Someone wanted the second half of the shift, and I'll cover for them next week. By the way, nice T-shirt." He tugged on the sleeve of the Oxford University T-shirt which was his.

"It was in the laundry room," Ruby said quickly in defense of her T-shirt choice.

Jason winked, then moved toward the couch and kissed Lisa on the top of the head. "I won't bother you all," he said before lifting his head and sniffing deeply. "Is that a Lisa pizza in the oven?"

Lisa stood, also walking on heels, she moved to Jason. "I made two pizzas just so you had left overs. Would you like some, fresh from the oven?"

Ruby watched as he licked his lips and nodded, as if the offer had made him unable to talk and his mouth water.

Of course she understood the reaction. Lisa was a food blogger and an amazing cook. They were all lucky when she wanted to cook for them—even pizza.

Lisa linked her arm with her brother's. "C'mon. Mama Rose would want me to take care of you."

Ruby watched until they disappeared into the kitchen before she plopped back down on the couch next to Mindy.

"I'm going to go change her," Tina said, lifting her daughter onto her shoulder and righting herself back into her T-shirt.

They both watched Tina go toward Ruby's bedroom, and when she was out of sight, Mindy pulled back and slapped Ruby on the arm.

"What the hell was that for?" she gritted her teeth.

"What's going on with you?" Mindy whispered loudly.

"I have no idea what the hell you're talking about."

Mindy sat there staring at her from behind the cracked pink champagne mask. Her eyes were wide, and the smile on her lips cracked the sides of the mask even further.

"You and Jason. What's going on between you?"

Ruby stared at her, and then turned her eyes toward the kitchen where she could hear the muffled sounds of Lisa and Jason talking.

"Nothing is going on between us. Why did you hit me?"

"What's going on?" she asked again.

"Nothing."

Pieces of Mindy's mask were falling off into her lap. "There will be," she said. "Did you see how he looked at you?"

"Like his roommate in a facial mask?"

"Like his roommate in his T-shirt. That's a sexy thing, you know. Wearing the roommate's T-shirt."

Ruby shook her head. "It's only sexy if you're wearing in in lieu of clothing."

"So when we leave…"

"I'll put the T-shirt in the hamper and wash it. Then it'll go back with his laundry."

Mindy shook her head. "I'm not one to say don't get involved with the guy *next door*," she laughed since that was exactly what Mindy had done, and now she and Vic were engaged. "I have to take this mask off."

Mindy stood and started toward the bathroom, before she turned and looked at Ruby. "You could do worse." She winked, and disappeared as she closed the bathroom door behind her.

Ruby sat back, and let out a breath.

She ran a hand over the T-shirt and thought of Jason in it. He'd worn it when he'd moved in, and again just the other day when he'd worked out.

It hadn't appeared that he was upset that she had it on, but admittedly, Ruby, in her pathetic state of singlehood, found it comforting to wear his T-shirts—should one end up left in the dryer.

Lisa and Jason walked back through the living room. He carried a plate in his hand and a bottle of water.

"Thanks for letting me crash your party," he said.

"You live here. It's not crashing," Ruby said. "Unless you stay for the movie."

Jason looked at the screen. *"Mama Mia?"*

Ruby nodded.

"That's a good one. Maybe one of these days when we're both off, we can watch it. For now, I'm taking my coveted pizza to my room. I'm going to take a shower, and go to bed for a day."

He kissed Lisa on the cheek. "Love you, sis."

"I love you too."

As he passed by the back of the couch, Jason leaned down and kissed the top of Ruby's head, much the same as he had to Lisa when he'd walked in.

"Night roomie in my T-shirt," he whispered in her ear.

Everything inside of Ruby went liquid at his breath against her skin.

Why had that seemed like such an intimate gesture? It was the norm where they were concerned, but that was the first time it swelled into to heat in her belly.

She really needed to think about dating again. If she didn't, she was going to cost herself another roommate.

PLEASE REVIEW

We hope you enjoyed *The Rom Com Movie Club - Book Two* by Bernadette Marie. If you did, we would ask that you please rate and review this title. Every review helps our authors.

Rate and Review: The Rom Com Movie Club - Book Two

MEET THE AUTHOR

Bestselling author Bernadette Marie began writing in the eighth grade. She sent off her epic family saga at the age of sixteen, but it was years before she would publish and eventually find her home in contemporary romance, and at the top of the charts.

The married mother of five promises romances with a Happily Ever After always...and says she can write it because she lives it. She also claims that her books are the antidote to anything heavy you might read.

Obsessed with the art of writing and the business of publishing, a chronic entrepreneur, Bernadette Marie established her own publishing house, 5 Prince Publishing, in 2011 to bring her own work to market as well as offer an opportunity for fresh voices in fiction to find a home as well. To date she has published the works of over sixty other authors.

When not immersed in the writing/publishing world, Bernadette Marie can be found spending time with her family, traveling (mostly to Disney parks), and running multiple businesses. An avid martial artist, Bernadette Marie is a second degree black belt and certified instructor in Tang Soo Do, and loves Tai Chi. She's a lover of a good stout craft beer, she might also have an unhealthy addiction to chocolate.

OTHER TITLES FROM

5 PRINCE PUBLISHING

www.5princebooks.com

A Crossbow Christmas *Ann Swann*
Hot For Teacher *Felicia Carparelli*
The Happily Ever After Bookstore *Bernadette Marie*
Perfect Mrs Claus *Barbara Matteson*
Princess of Prias *Courtney Davis*
Paige and the Reluctant Artist *Darci Garcia*
A Spider in the Garden *Courtney Davis*
Megan's Choice *Darci Garcia*
Something New *Bernadette Marie*
Something Forbidden *Bernadette Marie*
Something Found *Bernadette Marie*
Something Discovered *Bernadette Marie*
Something Lost *Bernadette Marie*
Ashes of Aldyr *Russell Archey*
Telephone Road *Ann Swann*
Paige Devereaux *Bernadette Marie*
Max Devereaux *Bernadette Marie*
Christmas Cookies on a Cruise Ship *Parker Fairchild*

Chase Devereaux *Bernadette Marie*
Kennedy Devereaux *Bernadette Marie*
The Seven Spires *Russell Archey*
At Last *Bernadette Marie*
Masterpiece *Bernadette Marie*
A Tropical Christmas *Bernadette Marie*
Corporate Christmas *Bernadette Marie*
Faith Through Falling Snow *Sandy Sinnett*
Walker Defense *Bernadette Marie*
Clash of the Cheerleaders *April Marcom*
Stevie-Girl and the Phantom of Forever *Ann Swann*
The Last Goodbye *Bernadette Marie*
The Gingerbread Curse *April Marcom*

www.ingramcontent.com/pod-product-compliance
Lightning Source LLC
Chambersburg PA
CBHW030646020726
47493CB00006B/1901